SHAKEN TO THE CORE

A Novel

Also by Dara Levan

It Could Be Worse

"*Shaken to the Core* is a beautiful rendering of love and loss, capturing the quiet, devastating ways each reshapes who we are. With emotional precision and deep compassion, Dara Levan traces how grief can fracture a life—and how love, even in its absence, continues to transform us."

—**Jane L. Rosen,** author of
The Fire Island trilogy

"Dara Levan's *Shaken to the Core* is a tender story of love, loss, and perseverance, a tale reminding readers at each surprising turn that regardless of what the universe dishes out, we all have choices."

—**Corie Adjmi,** *USA Today*
bestselling author of *The Marriage Box*

"In *Shaken to the Core,* Dara Levan crafts an emotionally astute portrait of a woman reshaped by sudden loss. As she uncovers her mom's old journals and in them, her long-buried dreams, Joy begins to see that motherhood isn't just about biology—it's about memory, courage, and the fierce desire to nurture something that outlives us. With warmth, humor, and emotional honesty, this uplifting novel reminds us that when life breaks our hearts, it can rebuild them even stronger and better than they were before."

—**Gila Pffefer,** award-winning author of
Nearly Departed

SHAKEN TO THE CORE

A Novel

DARA LEVAN

A REGALO PRESS BOOK
ISBN: 979-8-89565-253-4
ISBN (eBook): 979-8-89565-254-1

Shaken to the Core:
A Novel
© 2026 by Dara Levan
All Rights Reserved

Cover Design by Jim Villaflores

Publishing Team:
Founder and Publisher – Gretchen Young
Managing Editor – Caitlin Burdette
Production Manager – Kate Harris
Production Editor – Rachel Paul

As part of the mission of Regalo Press, a donation is being made to the Parkinson's Foundation, as chosen by the author. Find out more about this organization at www.parkinson.org.

This book, as well as any other Regalo Press publications, may be purchased in bulk quantities at a special discounted rate. Contact orders@regalopress.com for more information.

Regalo Press
New York • Nashville
regalopress.com

Published in the United States of America
1 2 3 4 5 6 7 8 9 10

For my late mother-in-law, Terri Levan Katz.
She left too soon, leaving a legacy of light and love.

CHAPTER 1

Daylight can be deceiving. Resting on my forearms and sinking into the sand, I watched the waves lap the shore. She wouldn't want us sitting around the house, moping and morose. That's why we decided to gather here instead. My mother loved lounging at the beach, jotting thoughts in one of her journals, and jogging near the coastline. I smiled, remembering how my brother Julian and I would giggle when the frothy surf tickled our toes. My dad preferred to sit in the shade and observe from a distance.

Sweat drizzled down my long-sleeved sun shirt as I smoothed the oversized, turquoise towel. My husband, Andre, suggested we all meet here before sunset—my mom's favorite time of day—and the others would be here soon. His brothers would likely be late. They were on Miami time; being punctual is considered early. My in-laws, Carmen and Carlos, called it Colombian time instead. They wouldn't be here today; Andre thankfully had handled that because I didn't have the stamina for my well-meaning mother-in-law, who could sometimes be easily offended.

I closed my eyes and rested my head on the towel. Glimmers of sun rays filtered between the ominous clouds, creating ideal lighting for taking photos.

I wished I'd taken more of my mother.

"*¿Estás despierta?*" Andre asked. His voice soothed me in any language.

I looked up, squinting at my six-foot-four, sculpted husband.

"Here, drink this or you'll get dehydrated," he said, handing me a cold bottle of coconut water. Then he reached for my hand and pulled me to my feet.

"Thank you, my love," I said, feeling a bit dizzy. Andre brushed my light brown bangs out of my eyes. In Vermont, they behaved. In Florida, they revolted, mushrooming and frizzy. I was growing them out, anyway. Too much maintenance and I didn't have the patience, especially in recent weeks, to deal with a flat iron. Though I missed living near my dad, my in-laws, and others, the humidity was one reason we moved to Burlington.

A shrill shriek I'd know anywhere pierced the muggy, thick air. I had no idea my favorite first cousin would be here. Scrambling to my feet, I nearly knocked her over.

"Tali! Oh, it's good to see you. I was a freaking mess at the funeral. I don't remember much other than my cell phone almost dropping into the casket—thank goodness Mel caught it," I said. "I'm so happy you're here."

She tucked a curly strand of hair behind my ear and grinned.

"Like a scene from a twisted sitcom, right? Not gonna lie, I thought for a second you did that on purpose. Then I saw your face. You're always making us laugh," Tali replied. I squeezed her tighter and looked over her shoulder.

Cousins of all ages stampeded toward me, the older ones herding their children. One tripped, another collided with her big brother, and I felt the heaviness I'd been holding all morning lift.

"Auntie Joy!"

"Hey there, cuz!"

"So happy to hug you!"

I smiled, not sure who to respond to first. And, just like the shiva last month, I was beginning to realize we need people most when we least expect it. We decided to hang at the beach this afternoon before the estate sale tomorrow, which I'd been dreading for days.

As I crouched down to meet my five-year-old nephew, he threw his little arms around me, nestling his damp head into my neck. Then he dashed toward the water and joined the others, splashing and swimming in the ocean like a pod of dolphins. I looked up at the darkening sky, concerned about the impending storm.

Tali dropped her beach bag, took off her wide-brimmed hat, and motioned for us to sit. She twisted her honey-blonde hair and clipped it on top of her head. We sat side by side on the towel and stretched our legs out in front of us.

"How're you holding up?" she asked, already knowing the answer. That's the thing about cousins—at least mine—we have some sort of telepathy.

I rolled my eyes. "Best day ever, T! If I took a shot for every time I see that look, you know the one—the 'poor pitiful griever' —I'd be wasted, and it's not even noon." We both snorted.

"Well, at least you've still got your sense of humor. I was worried the last time we spoke," Tali admitted.

As if on cue, our other cousin trotted toward us. She's the youngest adult-ish one of our crew.

"Holy shit! I just remembered something hysterical!" she exclaimed. I tried to raise an eyebrow; Andre had mastered this expression.

"I'll give you a hint," she grinned. "It may involve a culinary concoction at your house."

Tali got it.

"Joy doesn't remember, Rach. It was back in high school, tenth grade, I think. Anyway, we baked brownies between pretending to do our math homework and—"

"Aunt Allegra snarfed one down—she was hungry after one of her long runs. She was training for a half-marathon," Rachel interrupted. "A few hours later, she ate popcorn, pretzels, pretty much everything in sight."

I spit out the water I was sipping.

"She was high. I don't think we ever told Aunt Allegra that our special ingredient was weed! She'd be so mad cause, you know, she only drank wine on Shabbat or other special occasions," Tali said, giggling. "Anything mind altering, especially if unregulated or illegal, was off-limits."

I laughed, wiping the corners of my eyes. "I almost donated that pan! So glad you remembered, Rach. I'm taking that back to Burlington with me."

I thought I'd need an inhaler from laughing so hard. Tali even wheezed a bit. After I caught my breath, I leaned back on my hands, looked up at the sky, and wondered if my mom could hear us.

The brief drizzle had stopped, and the clouds parted. A sliver of sunshine shone on my face. I turned my head slightly, certain I was seeing things. The girls noticed and followed my gaze.

"Do you see that, too?" I stood slowly, pointing just beyond a big, billowy cloud.

"Holy crap."

"Whoa."

I guess that was a yes. The most vibrant rainbow I'd ever seen painted the sky. I'd never been one to believe in life beyond what I could see. Mom always said souls never die. Maybe she was right. After all, she is—was—a therapist, yogi, and eternal optimist.

Maybe she was letting me know I'd be able to feel her presence in a different form.

CHAPTER 2 

The weather had shifted slightly and so did my mood. Today the sky was a pastel blue with streaks of cottony white striated across it. My mom's lavender, metal watch stopped ticking as if it knew. It hung heavily on my sweaty wrist. I refolded the nubby sweatshirts, arranging them from light to dark. I straightened the hangers, restacked the books, and triple-checked that the belongings were displayed in an organized, methodical manner.

She didn't say goodbye. No time to plan, to prepare, to process. How could her abundant, beautiful life be reduced to one small room of stuff? Are we what we leave behind?

"Joy!" A baritone voice startled me. "People are arriving, *mi amor.*" In what seemed like seconds, Andre had his arm around me, leading me toward the front of the room in the shed. *What if we weren't ready yet? Would I ever be ready?*

I molded my mouth into something resembling a smile and gripped the rusty brass knob.

"The prices are marked on round, red stickers. If you have any questions, please ask me or my husband," I announced, leaning into Andre's sturdy hand. He got the cue and followed the first person toward the back of the room.

I exhaled and felt grateful I wasn't alone. Andre's parents joined him and showed the strangers my mother's belongings. I couldn't bear to watch random people pick through her precious items. The half-empty bottle of perfume. The cozy sweats, running shorts, vibrant yoga clothes. Her favorite pewter clock that had sat on her desk for as long as I could remember. I'd kept her jewelry, crystal heart, ladybug paperweight, and other items I just couldn't let go. My mom would want me to be practical. I could imagine her saying, "Honey, it's just stuff."

Yet right now, it felt like everything. It's all I had left.

As I stepped back outside, I glanced at the coconut palm tree, its brown fronds swaying like hands waving goodbye. I wondered how many storms it had weathered and yet somehow survived. Miami's version of fall blanched in comparison to the spectrum of colors in Vermont. I couldn't wait to get back home.

I'd arranged the items by theme and function. Holiday decorations lined the left wall, clothing hung on racks to the right, kitchenware stacked in the middle, and miscellaneous items, like books and tchotchkes (my mom's favorite Yiddish word for trinkets), were displayed on tables at the back. I made sure there were intentional spaces for people to meander, so they didn't break anything.

"*Mija, tengo una pregunta,*" my mother-in-law said from a distance. I loved that she and my father-in-law called me their daughter. Until recently. Now it stung. I didn't respond.

My in-laws were such sweet people who loved me as their own. Andre had introduced me to them during one of our college breaks and we clicked immediately. His four younger brothers also embraced me as if I were the sister they'd never had. I knew how lucky I was.

I heard Carmen call my name. Better than "hija"—especially surrounded by my mom's stuff.

It felt wrong.

All of it.

I jumped to my feet and brushed the dirt off my thighs as I walked back to the shed. Carmen glanced at me, her cheeks flushed from the heat. Her gold bangles jingled as she took off her glossy black Gucci sunglasses.

"The truck is leaving soon. I'll keep this for your babies," she said, draping the yellow and green knit blanket over her tanned forearm. "We hope we'll use this sooner than later."

"Wait. What? The sale is over?" I chewed on my lower lip.

Carmen took my hand in hers.

"You know my boys. They want to get back for the game. Colombia is playing Argentina in the soccer finals. *Dios mio—men,*" she sighed. "I brought my own car. I'll be here as long as you want. Andre is staying, too."

He's my husband, I wanted to scream. *He better not leave!* I plastered a smile on my face.

"Gracias, Carmen. I don't know what I'd do without you and Carlos, especially these past few weeks." She held me close and kissed my cheeks, one at a time.

"We love you like a daughter, Joy. And if you need us, we'll be on the next plane once you're back in Burlington. Or we'll send you a ticket—you can come to Miami for a weekend of shopping and a spa day," she said. Carmen would move into our house if I asked.

"You're the sweetest," I managed, trying to swallow the lump that'd formed in my throat. The pesky pebble, I called it. I'd somehow kept it away for an entire morning. That was progress, I suppose. I heard a loud engine and beeping, like a vehicle reversing. I excused myself and bolted toward the massive truck. I motioned for the driver to lower his window.

"Hi. I wanted to thank you for your kindness and patience," I said, clearing my throat. "You've made this painful process somehow a bit better. I'd like to take one last look before you leave."

The stocky man wiped sweat from his sunburnt forehead. "It's why we're here. If it makes you feel any better, your mom's stuff is going to a good cause," he said, opening the door and escorting me toward the back.

I scanned the haphazardly tossed cardboard boxes, fighting the urge to straighten them. I spotted a small open box under a tower of others. I peeked inside, saw a bunch of tattered books, and lifted them. A purple, leather journal was jammed between my mom's old Oxford dictionary and a Carl Jung biography. I gingerly pulled it from the pile and slid it into my canvas backpack.

I'd given my sister-in-law most of the holiday decor, except for the Thanksgiving projects my mom insisted we create every year. Carmen said she'd ship those and other items to us. I also kept a menorah, the one my mom received as a gift from her best friends on her wedding day. Unlike the others she collected, this one had an intricate celestial scene with what looked like animals from Noah's ark painted on porcelain. I'd wrapped it in newspaper and made a mental note to ask Andre to secure the menorah before we left in the morning, worried that it would break in my luggage.

My mom would be thrilled that we donated her belongings and the money we made from the estate sale to organizations close to her heart. And by doing so, I felt in some way she was close to mine.

CHAPTER 3

"Hurry up! We might miss our flight," Andre shouted, as he schlepped our luggage through the sliding doors. I adjusted my backpack, trying to find a spot on my shoulders that didn't ache. His family thought arriving at the airport an hour before a flight was sufficient. I didn't mind a sprint. And that last hug from Carmen lingered as if her arms were still around me.

My husband hadn't inherited his parents' perpetually tardy timeline. I loved the wiggle room. Andre? Not so much.

We checked in and he guessed correctly that our luggage was under fifty pounds. Then Andre grabbed my hand. "We need to pick up the pace. Our gate just changed," he said.

The swarm of passengers buzzed around us. I heard a chorus of Spanish, Portuguese, Creole, among other lyrical languages I couldn't discern. I loved Vermont but missed the diverse soundtrack of my hometown.

A tall, slender woman offered us sanitizing wipes as we boarded the airplane. I avoided her gaze, heading straight to our seats. As I settled into the wide chair, I exhaled and thanked my husband, grateful to be in first class. Andre cleaned every inch of the seatbelt, the tray table, and even the buttons. The two square towelettes weren't enough for him; he used the lemon-scented Lysol wipes from his satchel, too.

Somehow, even the extra space still felt suffocating. I dabbed peppermint essential oil on my temples, breathing deeply and wrapping my mom's cashmere pashmina around me. After a bumpy takeoff, the pilot announced that it'd be a smooth ride. I adjusted my headphones, rested my head on the cool window, and watched the Miami skyline fade as we ascended. A tear streamed down my check like an icicle melting.

As we soared higher, the sky cleared, and I thought about being between two worlds. The one where we'd lived while my mother was still alive. And how I'd move forward without her.

"*Mi amor*, we're home," Andre said, gently rubbing the back of my neck. "You passed out immediately! You must be exhausted."

I nodded groggily and leaned forward to retrieve my backpack from the seat in front of me. Standing too quickly, I bumped my head on the overhead compartment. Well, that's one way to awaken from a deep sleep. As we exited the plane, a chilly breeze blew in through that narrow spot just between the runway and entrance, so refreshing and much needed, a stark contrast to the mugginess of Miami. Dragging the carry-on behind me, I moved like a sloth toward the baggage claim area.

"I'm over here, Joy!" I turned my head toward the sparkly sound of my best friend's voice. We'd met our freshman year of college in the dank dorms. She made everything brighter. I wasn't expecting her to park the car and come into the airport.

I didn't know until this moment how much I needed her, sensation starting to return to my body like Novocain wearing off after having a cavity filled. My backpack fell to the floor as I sprinted toward her. I noticed a glimmery gemstone dangling from her neck as I got closer.

"Oh Mel, thanks for picking us up!" I hugged her, feeling her steady heart beating against my chest.

"Of course! You seriously think I'd let you take an Uber home?"

I dropped my arms and squinted from behind my cat-eye glasses. I pointed to the opalescent green gemstone. "Is this a new design? I love how you wrapped the wire around it!"

Mel grinned and shook her head. "Only you'd notice this with all you've been through. Yea, it's a stone I sourced from Australia—it is one of a kind. But I don't want to talk about me. We need to catch up," she replied.

Andre hauled the luggage toward us and swooped Mel up in a massive hug. "You're the best. Muchas gracias! Did you tell her yet?" he asked. I peered at them quizzically.

"No, I thought you did," Mel said, shaking her head.

"What have you two concocted?" I asked. They smiled conspiratorially at each other.

"I figured you'd like some time with Mel. I'll head home with our stuff, start the laundry, and unpack," Andre said, leaning down to kiss my cheek.

I encircled my arms around his trim waist, squeezing so hard he laughed and said, "I guess this was a good call?"

As Mel drove toward Lake Champlain, I marveled at the crimson, gold, and pumpkin-colored leaves fluttering in the wind. I thought about how some detach from branches, falling gracefully to the ground. Others linger on tree limbs, holding on a bit longer.

We parked and Mel opened the trunk on her GMC truck. I thought we were eating at Skinny Pancake. I'd been craving a whole wheat crepe stuffed with goat cheese and kale.

"What are you doing?" I asked, stepping on wet leaves strewn on the ground.

"You'll see soon," Mel chirped. "Here, take this please." She handed me a fleece, striped blanket—the one we'd sat on during tons of summer concerts. Mel motioned for me to follow her.

"Right here, this is the spot." She pointed to the sprawling, emerald lawn. Then I saw the woven basket in her left hand.

"You are the sweetest," I said, smiling bigger than I had in weeks. I unfolded the blanket and placed it on the grass. "What's in there?"

"Though I'd like to take credit for this brilliant idea, Andre called me a few days ago and suggested it. He adores you, Joy." Mel lifted the lid and took out napkins, utensils, and mugs.

I smiled again, feeling hopeful that my mouth remembered how to form this expression twice in a row.

"We're all lucky, right? Andre and Jake are buddies. I can't imagine how things would be if we didn't meet years ago at Middlebury. I knew we'd be forever friends; who knew the guys would connect, too?"

She handed me a stout Yeti as she finished setting up the spread. My eyes widened—there were the crepes I had craved, complete with sides of bacon and maple syrup. I cracked open the lid and inhaled the steamy dark roast from Vermont Artisan Coffee. I was home.

We took bites between interrupting each other like two sisters. Mel had a way of creating space as effortlessly as she created jewelry. I didn't feel compelled to fill the quiet gaps with chatter or jokes as I did with other friends. A golden retriever chased a frisbee and caught it in his mouth midair. Children frolicked on the lawn, playing with each other as their parents sipped cold cans of cider. A girl loosened the faded flannel shirt around her waist and put her head on the shoulder of the boy next to her. They seemed smitten. I recognized that look of young love, remembering when Andre gazed at me like that.

"Joy? Where'd you go, my friend?" Mel asked.

"I'm right here. What's in that mug?" I retorted, snatching it out of her hands and sniffing it.

"You crack me up! Just espresso and no, it's not spiked. But not gonna lie, I briefly thought about adding a shot of scotch to yours. Andre nixed that idea." Mel rolled her eyes. "Want to go for a walk? We won't have many days left of this stunning weather."

I leapt to my feet and followed her toward the placid, shimmering lake. Sailboats swayed in the distance. Concentric ripples of water bathed the shoreline and joined the rustling of leaves, a soothing sonata between seasons. An older woman with white hair in a braid linked arms with a girl who looked like she was about eight years old.

Mel must've seen the duo, too, because I felt her arm around my shoulder. *How are there more*, I thought, as I dabbed the tears streaming down my face.

"Shit, I'm sorry. This has been such a reprieve from the past month and I'm ruining it!" I sniffed.

Mel stopped abruptly and planted her hands on her hips.

"Listen to me. This sucks. And I'm here for it all, always. Don't you ever apologize for being human," she said firmly. I knew she meant it.

We found an unoccupied swing, a rarity especially this time of year. The wood planks creaked as we sat down. Mel removed her cardigan and took a sleeve, wiping the tip of my nose with it. I'd seen her do this with whatever was nearby when her daughter had a meltdown.

I'd usually find it gross, but right now it was just what I needed. We swung our legs up and down, synchronized, and I continued to catch her up on all that'd transpired. I inhaled fall—a fusion of fresh apples, pumpkin spice, and burning birch wood. Sunlight sparkled on the water and seagulls soared above it. For a second, I contemplated jumping in fully clothed.

Mel's words resounded like wind chimes, bringing me back to reality.

"So, tell me about that necklace!" I asked, intrigued by the shimmery stone.

"I've been searching tons of sites for an opal. Certain shape, certain size, you know when I'm on a mission. Then this green one found me! Isn't it incredible?" Mel took a breath. "I've never worked with wire before and figured I am reaching the end of my thirties. No time like the present."

Truer words have never been spoken. It's wild how a cliché can suddenly evoke deeper meaning. The temperature had dropped, but I didn't think that's why I shivered.

"I need to head back soon. Thank you for such a healing afternoon. I have a family portrait session near Shelburne tomorrow; these kids love animals. I'm both dreading and looking forward to diving back into my work," I said. "I need to get some rest because right now, I can't fathom holding my Nikon without dropping it."

———

"Something smells good!" I shouted. I tossed my backpack in the mudroom and took off my brown boots. A gorgeous sight greeted me—Andre in his plaid pajama pants frying chicken cutlets with veggies from our garden. He'd wisely suggested that we freeze the zucchini and green beans. Andre was a wizard with his hands, whether designing architectural plans, whipping up a decadent meal, or kicking my ass on the tennis court.

"Hola, mi amor. How was your time with Mel?" Andre lowered the heat on the gas stove.

"I'm so grateful that you two planned that surprise. I would've said no if you asked in advance," I replied, reaching up to wrap my arms around his neck. "I don't know what I'd do without you."

I plated the food on square, ceramic dishes. I grabbed a grater and a block of aged parmesan, watching the pieces fall onto the cutting board. Then I sprinkled the shavings on the vegetables. We sat down as the sun began to set.

"I'm so irritated with Robert," Andre grumbled. "How hard is it to review a few drafts? He keeps making stupid mistakes. I don't know if he'll be with the firm long term. I leave for a freaking week-end, and it's as if I've been gone for a century." Andre's hand shook as it rested on the table. It stopped when he reached for the fork and speared a chunk of chicken.

"That's frustrating, honey. I hear you," I murmured and kept chewing. I wanted to scream *at least your mom is alive!* Instead, I continued to shove food in my mouth.

"I have a shoot early in the morning. I need to get to bed soon. Thanks again for today and for everything," I said, kissing his full lips.

My eyelids drooped as if invisible weights had lodged themselves in there. I put my backpack in the corner of my closet, shrugged out of my sweatshirt, and ambled to the bathroom. Everything felt heavy, even the toothbrush. I had to coax my feet to move, my hands to turn the faucet, my mouth to open. Sounds seemed louder, irritating when once soothing, like my whole sensory system had short-circuited. Andre was watching the news while cleaning the pots; the clanging and clamoring traveled, unwelcome, into my quiet bedroom. My entire body felt frayed and fried.

After dousing my face in freezing water, I stared at the bags under my eyes. My skin looked pasty, even paler than usual. My cheeks felt puffy and swollen. I patted my face with a gray hand towel and blinked several times. Nope, still there. A face I hardly recognized stared back at me.

I plodded toward the bed, thankful we'd recently bought a new, luxurious duvet. I didn't know how I'd hold a camera in my hands tomorrow or focus, let alone reengage with the world. I pulled the covers up to my neck as my head sank into the down pillow.

———

"Good morning, mi amor!" Andre boomed. "I crawled into bed last night, and you didn't budge. I hope you feel rested today," he said, handing me a cup of coffee.

I stretched my arms, one eye open, and struggled to sit up.

"You're the best. I think I need an IV full of caffeine. Can you make that happen?"

Andre laughed. "I didn't want to wake you."

I bolted upright, saw the time, and dashed to the shower. I never sleep this late.

"Glad you did, honey. I might've slept until next year!" I shouted.

Andre somehow awoke without an alarm as if he'd installed a permanent timer in his brain. He'd designed his life, each phase of it, intentionally and precisely. When we were at Middlebury, he'd wake up early, even after a night partying. I'd be nursing a hangover while he'd already gone to the gym, studied for an exam, and eaten two meals. I wished he'd sleep in sometimes, snuggle with me, and turn off that busy brain of his.

I poured the rest of the coffee into a thermos, burning my finger in the process, and double-checked that my lenses were in the bag. Thankfully, I'd left the filter, tripod, and other equipment in my trunk. I stopped by the local coffee shop to pick up a turkey wrap and an oatmeal chocolate chip cookie. My favorite barista, Sage, turned her head in my direction, smiling hesitantly as she poured an espresso into a cup. I marveled at her ability to fulfill complicated coffee orders while brewing a variety of blends. She seemed to have endless patience with picky customers' polite, albeit specific, requests.

"Hey there, Joy! How've you been?" She normally looked directly at me. Today she fixed her gaze on the cash register. "Glad to see you're back home. I'm so sorry about your mom." I'd considered going to a different place, hoping to avoid this subject.

"Thanks, Sage. I see you have a long line." I mumbled my order, and she slid the premade wrap and cookie across the bar to me.

In the car, I was reminded of another reason I loved living in Burlington—traffic—and the lack thereof. Unless we had a snowstorm, driving here was peaceful. I blasted Noah Kahan from the radio, trying to distract myself with his soothing songs. A Vermont native, his music spoke to my soul.

The drive took longer than the last time I'd been at the farm. As I pulled into the parking lot, I saw a boy jumping up and down. He tossed his long, striped scarf in the air while his older sister held her mom's hand.

"Hi everyone! I'm Joy!" The little boy spun in circles and sang "Old MacDonald Had a Farm." I quietly joined him.

"You know that song, too?" he squealed.

"I sure do! It's one of my favorites," I replied.

I pointed beyond where we stood. "Do you see the mountains? Let's go that way and we can keep singing."

The mom motioned to me, indicating her kids should walk ahead.

"I'm absolutely amazed," Eden said. An expression I couldn't decipher flashed on her face.

"You've never met a singing photographer?" I said.

"No, no. Jacob doesn't warm up to people that easily. He's shy, and, well, he can get overwhelmed by the slightest sounds," she replied, admiring her little boy from afar.

"This is a serene space you chose," I said. "The lighting is perfect—we should start shooting soon. Will your partner be joining us?"

Tears pooled in her hazel eyes. "I thought I told you. He died two years ago. My therapist suggested one way to move forward is to take a portrait. I don't know if I'll ever feel complete as a family of three." I handed her a tissue and the pebble in my throat returned.

"I'm so, so sorry. I understand, in some ways, how you feel. Let's make this a super special afternoon for all of you," I said. *Really? Talk about ripping off the Band-Aid.* I tried to compose myself, looking away and rummaging in my bag.

The little boy flapped his hands in the distance. His sister twirled her thick, blonde braids. I asked Eden if she was ready. She reapplied mauve lip gloss and flattened the collar on her chambray shirt.

I loved this time of the day. The light shone through the leaves, spotlighting fall's fiery orange, auburn, mustard, and plum hues. The sun melted like molten lava across the cloudless sky, the majestic mountains a perfect backdrop for this sweet trio.

"Look over here!" *Click.*

"Now join hands!" *Click.*

"Walk toward the goats!" *Click.*

Eden's smile broadened as her kids giggled and chattered. The little boy had more songs in his repertoire—"The Wheels on the Bus" and "The Itsy-Bitsy Spider." I sighed, wistful and still yearning for a child of my own. Eden shared that she'd chosen this area because her late husband was a third-generation Vermont farmer. And the kids, especially her son, adored animals.

I'd worked at a corporate company, taking photos for their social media and helping with branding as well. Though the income was steady, I felt creatively suffocated and confined. A few years ago, I decided to launch my own business. We'd gotten accustomed to an untethered life after moving here. This offered even more flexibility so Andre could plan trips for us and travel all over the world. He owned his architectural firm. He had the brilliant idea (that honestly, I doubted at first) to bring the tropics to the mountains. Who knew that Vermonters would love a home with a tropical vibe?

As the sun slowly sank behind the mountains, I snapped a few more images, capturing the lingering light that streamed through the labyrinth of branches. I inhaled the brisk air, grateful to be back. And again, I thought about the one time that death is beautiful. These maples, gracefully letting go of their leaves, the radiant colors, deceptively alive yet dying.

My mom, only sixty-two years old, healthy, vibrant, and now gone. The headache had come on suddenly, intensifying rapidly. Thankful for the drive home, I wondered if I'd ever get through a day with dry eyes.

CHAPTER 4 

I rocked back and forth in the cherrywood chair—the same one where my mother held me when I was a baby and lulled me to sleep. Cradling the curved arms with my fingers, I closed my eyes and tried to imagine my mom as a young woman. She had me in her twenties and this antique rocker was her mother's. I never thought I'd be sitting in it here in Vermont. I listened to wind coax the leaves to the ground. Most of the trees had let go. The ones that remained had turned brown. Stick season was here, a brief intermission between autumn and winter.

The ambiance matched my mood: bleak, barren, broken.

"Mind if I join you?" Andre asked. The caning creaked as I leaned back and looked up at his olive face, noticing he'd missed a patch of hair on his chin. Strange because he shaved three times each morning, with different blades, one of his many rituals.

"Sure. I can't believe it's already November, honey. How can it be two months since—"

He knew the question and answered it before I could finish.

"I woke up thinking about her, too. I also had an idea, just the thing to cheer you up!" Andre winked.

"Ice cream for breakfast? A planet I can teleport to until I feel happy again? What?" I snarked.

"Not exactly what I had in mind. I booked a night at that bed and breakfast in Middlebury. The one where we—"

"Oh honey! What a great idea. When do we leave?"

"As soon as you're ready. I already packed your bag, supplements, travel camera, and snacks," he said. "Though I don't think you'll need much clothing."

I stood up and caught my toe on the rough edge of the rocking chair. Then I hobbled over to him as we laughed. Speaking of shaving, I realized that I'd grown a bush in certain places. Even showering took effort lately. I told Andre I would need about an hour and then we'd leave.

We cruised south on US-7, the Audi humming as we spoke. Or, really, I listened to Andre tell me about his latest idea, a Key West–inspired plan and collaboration with a local interior designer. Something about flamingos, white wicker, plantation shuttered windows?

I turned down the dial on the radio; his words competing with the blaring tunes frazzled my nerves. My internal system could only tolerate a certain decibel until it hurt.

Andre cranked it back up.

"Please. It's too much," I said, clenching my jaw.

"What's too much? You love Bob Dylan." I shook my head. *He doesn't get it.*

"It's one or the other—you talking or the music. I can't handle both," I muttered.

Andre exhaled loudly and stopped speaking. Terrific. Great way to kick off a romantic getaway.

He approached Main Street, then made a right turn. The road narrowed and majestic evergreen trees lined the path. A squirrel scampered up a thick trunk and onto a long branch. Then the inn appeared, quaint and welcoming, just as I remembered it. I squeezed Andre's hand, hoping he'd feel the gratitude that I couldn't put into words, yet.

"Damn it. I thought we'd avoid the peepers," Andre said, rolling his eyes. "Don't these tourists know peak season was last month? Ugh."

I stared ahead, noting the four gargantuan buses ahead of us.

"They're probably just here for a little while. Maybe it's an outing from a local assisted living facility? Don't worry about it," I said.

A petite, white-haired woman greeted us at the front desk.

"We're so glad you are here. Welcome!" She unfolded a map of the area, highlighting the coffee shops, galleries, trails, and historic homes. Andre preferred to figure this out on his own, but he pretended to listen.

"I'll have Bob show you to your room. We upgraded you, by the way. Heard from a lil bird it's a special weekend," she said, smiling brightly. Sweet, yet I felt nauseated. How did she have the right to be so chipper?

When we walked through the molded, oak doors, my spirits lifted.

"You like, mi amor?" Andre circled his hands around my waist.

"Wow," I managed, gawking at the mahogany four-poster bed in front of me. An intricate quilt with dainty flowers in all shades of green covered the king mattress. Oval, antique nightstands flanked the bed, each one with a wrought iron lamp. An opulent chandelier hung in the middle with a patina finish and oblong crystals.

I pulled off my high boots, noting I needed a new pair after seeing the tear in the heel. I ran my fingers over the blush-colored toile wallpaper. It looked newer than the hundred-year-old inn. Maybe they'd updated it since our last visit?

"It's so nice that they gave us this spectacular room," I said.

"I phoned in a favor. I know an architect in the area, a friend of a friend, and he made it happen." Andre led me toward the chenille settee, which dipped in the middle. The maple frame had softened to a deep honey. He rearranged the square, tasseled pillows and patted the space next to him.

"Isn't this amazing? I love how they upholstered it. Windsor with a modern twist," he remarked. "And the detail on the crown molding is exquisite!"

"I totally knew that," I snorted. "Let's explore the property. I wonder if anything's changed?"

We donned our hiking boots and headed toward the lobby. I nudged Andre to take the map. He refused, of course. This place, these woods, held so many memories. We walked down an easy trail, and I noticed Andre's right thumb twitching. I wondered if that was a new tic, maybe all the stress from the past few months?

I laced my fingers through his, and we strolled over the first bridge. Admiring the faded, red roof, I slowed down to read the plaque affixed to it. I loved covered bridges and wondered how many people had walked the same path before us. Our lug soles gripped the damp wood; it must've rained earlier. A few droplets lingered on a spruce—I watched until they landed on the dank dirt. We continued to walk, both lost in our own thoughts, as the planks groaned under our feet.

To the left, a rush of water roared through the rocks. Taking out my digital camera, I paused to take a few photos. The landscape in our state shifted unpredictably between seasons. Even the most knowledgeable meteorologists couldn't predict the weather with total accuracy. This year, the colors popped earlier because the temps plummeted. Mocha brown maple leaves floated in the water, some making their way downstream, others plastering stones like papier-mâché.

"Here we are," Andre said. He gently took my camera and slipped it into his pocket. I tried not to grimace because I just spotted a cardinal flying above us.

"This is the bridge. The one where we first kissed," Andre said, bringing me closer. I rested my head on his broad chest, his strong heart beating through his sweater. He lifted my chin until our eyes met, the tips of our noses touched, and he kissed me deeply.

"I love you, Joy. This has been such a tough time—thank you for agreeing to come here," Andre said, his eyes dewy. "I wasn't sure you'd be up for it." His mouth inches from me, he kissed me again, this time more fervently. Andre's full lips melded against mine as I gripped the back of his head in my hands. Tracing the cleft in his chin with my finger, I saw the darkening sky that threatened to drench us.

"I know, let's head back before we get soaked. I should've brought an umbrella," Andre said. We doubled the tempo, walking briskly back to the inn. "I made a reservation for dinner, later than our usual, at 8 p.m. And we won't have to drive anywhere," he added.

I sighed with relief. Though it was a peaceful afternoon, I needed some time to myself.

But Andre had other plans.

When we entered the room, a delectable display greeted us: a bottle of champagne accompanied by two glasses and a plate of the most enormous chocolate-covered strawberries I'd ever seen. As I got closer, I saw a note and snatched it before Andre could.

"Happy anniversary and wishing you a memorable stay." The flowery writing matched the energy of the kind woman at the front desk. I froze and flipped through the pages of my internal scrapbook. *What did I forget? Shit. I was officially confused.*

"Damn it! Those weren't supposed to arrive until after dinner!" Andre huffed.

"This is so sweet—see what I did there?" I quipped, reaching for the juiciest one. "Oh, this is heavenly." I chattered about the berries that I swear had been injected with steroids. And hoped my hubby wouldn't ask about the anniversary I'd apparently forgotten about. He opened his mouth to say something, and I popped a strawberry into it—stem, leaves, and all. Andre sighed in defeat and looked at his stainless-steel Rolex.

"I didn't realize how late it got, mi amor. Do you want to take a nap or maybe we can move up dinner?" I already knew what he wanted. And why delay uncorking an expensive bottle of champagne that was chilled to perfection?

"Let's pop open that bubbly, and I'll let you know." I pointed to the silver ice bucket. Then I reached for my pajamas.

We'd saved the corks from our first date and other special occasions. Milestone birthdays, anniversaries, my first solo gig, his project that landed on the cover of *Vermont Magazine*.

I downed the first glass, relishing the bubbles as they tickled the inside of my cheeks. Andre disappeared while I looked at the dismal, dark sky. I poured myself a bit more and heard running water.

Carefully placing the flute on the mirrored tray, I inched closer to the bathroom and gasped. Fuchsia flower petals formed a path to the most stunning bathtub I'd ever seen. White porcelain, clawed feet, and an old-fashioned handheld faucet. But my naked husband floating in the oval tub, his chocolate brown hair curling at the nape of his neck, was like viewing a sculpture at the Louvre.

Andre's lips lifted in the corners. "Care to join me?"

The second serving of champagne had kicked in and my heartbeat doubled. I shimmied out of my mulberry silk pajama pants, didn't bother unbuttoning the top, slipped it over my head, and dipped a toe in the water. Andre held out his hand as I stepped into the deep tub. He positioned me in front of him and twirled the ends of my chestnut, corkscrew curls.

Candlelight danced in the corner, a smoky scent that reminded me of camping in the woods. I exhaled and relaxed into the warm water, making ripples with my right hand. With my left, I stroked the dusting of hair on Andre's thigh, moving upward until he moaned.

"Is there anything you didn't think of honey?" I murmured, turning around slowly. I scooted backward, occupying the little space that was left and closing the gap between us. Andre adjusted his long, muscular legs and dangled one over the edge of the tub.

His sensual smile warmed my core as he moved his eyes from my face to the taut hills on my chest. Andre bit his lower lip. I traced the line of his square jaw with my index finger. I grazed the patch of bristly hair near his chin with my lips and his breath hitched. He eased me onto his lap and the pulsing between my thighs that I hadn't felt in weeks quickened; I slowly stroked his length, feeling it harden in my hands.

"I don't know how much longer I can—"

I covered his mouth with mine and parted his lips with my tongue. Teasing, taunting, until he moaned again. Our desire building between uneven breaths.

"Now, please, I can't—" He entered me, cautiously, unsure. We hadn't been intimate since my mom died. I took all of him into me, gripping his broad shoulders and rocking rhythmically on top of him. He shook inside of me as I groaned louder. His long fingers cupped my mouth, but nothing could mute the sounds coming from my lips. I leaned back a little, moving his hand to the spot that had long been ignored. Again and again, until we couldn't catch our breaths.

He dried me off with a plush towel as we looked at each other, the mirror reflecting an ease I hadn't seen in my eyes lately. I took a hand towel from the glass shelf above the toilet, wiping the water that'd splattered from the bathtub.

"I'm not done with you yet," Andre breathed into my ear. He slipped me into a terrycloth bathrobe, put one on himself, and led me to the fireplace. I guess they did update the place because this was electric. My pulse started to return to normal.

I touched the shriveled skin on the pads of my fingers.

"Oh no! Did we miss our reservation?" I looked at Andre.

"That's what room service is for," he replied, brushing my cheek with the back of his hand.

I couldn't believe it, but the pulsing picked up again. Softer, below my belly, undeniable desire. I untied his robe and let it fall to the floor. This time we savored each other, like two souls reuniting after years apart. Andre trailed tiny kisses from my forehead to the crook in my neck and continued to caress every inch of my bare skin. Then we quieted, our bodies and ourselves, laying bare on the plush carpet. Andre's heartbeat thrummed, slowing, regulating, as he drifted to sleep.

When he started to snore, I began to sob uncontrollably. I pressed the cuffed, thick sleeve of my robe over my mouth. He was right next to me.

Why did I feel so alone?

⸺

Sunlight streamed through a gap between the gold, damask curtains. Stunning but terribly, annoyingly impractical. Dreams fragmented my sleep, a jagged mosaic of disturbing, disruptive snapshots. I couldn't remember the details. Nor did I want to. I liked my room totally dark, and when we'd travel, I usually joined drapes together with a hair clip. These particular ones were posh; I worried I'd damage them. Andre could sleep in a mob with fluorescent lights. The back of my neck damp and my hair disheveled, I stared at the ceiling wondering why I still hadn't dreamt about my mom. Frustrating because I'd read that people who have passed away can visit during dreamtime.

Andre rolled over and faced me, his eyelids heavy and gaze smoldering.

"Morning, gorgeous," he said, yawning audibly. "How'd you sleep?"

"I don't know how to answer that question." I pulled at a loose thread on the quilt.

"*¿Que pasa?*" Andre gently turned my face toward him.

"I honestly haven't slept well in weeks. Weird dreams I can't recall—it's like clips of a horror movie and then the screen goes blank," I said.

He rubbed his eyes and tilted his head. "Were you crying?"

"Maybe," I whispered.

"Did I hurt you last night?" he asked hesitantly.

"No, no honey. Just a flood released that I can't even describe," I said, not wanting to ruin our morning. We had to pack up and drive home soon.

Andre stood and pulled back the curtains. I didn't budge. "Let's not waste the day!" he exclaimed. I wanted to smush the pillow over my face. Begrudgingly, I rolled to my side, stood up, threw clothes into a bag. Then I trudged to the restaurant and tried to enjoy the lavish breakfast.

I slowly spread the homemade jam onto crispy, sourdough bread. Nibbling at the crust, I let the plump blueberries linger, relishing the squishy sensation when they burst. It was the perfect accompaniment to fresh scrambled eggs from the nearby farm and brewed coffee from a local roastery. The waiter even offered to heat my oat milk! I lowered my chin near the steam, giving myself a quick java facial. Then I asked for an extra cup for the road.

CHAPTER 5

On the way back to Burlington, Andre peppered me with questions. Did he seriously think our staycation was a salve for the emptiness I felt inside? I listened, attempting to appear interested, until he went too far.

"Tell me you're kidding. You want us to host a Shabbat dinner next Friday night? And for colleagues?" I snapped. He turned his head and peered at me.

"What's the big deal?" he huffed. "We haven't done this in ages. Plus, I need to close a deal, and this would really help. You're so charming, mi amor."

He exited 1-89 near Williston, not our usual route. I noticed his thumb quivering.

"Where are you going?" I spat through clamped teeth.

"We are stopping by the office. I told you, I've been behind and need to finish a few things," Andre said.

I inhaled deeply and puffed my cheeks with air. Then exhaled slowly, just as Mom had taught me years ago. My husband was so consumed with the lengthy list in his head that he didn't notice. Thankfully, he just needed to pick up a set of plans, and we got back on the road.

We turned into our neighborhood, and I waved to Eliza, our next door neighbor. I admired her dexterity—the woman was amazing. She walked her two massive golden retrievers in one hand and sipped tea with the other. And she'd recently shared that she'd just celebrated her seventy-fifth birthday. Unreal! I asked her when we first moved to Vermont if it was just a lucky gene pool or if she had a potion for longevity.

Eliza smirked and said, "Come a bit closer, Joy." Then she stood, elongating all four foot, ten inches of her lithe body, and whispered one word in my ear: "whiskey."

I wondered why some people, even the unhealthy ones, live until their nineties despite how they choose to live. Others leave suddenly or at an unfairly young age. I guess some questions don't have answers.

I was glad we got back early. I'd admittedly been procrastinating; I had a slew of images to edit. The other project I needed to finish—the family has been so patient. They wanted the pictures for their holiday cards, and I had to hustle. But that would have to wait until the morning. First I'd clear the clutter in my house to make space for creative flow. A messy office made for a stagnant mind, at least for me.

We ordered organic burgers and truffle fries from a local joint. We devoured our food and split a bottle of Pinot Noir from our friend's winery. Then put the leftover lettuce in the garbage disposal. Andre disappeared into his home office, and I needed some downtime to synthesize my sundry emotions.

Joy and sorrow. Gratitude and grief. Elation and exhaustion.

All mixed with a tinge of guilt.

Why couldn't I appreciate my husband's kindness? His unwavering support, always and especially now, kept me going. I opened the bottom drawer, searching for my softest jammies. The ones with the holes near the neckline, frayed from overuse. The ones Andre's parents sent to me last Hanukkah.

I'd forgotten about my backpack that was shoved in the corner near the wool sweaters. My mind became like an old film projector, images suddenly splicing into a reel. I rummaged through the biggest compartment in the bag.

And that's when I saw it.

I eased down onto the wood floor and opened the purple diary. I hadn't noticed the day of the estate sale that it was locked. I examined it, running my fingers over every space. Then I turned it over, shocked to find the tiniest key tucked, almost imperceptibly, into the crease where the pages connected. I gingerly removed it, tearing a tiny piece of paper in the process. Shakily, I inserted the key into the lock, hearing a faint click like when I set my camera to silent mode. I turned each unlined page, captivated by my mom's teenage musings.

My foot tingled and got numb—I guess I'd been so immersed in reading my mom's innermost thoughts that I didn't move. I flipped onto my stomach and continued to read her cursive handwriting, some letters angled and even, others scrawly and smushed.

Talk about traveling through a time capsule. Each entry a doorway into the middle school version of my mother. The time she got her period at a bat mitzvah. A detailed description about her first kiss. The summer she'd stood up to a bully. Pages about toasting marshmallows and sliding them off the stick seconds before they became charred. And notes about her camp counselors—she loved one and the other, well, not so much.

She wrote about her best friend, Ruby, and their instant friendship. Bunkmates, campfires, performances, crushes on boys, swimming in the cold lake, even a pay phone at her camp in Michigan.

Mom journaled nightly; I remember how her eyes crinkled in the corners. She was enthralled with every independent bookshop we'd seek when we traveled as a family. She had half-written in journals scattered throughout my childhood home. I remember joking that she should consider assembling them to create an artful stack.

But I had no idea she'd started documenting her life during summers at Camp Intermezzo. She'd shared stories with me and my brother, Julian, about her summers in Northern Michigan but not in this detail. I read every one of her words, her memories, dehydrated from tears, wanting to quench my grief.

One line, dated July 4th, 1987, halted me:

"I want to own or run a camp one day. Being here is a second home for me and so many friends. Wouldn't it be amazing to work with kids in the summertime? I want to make a difference in their lives."

I read it. Reread it. I tried envisioning my mother as a budding teen, on the cusp of entering young adulthood.

Suddenly I was twelve again, hiding in the corner of the camp recreation room. It was the last night of the session. I'd finally confided in Remi, telling her about my crush. I still remember Mike's kelly-green eyes that dazzled me the second we met at the lake. But I never had the guts to tell him. After spilling the secret to Remi, she loaned me her favorite top and even her sparkly eyeshadow.

She gave me a few lines, which I rehearsed all week, so I didn't freeze and shrink into the comfort of silence.

All of the other girls seemed so confident. The flat-chested ones stuffed their bras with tissues. The busty ones wore plunging necklines. Me? I wanted to stay in the shadows and keep counting the wood rafters above my head.

"Joy! C'mon, the dance is almost over," Remi cooed, nudging me into the light. I inhaled slowly and exhaled through my nose, like my mom taught me to do when I got nervous before a test.

I remember inching closer. Just as I was about to tap Mike's shoulder, Remi swooped in front of me, fluttered her mascara-lacquered lashes at Mike, and threw her arms around his long neck. I turned on my heels, horrified and humiliated. As if being away from my parents didn't already tear at my heart. This torched it. I never went back.

The journal fell from my hands, a short descent to the planks of walnut wood beneath me. I gently closed it, for now. I lay with my head on my arms as an idea brewed. I wondered what Andre would think when I told him about it. I don't know how long I stayed there, but my husband's voice echoing from across the house interrupted my reverie.

"Found the perfect movie for us," he hollered. Our Sunday night tradition, the one where we left our phones by the door and picked a film or television show to watch together.

"I'll be right there," I replied. Sunday "wine downs" were my idea; it encouraged us to connect and be present. Though I didn't feel like budging, I slipped on cozy, thick socks and slogged to the family room. I currently couldn't decide if purchasing the sixty-five-inch television was brilliant or a bad idea. A gift for Andre's fortieth birthday, it'd become his latest obsession. The clarity, color, and contrast it displayed, especially when watching tennis matches or soccer games, made him happy. I preferred those qualities in diamonds.

"What'd you pick, honey?" I asked, sitting on our navy leather couch. I couldn't focus on the screen; my mind wandered, desperately wanting to dive back into my mom's diary.

"Glad it was my turn to choose this week. Just wait and see. You'll love it!" Andre put his arm around me, and I rested my head on his shoulder. He was still in his slacks and button-down shirt. The second I get home, I unhook my bra and other confining contraptions like buttons or snaps. I prefer loose dresses and cozy sweatshirts to skinny jeans and tight turtlenecks.

Andre held the remote like a magic wand, dotted with buttons that I didn't understand how to use. And I had no interest in learning. On and off seemed sufficient.

"Isn't the sound crisp?" He amped up the volume, psyched about the new Bose speakers he'd installed.

I nodded, pretending to give a shit. "Can we start the movie?" I yawned and poured the rest of the Pinot Noir into a stemmed glass.

Andre looked at me sideways.

"You sure you'll be awake after the first five minutes?" He grinned, eyeing the half-full glass.

I laughed. "Well, if this film is as fabulous as you say, it shouldn't be an issue!"

He nodded in agreement and changed the channel to Netflix. Andre had chosen a rom-com. About midway into the movie, I couldn't concentrate, especially after a poignant scene when the lead found out she was pregnant. She was shocked because it was unplanned, and she wasn't married. Andre still held the remote, which I teased him was ridiculous. We paid for subscriptions so there weren't any commercials. I slid it out of his hand.

"Hey! What're you doing?" he protested, dismayed that I had the control. I searched for the one of the only functions that I thought was necessary—the pause button. I took a deep breath and turned my head toward his befuddled face.

"I keep thinking about our weekend and how much it meant to me," I began, bolstered with bravery from the scene we'd just watched. "I've been thinking about something since Mom died." I stopped talking and flattened my bangs with my palm.

"You can tell me anything, mi amor. I kinda wish you'd wait until the movie was over, but this must be important. I've never seen you even touch the remote control," he said, pulling me toward him.

I looked at the deep cleft in his chin and clasped my hands together. I started slowly like a runner training for a marathon. My voice picked up speed as the words tumbled from my mouth.

"I feel like a piece of me is missing since Mom's been gone. Ever since that horrific call, I wake up shaking and sweaty—I can't believe I'll never see her again." My lips quivered. I wasn't sure I could continue.

"She'll always be with you, with us," Andre said, wrapping his arm around my shoulders.

I tried to organize my thoughts, knowing he wanted to finish the movie.

And I unpacked the box where I'd stored six words, the sentence I could no longer contain.

"I want to have a baby," I said unflinchingly.

Andre jerked backward and sprang from the couch. The remote hit the floor, and the cap popped off. Two double-A batteries rolled under the built-in pine cabinet in front of us.

"Are you freaking serious? I can't believe you'd even go there, Joy," Andre sputtered. He stood tall, all six foot, four inches of him vibrating with agitation.

I knew he'd be surprised but I didn't anticipate anger or annoyance. His fiery reaction fueled me with courage. I crossed my arms over my chest and glared at him.

"Honey, I need you to hear me," I tried to take his hand, but he yanked it away. "Please listen for a minute."

He reluctantly obliged but spoke before I did.

"Joy, we agreed years ago we wouldn't have kids," Andre said, struggling to stay calm. He knew I'd shut down—no matter what the topic—if he raised his voice. "Why now? How could you even go there?"

I tugged at my bangs and gnawed on the inside of my cheek.

"That's a fair question. And I'll answer it if you promise not to interrupt me again," I said, my confidence growing the way I hoped my belly would soon. Andre nodded and I placed my hand on his knee.

"I get that you're surprised," I began. "Honestly, I am as well. I've loved our untethered life—traveling around the world, never needing to depend on babysitters or dealing with middle-of-the-night tantrums. I remember even at the estate sale, you commented on my cousin's bratty kid. And I totally agreed—such a little pain in the ass."

Andre flashed a short-lived smile.

"Ever since my mom died, I can't stop thinking about legacy. Hers. Yours. Mine. Ours. And we're not getting any younger," I continued, pausing for a moment and studying his face. "I want to try again."

Andre looked down at his fists. He didn't respond so I kept going.

"Honey, I'm already in my late thirties. Our window is narrowing with every passing day; it's like my womb is murmuring, wanting to grow a little human. We could even name him or her after my mom!" I paused.

Andre opened his mouth and shut it quickly. The upper tips of his ears reddened. He finally looked at me, flecks of yellow blazing like a bonfire in his dark blue eyes.

"Joy, this isn't fair. I can't believe you're even going there. I'll always say yes if it matters to you. But what you're asking is a hard no. We tried and tried. All those rounds of IVF never worked and nearly bankrupted us. Thank goodness our parents helped out. And look what we've built since then!" His pupils dilated.

"I know the past few months have sucked. I miss your mom, too." He looked away and cleared his throat. "But having a baby won't change anything. I don't mean to be harsh—it is what it is," Andre said. I fought the urge to scream.

"I'm painfully aware, Andre. Speaking of change, that's my point. In a gazillion years, did either of us expect to get that call? How can you be so rigid? When we got married, do you remember what the rabbi shared with us? He said our Ketubah that we signed represents universal promises: for better or for worse, in sickness and in health, blah blah. But there's one other thing he said regarding marriage contracts. He cautioned us that the unexpected can, and will, happen. That we must be flexible." I inhaled deeply. "Just like when you're making a deal, there are times we'll need to renegotiate within our own relationship. And that time is now."

His ears deepened from blush to magenta.

"I hear you. I'm trying to, at least. But for fuck's sake, Joy, this is the one conversation we promised we'd never have again. My parents still don't even know the truth!" Andre faltered, his right hand trembling.

I slowly sank into the couch, feeling defeated but not ready to surrender. The cool, leather cushion buckled behind me.

"Andre, I can't and won't let this go. Maybe we need to consider a different way to do this? Adoption? Surrogacy? I mean, since when have we followed the crowd or lived conventionally? I think our family is still stunned that we left Miami to live here," I said.

His breathing slowed a bit. I was hopeful I'd made a breakthrough.

"I love you. I love what we've built here in Vermont. I love our friends, who you always call our chosen family," Andre began, his words wobbling. "I can't believe you're willing to give up our freedom, especially at our age." He spoke as if we were octogenarians. *Spare me the drama.*

"If we've learned anything at all these past few months, it's that we have so much less control over the future than either of us realized." I rubbed my belly, longing to fill the space with a heartbeat, a little being. "I keep thinking, what if something happens to you? Just the thought—" my voice cracked.

Andre wrapped his arms around me. We held each other, not moving for a few minutes. I pushed him away and his expression had shifted like storm clouds passing in the sky.

"Joy, I'm not going anywhere. You know I eat clean and weight train so I can keep kicking your ass at tennis." Andre also reminded me that his grandparents not only survived the Holocaust but lived into their nineties.

I felt a bit better, but my stomach ached, as if my body was already fertile, preparing for a potential baby. I twirled the tiny curl at the nape of my neck.

"Andre, I want a baby. I want to try again. It's like my mom is sending a message right to my womb. I've heard stories from clients about miracle babies. I've also read about new methods, more efficient and easier, to help us conceive. And if we can't after a few months—"

"All the specialists, the mood swings, the lab tests. Every single doctor, even the best ones we saw in New York City, they told us it's impossible." Andre voice lowered to barely a whisper.

"But it's been so long. What if—"

"I am done with this conversation. You promised to never speak of this again; it's not happening. Not now. Not ever. This part of me is broken. I can't fix it. I can't fix me," Andre bellowed, his high cheekbones burning with shame.

I turned away, fisted my palms, and willed my mouth to stay shut like a padlocked door. I stood, stomped up the stairs, and brushed my teeth so vigorously I might've stripped the enamel. We hadn't gone to bed angry at each other since we started dating.

I pretended to be asleep when Andre padded into the room. I heard him murmur "*te amo*" as he tucked himself under the covers.

I wanted to say "I love you, too" but stayed quiet because I didn't trust my mouth to stop there.

Insomnia won tonight. I tossed and turned, feeling empty inside. I brightened the light on my phone and pointed it at the bedside table next to me. I pulled on the tiny, iron knob and reached for my sketchbook. The pages were blank, another failed New Year's resolution. I ran my fingers toward the back of the shallow drawer and found the felt pen.

Carefully climbing out of bed, I walked to the bathroom and sat on the plush bathmat. Then I took off the cap and started to write.

CHAPTER 6 

Dear Mom,

I miss you. It's like a limb was severed from my soul. How could you leave without saying goodbye? And during our favorite season. I wish you could see the colors—they're brighter than ever. Fall usually inspires me. Elevates me. Enthralls me.

It's the one time death is beautiful.

But now it's a reminder that you're gone. Watching the leaves float to the ground as I wail.

And holy shit, I just found your camp journal. (I know you don't like when I swear—can you hear me wherever you are?) I almost donated it with a bunch of books that, honestly, I've never seen you or Dad read. Maybe you got them on a whim at one of those Sunday garage sales? Thank G-d I grabbed it before the truck left the driveway at the estate sale. I'm reading it and trying to imagine your fourteen-year-old voice. Seeing your heart and rainbow doodles, your bubbly handwriting. You never told me that one of your childhood dreams was to run a camp!

Anyway, I'm SO mad at Andre. And mad that I can't tell you about it. You'd be my first call. Do you know I reached for the phone and dialed your number? Dad must've disconnected it already. You'd calm me down, I know it. Livid is an under-statement. Writing to you is the closest I'll get, it seems, right now. I mean, forever?

I remember you journaling and telling your patients how much it helps to release emotions on the page. I hope it helps; I've never felt pain like this before. I promised this would be the year I start drawing again. Of course, it's nearly wintertime and I didn't sketch one thing. So busy taking photos of families and pregnant women.

So, here's my first entry in what will become a journal. I bought it from Mel's friend—you know, the one who has that adorable bookshop on Church Street? The cover is faux leather and forest green with a lake on the front. There are cute cows and baby sheep in the background, too. You'd love it. Shit, here come the tears. Again. And the swear words.

Back to Andre. Frickin' a-hole. Why? I know you'd ask. Remember we agreed years ago that we wouldn't have kids? We love traveling, living our full, fun lives. And besides, with all his little cousins, the nieces/nephews, we figured we can always borrow them and send them back! (Yea, still have my humor. It's harder to find these days but it keeps me going.) And he's trying. I know he is. Took me away to a quaint B & B. Farm-to-table food with cheese and milk from the goats on-site. It's near Middlebury—beyond breathtaking with a canopy of maple trees and tons of hiking trails. We hadn't been there in years; it was renovated and still charming.

If only I could find a way to reconstruct my splintered heart. We stayed in a quaint room and even took a yoga class. I thought about you on the mat during shavasana, visualizing you doing a downward dog in the middle of the kitchen when I was younger.

We really connected in all ways. Big. Time. It got me thinking about what we leave behind, and, who. It's been forever since Andre and I talked about having kids. And I remember you (and our rabbi) telling me how marriage includes a contract between two people. Sometimes it needs to be amended and revisited, right? With that in mind, I told Andre I wanted a baby. Desperately.

Mom, he shut me down. Frustrated. Angry. Explosive. My nervous system can't handle that now. Maybe ever. Weird, too, his hand started shaking along with his voice. I can't remember the last time I heard Andre combust with such intensity. And it hurt me viscerally, like my chest squeezed and it was hard to breathe. He didn't even consider the surrogate or adoption idea! His parents still don't know that he's the reason we can't conceive. You're the only one who knows. Knew. Ugh. How will I ever get used to talking to you in past tense? All of this feels wrong.

I keep thinking about what if I died suddenly. I really thought I'd accepted not having children. After all, the kids and pregnant moms I photograph were always enough. Kids can hold you back in certain ways—I see so many parents struggling. And Andre's built a thriving architectural firm. My little biz is booming, too.

Why doesn't a party of two feel like enough anymore?

CHAPTER 7

The small alarm next to my bed blared like a bear horn in dense woods. It sounded more obnoxious and louder than usual. I rarely hit snooze, but I realized that I did today after seeing the numbers on the clock. My head felt like a massive boulder; lifting it off the pillow required extra effort. I rubbed my eyes, squinting at the rare glimmer of sunlight that projected horizontal lines onto the taupe, cotton duvet.

Damn it. He was working from home today. I didn't want to see Andre until I could process all that happened last night. Just rewinding the words and replaying them annoyed me—who knew anger could be just as effective as espresso? This was one emotion that felt foreign to me.

I donned the fleece leggings and long-sleeve zip up that draped over the chair, smirking because my routine was one of Andre's pet peeves. He couldn't understand why laying out my workout clothes before bed motivated me. He thought clothes belonged in neat, perfectly folded piles, and out of sight. Whatever.

Heading toward the mudroom, my shoulders lowered when I saw that Andre had already started his day. I hoped my mood would lift so I could rearrange my current resting bitch face. I double-laced my sneakers and texted him, "GM. I'm heading out for a run. See you later."

Cold wind whipped through the few leaves that somehow still clung onto branches. I pulled down the wool beanie to cover my ears and bent over, trying to touch my toes. My hamstrings felt taut like a tennis racket strung too tight. I stretched longer than usual—the last thing I needed right now was to pull a muscle.

I started off slowly, passing by the barren birch and maple trees that lined our street. Stick season had officially arrived along with freezing temps. Though we'd lived here for years, I still detested nature's nebulous indecision. It's impossible for humans or animals to prepare for this unpredictable time. I loved when it snowed because it brightened the landscape. This in between—the lush green mountains morphing to a sludgy brown and crunchy leaves becoming soggy—didn't exactly uplift me.

My neighbor recently told me that a trail had been cleared just behind her house and that I could use it whenever I'd like. As I approached her two-story brick home, she raised the shades and smiled. I waved back. She cracked open her front door, dressed in a plush cranberry-colored robe with her newborn on her hip.

"Hey there, Joy! It's good to see you out this way. I hope you and Andre are doing well," she piped as her baby boy sneezed. His tiny rosebud mouth formed into an oval while he yawned.

Her compassion hit me like a punch in the gut—a double doozy between missing my mom and now seeing my neighbor's adorable newborn. Normally, this would've been a lovely morning chat. Today I had to swallow the lump that returned in my throat, clearing it before I spoke.

"We're doing alright, thanks! Have a great day!" I forced myself to find the energy that seemed to have evaporated into the fog, deciding to walk until locating the obscure entrance to the trail. I relied on my phone trails app, briefly wondering how I'd find my way home if it failed.

I heard water trickling and headed in the direction of the serene sound. The path appeared between resplendent evergreen trees interspersed with pines and fir. These trees didn't shed and being enveloped in deep green nourished me. As the trail widened, I spotted a small waterfall and jogged in that direction.

Wishing I'd brought my camera, I watched the water cascade over rocks of all sizes and shapes. Then it journeyed downstream just as a little light gleamed on it. A teeny, partial rainbow appeared and, as I stared in awe, it faded away. I touched the smooth stones next to my feet and slipped a flat, oval one into my pocket.

I continued to explore the trail, the Adirondacks to my left and the river to my right. Thin sheets of ice framed the outer banks of the narrow stream. It seemed quieter than usual—I didn't hear or see many birds. I breathed in deeply, my body joining this pause between seasons: nature's and my own.

Glancing at my watch, I was pleased to see that I'd completed four miles. Less than my norm but not bad given how depleted I felt. Wiping my forehead with the back of my hand, I clicked the key fob and opened the trunk as I approached my home. I loved cruising around in this vehicle—a souped-up Bronco, including the "oh shit" handles if I wanted to go off road. And it had ample storage for my camera equipment. Though some of the native Vermonters I knew thought this was bougie; a truck for them often involved a flatbed in the back.

It was December tomorrow, which I could barely believe, so I suppose it wasn't too early to use the seat warmer. I started the engine, pushed the button, and asked Siri to call my bestie. She answered on the second ring.

"Morning sunshine!" Mel said. I heard dishes clanging and guessed she was cleaning up after bringing her kids to school. Just like Andre, Mel popped out of bed like a groundhog in the spring. She didn't even need an ounce of caffeine.

"Hey *chica.* Just on my way home from a workout. Or, really, a *ralk/wun,*" I laughed. "We must go back to this area one day soon—it is stunning. I'll bring my camera next time."

Mel giggled and I heard her labrador retriever, Bernie, barking in the background.

"You know I don't run. Happy to go for a stroll, though!" she said. "What do I hear in your voice, my friend?"

"Nothing. Just tired from reentering reality and still not sleeping well," I replied, hoping she'd stop there.

"Bullshit. Spill the tea." Mel's pitch rose an octave.

That's the thing about forever friends. They can see beneath the veil and often know us better than we know ourselves. I decided to pass my house and park at a nearby gas station. I had a feeling this wouldn't be a quick chat.

"Is it that obvious?" I muttered. Mel didn't respond, carving space for me to keep talking.

I started to tell her about my intense longing for a baby and how Andre reacted. My neck tensed and my heart pounded as I continued to share. She cut me off.

"How dare he! What a total jerk, Joy! And the timing, too. Oh, sweetheart," Mel said, validating my agitation. "Where are you? Do you want to come over? I'm alone or we can meet at the shop in a few hours."

I sniffed and blotted my eyes with a crumbled napkin.

"You're the sweetest, and I appreciate it. I'll be okay," I said.

"This really stinks. All of it. I'm so sorry. Do you think he'll reconsider?" Mel asked.

We shared nearly everything from the days we dated college boys, to deaths, marriages, and more. This was one of the only secrets I'd ever kept from Mel. Just like Andre's parents, she didn't know that he was infertile. I almost blurted it out but chugged the rest of my water instead.

"He will not. A hard, definitive hell no. And I understand—we agreed no kids and I thought I'd made peace with that decision. But I never expected my mom wouldn't be here. It's like my lens has been forever altered. I can't explain it," I gushed, feeling a bit lighter as the words flowed from my mouth.

"How will my mom live on if we don't start our own family? I even brought up adoption and he vetoed that, too." A fresh flood of frustration surged.

Mel sighed audibly.

"I wish I knew what to say. Nothing feels right about this and it's so much to process. I won't even pretend to imagine how you feel. Just know you are never, ever alone," she said, likely thinking about her own adorable children. I loved being Auntie Joy to Andre's nieces and nephews. And Mel's kids also called me by this endearing term.

Then why did I feel so lonely?

On the way home, I thought about how fortunate I was to have such a loyal friend. "Framily," I called her. I couldn't find my center. The world kept spinning on its axis while my own stalled. I wanted everyone to join my misery, to slam on the brakes, to be in it with me. Carmen called me every single day now, which was thoughtful yet strangely annoying. Even Carlos sent me texts when he didn't before. Neighbors dropped off meals now and then. And my clients were so compassionate, always asking how I was doing.

I had started to assemble an arsenal of answers.

"Taking it one day at a time."

"I'm doing okay."

"You're kind to check in."

I mean, who really wanted to hear the truth? Who wanted to hear that most days I had to stitch myself together with invisible thread? Life must go on, even if my lovely husband didn't want to create a new one, or, even try. I avoided him and went straight into a long, steamy shower.

As I lathered shampoo on my scalp, an idea began to form like photo paper being dipped into developer. By the time I blew-dry my hair, it became clear, and images materialized in my mind. I couldn't wait to tell Andre about it!

"Oh my gosh, honey!" I shrieked, scampering toward his office.

He held up a hand. I didn't want to wait. Adrenaline coursed through me—if he didn't hang up soon, I might need to call Mel and tell her first. I hadn't felt this kind of passion in ages. I paced the perimeter of his office like an impatient stallion locked in its stall.

Andre wrapped up the call and asked me to wait for another fifteen minutes. No chance.

"I have the most amazing idea!" I said, jumping into his lap and blocking his computer screen.

He scooted forward, attempting to get me upright. I refused to move.

"Okay, okay. It's good to see you so excited, mi amor. Tell me," Andre surrendered, putting down his ballpoint pen.

"Did I ever tell you that at the estate sale, just as the truck was about to leave, I took one more look in the boxes?" Andre shook his head.

"I totally forgot that I tossed a few things into my bag. Guess what I found?" I exclaimed.

"No clue. But I bet you're going to tell me," Andre smirked.

"Hell yes, I am. You know Mom journaled for years and taught her patients about mindfulness," I said eagerly. "Well, I had no idea she'd started writing her feelings on paper as a kid!"

"And?" Andre laughed.

"So, get this! I found her sleepaway camp diary from 1987!" I didn't blink. "This is like finding a treasure, a peek into parts of my mom's childhood, her life, I never knew."

He handed me a tissue from the pocket of his khaki pants. Perfectly pressed even after hours of sitting.

"That is incredible," he said, turning back toward his laptop.

Wait until he hears the rest, I thought. *He'll be gobsmacked.*

I planted my feet on the ground and continued to ramble.

"One of her entries stopped me in my tracks," I chattered, my pace increasing. "Andre, it was my mom's dream to run or own a summer camp!"

He huffed, clearly bored or ready to return to his work. I put my hand on his heart and peered at him.

"What if I found a sleepaway camp, a small one hopefully near our house? It's honestly been triggering to keep taking photos of families, especially the ones with pregnant moms. I love children and this could be a new chapter for me and maybe another way to carry on my mom's legacy," I paused to take a breath.

I knew I'd flooded Andre, pelting him with this exhilarating idea. I couldn't recall when I'd last felt so alive, energized, hopeful.

He gritted his teeth and asked, "What do you know about running a business? Besides, I thought you hated sleepaway camp."

Really, that's your response? Thanks for the encouragement, jackass.

"Well, I do have a photography company. I love learning and expanding my knowledge base," I snarked, wiping my sweaty palms on my pants. This wasn't what I expected from my typically supportive husband.

Andre rolled his eyes.

"Fine, whatever, I can see you've already made up your mind," he retorted. "But it has to make fiscal sense. And it's already December.

How do you expect to find a camp, purchase it, and learn about this industry in just six months?"

I twisted my yellow gold wedding band around and around before replying.

"Always Mr. Rational, eh? I see where you're coming from and get it. I keep thinking about my purpose in this lifetime," I said pensively. "It's like I knew you were the one, my *bashert*, my soulmate—without a doubt. Reading my mom's words from decades ago sparked something inside me."

Andre put his hands on my knees and gently squeezed them.

I touched his smooth, freshly shaven cheek, noticing he'd missed a small area, again. "I know you need to get back to work. I'll leave you with this one last thing: I've always believed that what's meant to be will present itself in a seamless, synchronous way. I need you to trust me. If I don't find a camp by, let's say late January, then I'll let it go. Promise."

Something in my gut guided me—I knew the right opportunity would appear at the perfect time. Maybe this is what my mom tried to teach me about listening to inner wisdom and the whispers within ourselves?

CHAPTER 8

WINTER

Dear Mom,

I'm sitting on the cream-colored cushion near the rectangular window and picking at the striped piping. I think it's time to reupholster it. This is where we'd sit, chatting for hours, and it's comforting to nestle into this nook. I miss you more every day.

I have an insanely wild and exciting idea! I couldn't stop thinking about your camp diary. I've read it at least four times. Sorry! I know it was locked, but truthfully, I could've busted it open even without the key. Clearly Andre and I aren't having kids, which I'm still stewing about. But I've gone from a boil to a simmer. I guess that's progress!

After reading about your childhood dream, a seed rooted itself somewhere inside me. Maybe I can create the camp I always wish I'd gone to where kids, no matter who they are or where they're from, feel safe and accepted. I want to purchase a sleep-away camp. I've been feeling uninspired and often sad after photo shoots. I shared this with Andre—he doubted my ability to negotiate and buy a business.

I'm starting to sense messages—maybe from you—in my dreams. I still can't see you, which makes the hole in my chest feel like a grotto of grief. I'm afraid that as time passes, I won't be able to hear your voice anymore. There's a palpable sensa-

tion that appears every time I think or talk about finding a camp. I'm starting to recognize a pattern, though I can't figure out a word for it. You'd describe something similar when meditating, I think.

I still can't believe you are gone. How will I ever get used to my life without you in it? Maybe I never will. I have friends who whine and complain about their parents. One is estranged from her self-absorbed mother. Another person said her father is an egotistical misogynist (her words, not mine!). If they only knew what it'd be like without them, maybe they'd be more accepting or tolerant. Then again, I can't imagine having toxic parents. I know you had to deal with them.

I've read books lately about grief, and it seems you learn to live with it. I'm not sure I agree.

Flurries are floating from the sky—it's the first snowfall. I'm watching with wonder as the flakes accumulate, some sticking to the ground, others disappearing. It's another first for me. The second I saw the weather report, I reached for my cell phone, eager to tell you about winter's arrival. I'd normally FaceTime because I know how much you also adored the snow.

Just breathing hurts, like I have a permanent flu that's taken residence in my lungs. When will the crater in my chest close?

CHAPTER 9

With the sketchbook tucked under my arm, I moseyed to the family room. The snowfall slowed and tiny particles glittered under the full moon's glow. Andre had started a fire and was reading *Architectural Digest*. He looked at me above his wire-rimmed glasses.

"Where've you been?" Andre closed the magazine and placed it on the square ottoman. "We need to meet Mel and Jake soon."

"I keep trying to draw landscapes, you know, my annual New Year's resolution?" I sighed. "Ever since Mom died, I can't get pictures on the page. Words instead of images seem to flow from my mind to my fingers. It's bizarre."

Andre reached for the pad and pen, placing it on the glass table next to him. Then he pulled me down beside him, and I put my head on his chest, listening to his heartbeat quicken as I pressed into him. I felt other parts grow firmer against my forearm.

"I need to say something," Andre murmured.

"Your body's already talking to me," I replied, my fingers fumbling with his belt buckle. He sucked air through his teeth.

"I am sorry. I want you to go for it, the camp, your dream, all of it," Andre said.

"That means the world to me. Now can we—"

He took my hand and led me toward the fireplace. I loved watching the wood burn, glimpsing hues of cobalt blue and tangerine as logs ignited. Andre tapped his phone and swooped me into his arms. One of his favorite Latin singers crooned from the surround sound speakers. We swayed to the Cumbia song, his palm pressing firmly into my back, my arms wrapped around his tanned neck. Andre drew circles with his hips as we glided across the family room. His agility on the tennis court or a makeshift dance floor made my body tingle.

"We may be late," I said huskily. "Should I call them?" I moved to his mouth, teasing his lower lip with the tip of my tongue.

He lowered the music and lowered me to the cowhide rug below us. Andre kissed the back of my ears, the crook in my neck, the inside of my wrists—all the places that ignited my insides. The fire crackled next to us, warming the room as heat blazed between our bodies.

"Holy shit, honey!" I purred, raking my fingers through his tousled hair.

"I mean, right? Damn, we've still got it." Andre gasped, lying naked and flat on his back.

This time I didn't cry. After climaxing three times, I felt relaxed and more connected to Andre than I had in a while.

We showered quickly, threw on our Patagonia puffer jackets, and headed to the bar.

"Hey! We're over here!" Jake waved from the back corner. As we got closer, I noticed two other couples at the high top. I was not up for socializing with new people.

Mel shot me a knowing look. I blushed like a teenager busted.

"Thanks for joining us!" She giggled, popping a handful of buttery popcorn in her mouth. I winked at her.

Jake introduced us to his friends, and I forced myself to engage. Everything took more effort these days, especially small talk with random folks. I was disappointed because we hadn't been out, just the four of us, in a while. After an hour, I started contemplating various excuses for why we needed to leave.

Andre wasn't reading the room—he was busy devouring a juicy burger. The others smacked their lips after eating barbecue chicken wings. One guy licked his fingers, which I found utterly disgusting. His girlfriend repeatedly remarked that the buffalo ones were too spicy while wiping her drippy nose. A family of five next to us were all on their phones—two preteens and a newborn in a car seat.

Why do people even have kids if they're going to ignore them? Didn't they realize how lucky they are? And who the hell brings a baby to a bar, in the winter, no less?

Mel saw my expression and suggested we go to the bathroom.

"You've had it, ya?" she said as we both reapplied lip balm.

"Is it that obvious?" I snorted.

"Just to me. I told Jake you might not be ready for mingling. He didn't listen—he thought it would be a good distraction. I should've pushed back harder," Mel said, putting her head on my shoulder. "But it sure looked like you had an appetizer before coming here!"

My cheeks flushed.

"Sometimes I wish you didn't know me so well," I laughed. "I will say make-up sex mixed with grief can really—"

"Okay, my friend, TMI. You can stop right there." Mel chortled, holding up her palm. "Let's tell them you have a migraine."

"Genius. You're the best," I said, wrapping a paper towel around the wrought iron handle and opening the door.

We said goodbye without much pushback. I mouthed "thank you" to Mel and exchanged pleasantries with the two couples. Besides, Jake and his buddies were on their third round of Zero Gravity beer. Andre stopped at one, as always, in control. We'd drink in college, but even then, he'd make sure to hydrate before, during, and after a night of partying.

Andre's zippy sports car was fun, but I preferred driving my truck in the winter. Thankfully, the roads were clear, and the snow had stopped. On the way home, I thought about the day we'd met. Growing up in Miami didn't prepare me for glacial temps. I remember overheating in my morning classes from overzealous layering, clearly needing a crash course in winter attire. I was a sweaty mess when I slid into my seat freshman year at Middlebury College.

We'd both declared our majors—mine was graphic design and his architecture. We had required classes together, one of which was Sketching and Drawing 101. I sat in the back, a bit quieter then. In new environments, I tended to listen more than talk. I guess it was from the days in elementary school when I was bullied. My mom brought me to several speech therapists; I had the toughest time saying the letter "r" at the beginning of words. By middle school, I told her I was done. That's when I fell in love with swimming and photography, spaces in which I could express myself without being teased.

The first assignment in this prerequisite class was to sketch a partial nude! I was horrified. I slunk into my seat, hoping it would transform into a tent that'd cover me. Since nobody raised their hands, the professor decided to pair students.

I heard "Andre and Joy" and missed the rest of the assignment. I flipped through the syllabus, scanning the page to figure out the last day I could drop a class. Shit. I'd missed the deadline by a week!

A large hand looking like it belonged to a professional basketball player pressed onto the middle of my desk. Mustard, nubuck laced-up Timberland boots positioned themselves in front of me, hip width apart. I looked up and stared into the most striking blue eyes I'd ever seen. And I lost all capacity for speech. I thought my neck would snap so I stood, dwarfed by this sculpted, sensuous student.

"Hi, I'm Andre. I guess we're partners?" He stuck out that gargantuan hand and shook my small clammy one.

"Um, yeah, so it seems," I managed, hoping my shaky voice wouldn't betray me.

"Please give me your phone number. Joy, right?"

He's hot, polite, and direct. OH G-d.

Andre texted me that night and we met for coffee the next day. I still remember his meticulous order—a double shot of espresso with a side of 2 percent steamed milk and a teaspoon of cinnamon. I had a cappuccino. He seemed totally comfortable in his own skin, which I discovered during our first sketching session when he swiftly undressed and tossed his shirt on the floor. I'd emailed the professor stating that in no uncertain terms would I be baring my skin to a stranger or anyone for that matter. He understood and made it a one-way assignment.

Andre, after years of swimming and being a goalie on his soccer team, had no problem being seen—with or without clothes. That was all I needed to see, and it didn't take much longer to discover the rest. We have been together ever since.

"Mi amor, what are you thinking about?" Andre pulled into our driveway and put the gear in park.

"How we met. Just visualizing that moment you peeled off your shirt, like it was no biggie. I thought I'd faint!"

"Oh, I remember that well." Andre laughed and fiddled with the keys. I watched his right hand and pointed my phone light at it. He couldn't seem to unlock the front door. I tried to help but he shooed me away. Stubborn, determined, and usually coordinated. He muttered something about WD40 because clearly rust needed to be removed. We went through the garage instead. I let it go, for now.

Raising the blinds in my bedroom the next morning, I stared at the speckles of glittery snow adorning the pines like fairy lights.

"Andre! Did you look outside, honey?" I shrieked.

"I've been up since 5 a.m. and just got back from my workout," he answered. "I made you a *café con leche*." I slipped my feet into slippers and joined him in the kitchen.

Tightening the tie on my mid-calf, silk robe, I tucked my legs under me and sipped the milky liquid. I loved that Andre had designed our home. The vast, rectangular windows showcased four acres of mostly deciduous trees, though now barren, that looked like stick figures standing proudly in front of the Adirondacks. These days could be illusory—subzero temps yet brightened with layers of pearly snow that glimmered intermittently, as if sensing it might melt at any moment.

Just like autumn, when leaves changed from greens and browns to plums and golds as they died, winter knew her time was ephemeral. I thought about snowflakes, each one on its own journey, falling and not knowing where it would land or how long it would be here.

"I'll be right back," I said, putting the handcrafted azure cup and saucer in the sink. I unzipped my messenger bag and found my old Pentax camera from college. Then I grabbed a cashmere scarf, wrapped it around my neck, put on waterproof boots, and slid open the glass door. What I didn't sketch, I'd capture on film. Looking through the viewfinder forced me to be present—with nature and with myself. My form of active meditation.

I dawdled in the backyard, tromping in the six inches of snow. A whoosh of wind stirred up snowflakes that dusted the cement as if a phantom ballerina pirouetted across it. The tips of my fingers reminded me about the frigid temperature. I wiggled my toes, but they refused to move, numb and not so happy. Putting on socks before stepping outside might've been a smart idea. I stomped on the rubber doormat to clean off my boots. Then I tugged them off and felt a tingly sensation in my calves.

"Are you bonkers, babe?" Andre said. "My gosh, you ran out there barely dressed—it's freezing today."

I grinned. "True. But I didn't want to miss the light—who knows how long it'll last." *Who knows how long any of us will*, I mused.

"What time do you finish today? I'll stop by the store on the way home and make *arepas* tonight. And we need to figure out the party details. Let's discuss over dinner," Andre said. Ever since the pandemic, he'd worked a hybrid schedule but still rented a modest office in town to meet with clients. While much of Andre's work was online, he preferred face-to-face meetings, insistent that Zoom couldn't replace in-person connection. The younger architects who worked for him felt otherwise.

"Thank you so much, sweetie. I have a long day ahead of me— this is a huge help," I said. He came home later that night with a bouquet of jewel-toned tulips, one of my favorite flowers. We chatted about our annual Hanukkah party, which normally would excite me. Why did my heart feel like an apple going through a juicer, squeezed and liquified?

I tried to focus on what Andre was saying while he meticulously chopped onions. It looked like a symmetrical smorgasbord of veggies—the peppers rectangular, the onions square, and the chicken pieces oblong. I couldn't even draw a straight line with a ruler; I barely made it through geometry.

"The little ones love making latkes, so let's make sure we get extra potatoes. I had an idea! What if we created a donut bar in the basement like an ice cream store? We could have a contest, and someone can win for most creative and other categories—they'd get extra chocolate gelt," Andre said in a low voice.

"I didn't hear that last part?" I said.

He repeated it. "I was also thinking it would be hilarious if we played a dreidel drinking game."

"Ha! That is brilliant! I love it," I snorted.

He nodded, jotting notes on the mini yellow legal pad next to the cutting board. "Glad you're looking forward to seeing the family."

I mean, not really, but I was excited to see my nieces and nephews.

Another week of taking photos of newborns, expectant mothers, and family portraits. I loved the solitude and serenity of the winter season. I preferred shooting outdoors, but the inclement, unpredictable weather necessitated going inside. So, I rented a studio space from Laurel, a local potter. I enjoyed being in the vicinity of another artist; when we had downtime, we'd banter and brainstorm ideas.

A couple, who'd been married for five years, had just heard back from an adoption agency. They scheduled a shoot to document the news that they'd finally be parents. We discussed possible settings and props.

"I've never had a client suggest this type of photo sesh," I said, smiling at the thirty-something couple sitting across from me. Their eyes met, and I saw Gabe—the one with the closely cropped beard—take his partner Eric's hand.

Their eyes shimmered as they both started to speak.

"It's felt like forever since we've been—" Gabe began, his voice cracking with emotion.

"We never thought this would happen for us. It's a dream come true!" Eric continued.

I asked them to share more about themselves and explained how my hope was that I'd be able to portray this moment, their journey, their story. They finished each other's sentences. Gabe made gestures that accompanied his tenor voice while Eric's lower timbre filled in the backstory of how they met. My mind wandered momentarily, again wishing that Andre would consider adoption.

We spent the entire afternoon together. They brought six outfits, all of which represented different phases of their lives. Just before dusk, we ventured outside near Lake Champlain. Eric explained this was the place where they'd first encountered each other, lovingly debating who first approached the other one. Low clouds mixed with a partial sunset provided filtered lighting—a photographer's dream backdrop and a lucky moment, especially in December.

Ice frosted the dense, steel water like the base layer of icing on a birthday cake. I loved witnessing Gabe's and Eric's excitement, their warmth a stark contrast to the bitter winds they didn't seem to notice. I shivered despite my heavy, floor-length coat. Both men wore powder blue turtlenecks, crew neck cashmere sweaters, and luxurious scarves—one cream and the other cerulean.

I couldn't wait to see these photos! As I packed up my equipment, I listened to them prattle. Their speech became unintelligible murmurs that melded and unified to form an ethereal connection that transcended words. In many ways, it was similar to how Andre and I spoke to each other.

On the way home, the pebble bobbled back up. It hadn't visited in nearly a week—the longest since my mom died. I was content, dare I say even happy, a few hours earlier. I tried clearing my throat. I swallowed hard. But the stone of sorrow wouldn't budge. Work only temporarily dulled the pain and distracted me from the constant ache of missing my mom.

I felt deflated, as if I'd filled myself with emotional helium that only lasted so long. Today a new feeling, one I rarely experienced, had poked at me like a pesky gnat. *Maybe this was how jealousy felt?*

I shuddered, not recognizing myself, and wondered if I ever would feel normal again.

CHAPTER 10 

Jubilant squeals joined the repeated ringing of the doorbell. Despite our solid, thick front door, I heard our nieces and nephews before opening it.

"Auntie Joy!"

"Uncle Andre!"

Hat-covered heads huddled together like a football team before a game.

"Natalia—take off your coat!" My sister-in-law shouted.

"*Tranquilos por favor*," Andre said while he picked up one kid and lifted him onto his broad shoulders. The others ignored him, plowing past their uncle like linebackers. What do you expect after a long travel day from young Floridians seeing snow for the first time?

I did appreciate Andre's brother running interference and making sure all children entered our home without shoes. The clean freak gene, thankfully, was inherited by nearly all of Andre's siblings. Usually, we'd go to Carmen and Carlos' house. I'd asked the family to gather in Vermont this year; I couldn't stomach going back to Miami.

"Mija, how lovely you look!" Carmen hugged me tightly. I felt a light squeeze on my upper arm, which I recognized immediately. Carlos exuded a quiet strength; he knew after forty years of marriage that getting in a sentence between Carmen's exuberant paragraphs could be challenging. I glanced at him and grinned. In return, he winked before strolling over to his son.

"Andre, need any help grating those potatoes?" Carlos asked.

"*¡No es necesario, papi, pero gracias!*" Andre replied. "It's all done." I heard him tell Carlos about the donut bar surprise. The kids had scurried to the basement, which was like a wonder-filled cave of board games and bean bags. We locked up the liquor, not that the children would even be interested—yet. The eldest had just turned fourteen, but I wasn't taking any chances. Not everyone could make it, so choosing beds didn't require the usual pick-a-number-from-the-mason-jar scenario. I could hear squeals and screeches from up here.

A warm hand covered mine.

"It's so good to see you, Carmen. Thank you for trekking north. I know it's not easy with Carlos's back pain." I smiled at my mother-in-law. She had a dimple on her rosy left cheek, just like Andre, and it deepened as her smile widened.

"I worry about you," she said as she studied me with a mixture of love and pity.

"I'm fine, really!" My pitch escalated.

"Let's sit down and catch up." Carmen repositioned her Louis Vuitton tote on her shoulder. I didn't miss the showy, branded fashion of South Florida. Carmen still thought that's why we moved up here, to escape the glitz and grandiose lifestyle in Miami. She searched through her bag and withdrew a small box wrapped in shimmery, silver paper. Carmen insisted I read the card first.

Dearest Joy,

You're mi hija, my daughter, as I said the day we met. I thought of you the second I saw this and hope you feel our love from across the miles. Happy Hanukkah to the woman who brings such light to our entire family.

Con mucho cariño,
Carmen and Carlos

A tear dropped onto the card and spread across the little hand-drawn heart.

"Oh Carmen!" I exclaimed, throwing my arms around her petite body. "May I open the ridiculously unnecessary gift?"

She nodded eagerly.

I slowly untied the shiny satin bow. Then I smiled, thinking about my uncle Jack who always said, "Save the paper!" The wrapping itself was so stunning that I hesitated before removing the tape, not wanting to disassemble its beauty.

As I gingerly lifted the top off the box, my breath hitched. A dainty, elegant gold heart nestled in the box like a baby bird napping in a nest. I touched it with my finger and noticed the tiniest hinge I'd ever seen.

It was a locket. I couldn't meet my sweet mother-in-law's eyes. But she knew me too well.

"I didn't mean to upset you." Carmen took my hands in hers. I still didn't look up, fixing my gaze on the stunning piece. "I saw this in a boutique in Miami Beach and immediately thought of you. I hoped it would bring you joy; maybe you could put a photo of you and your mom in it."

That's all I needed to hear. A downpour streamed from my eyes and nose. *What the hell is wrong with me? I'm the luckiest woman in the world!* Carmen, thank goodness, didn't call me her hija—daughter—this time. In fact, she said nothing, patiently waiting while I centered myself. Then she lifted my chin to look at her.

"Maybe, in time, this helps mend your heart? When my mother died, wearing her precious jewels made me feel less alone," Carmen said, with her singsong cadence, as if she were speaking in Spanish. "I love you and understand if you don't want this around your neck yet."

She handed me a tissue with a smidgen of coral lipstick in the corner. I blotted my eyes with the unused part and blew my nose. Then I rested my head on her shoulder. We sat like that until the kids bounded up the stairs.

Just before the youngest nearly nose-dived into the antique armoire, Carmen whispered in my ear, "One day, you and Andre will have a house full of *niños*—Carlos and I can't wait!"

I inhaled deeply, thankful she couldn't see my flushed cheeks and ruddy neck.

"It's dinner time!" Andre hollered from the kitchen. I admired my stunning husband, who I found especially sexy right now with his tousled hair, rolled up sleeves, and a dishtowel slung over his shoulder. Too bad the family was there, but thank goodness none of them were clairvoyant—the thoughts in my head were definitely not PG.

The kids gobbled up Andre's brisket, chicken wings, and *patacones*. We had a nontraditional meal, a Colombian-infused Hanukkah buffet. We always made sure to include fried food, which represented the miracle of this holiday. The oil that was supposed to last one day lasted eight according to the Maccabee story.

Our youngest nephew missed his latke and a heaping spoonful of my homemade applesauce landed on the needlepoint instead of his plate.

"Pablito! Please be more careful—that rug cost a fortune," Andre grumbled, returning to the table with stain remover and a roll of paper towels. I noticed his index finger shaking slightly before he squeezed the spray bottle. Liquid dribbled from the plastic opening. Frustrated and irritated, Andre gave up and removed the top before soaking the stain. I looked toward the head of the table and saw Carlos staring at me, his amber eyes asking silent questions.

"Let me help, sweetie. I've got this. Go sit down," I said and started to collect the dirty plates and utensils. I was glad I'd won this debate regarding fancy china versus festive paper. I loved these kiddos, but they made a mess.

"Natalia, Joseph, Pablo, Tamara! Get up and help your Aunt Joy, please," Alejandro said. I mouthed "gracias" to Andre's brother while the quartet of kids sprang into action. They ranged in age from six to fourteen. I admired how kind and polite they all were. I knew this sadly wasn't the norm these days. Many families I'd photographed were distracted by checking their texts, scrolling on social media, and posting live updates; I often had to encourage them to detach from their devices. Recently, I had included a fine print line about leaving electronics in the car or on silent in my pre-photo prep material. Capturing the nuances of human emotions seemed increasingly more difficult.

The kids played hide-and-go-seek, respecting that our bedroom was off-limits. Joseph, the eldest, made sure to monitor his younger cousins' moves. The little one, Natalia, tended to wander. I always thought she'd love living here in Burlington. I mentioned this once to Andre, that maybe each child could take turns staying with us. We'd have a blast taking them skiing, to Jay Peak's indoor water park, or simply exploring the trails. He grimaced and said something about it being a fun idea but also remarked "what a handful that would be."

I removed my external flash and took a few pics of the adults connecting. I adored these moments—nobody noticed, people didn't pose, and I relished capturing the presence. Glancing at the Dali-esque, oval clock, I saw the time and put down my camera. We used to give all the kids gifts. But a few years ago, I decided they didn't need more material possessions. We asked each child to identify a charity that interested them, and we donated checks in their names instead.

"Everyone please come to the basement. Uncle Andre and I have a surprise for you all!" I yelled, cupping my hands around the sides of my mouth.

The kids dashed past me and skipped down the stairs. I'm glad we decided to put a rug over the wood. I envisioned broken bones if they slipped! Andre didn't think the aesthetic worked with the rest of our home, but I insisted. Besides, it also provided a soft landing for any of our friends who over-imbibed and had to stagger up the stairs.

We tried to make *sufganiyot* before the family arrived, dropping balls of dough into a deep pot of oil. The pungent smell irritated Andre—I didn't disagree. Plus, I found another splatter on our formerly pristine ceiling. Our local bakery had delicious donuts, so we ordered a few dozen. We put a few of the apple cider ones aside, knowing it was Carmen's favorite flavor and a Vermont classic.

Andre had precisely lined up blue and silver bowls on the blanched, oak bar. He wisely put a plastic, sapphire tablecloth on top of it before arranging the festive smorgasbord. The kids already spotted the jelly donuts, gesticulating impatiently and wondering why they had to wait. I asked them to sit down in a semi-circle.

"Uncle Andre and I thought it would be fun to have a donut decorating contest! Adults versus kids. And then we can have our dance party, okay?"

They bleated like baby goats looking to munch on a mound of hay. I laughed and held up my hand.

"I guess that's a yes?" Natalia gripped my lower legs with her small, chubby hands.

We had to light the menorah, which had been in a box for months along with a hodgepodge of mementos my mom had accumulated. The lid of the lilac container was bulging and about to pop off at any moment. I removed the top as a flood of memories nearly knocked me over.

"Auntie Joy, are you okay?" Pablo asked as he tugged on my arm, looking at me with wide, worried eyes.

"Yes, sweetheart. I just haven't seen this stuff in a long time," I lied, grateful for the hum of conversations. I noticed a crack in the back corner of the container. My mom, organized and sentimental, had written dates on masking tape that stuck to the top of each Ziplock baggie. A curated box that spanned decades. She'd always said, "I'll keep this or that for when you have kids, Joy."

I wiped the corner of my eye. There'd be time to go through this storage box and all the others another day. Right now, I needed to get the menorah, the one we'd used for generations. And I needed to get through the remainder of the night. It rested on its side just below my preschool projects near a barely discernible piece of canary yellow construction paper with what looked like a sketch of latkes. I grabbed the bag filled with primary colored, plastic dreidels and gave it to my nieces and nephews.

Touching the bubble wrap that hugged the *hanukkiah*, I remembered how my great grandmother would always correct us. "My *shayna punim,* a menorah has seven candles. For Chanukah (there are tons of ways to spell this word—she preferred this one), we use nine. The tallest one, the *shamash*, is the helper candle that lights all the others."

I could still hear her soulful, Polish accent. She'd become part of my inner tapestry, threads of love and lessons woven within me. I worried I might not be able to remember my mom's voice. I shook my head like a puppy after a bath, trying to shake off these thoughts.

"Aunt Joy, what's that in the back?"

Pablo's pubescent pitch pulled me back to the present.

"What are you pointing to, sweetie?" I cleared my throat and turned to face him.

"This!" He reached forward and scooped up a mesh bag.

I grinned. "That's Hanukkah gelt—it may be a decade old."

"Yummy. Chocolate always tastes good!"

The kid had a point. I told him to go find his cousins and share the goodies with them. I grabbed a stout crystal glass and lightly tapped on it with a knife.

"Time to light the menorah!" I exclaimed. The kids barreled toward me from the game room on the other side of the basement. Andre and the other adults kept yapping. Smart little ones: They knew after the candles were lit, it would be time to decorate donuts and then devour them.

Striking a match, I loudly called Andre's name. "C'mon, honey. We are ready. Please come here," I said, getting irritated that the children seemed to listen more than their parents and grandparents.

We'd spent the first part of Hanukkah alone, deliberating having friends over, but I wasn't ready yet. I already drew from my emotional reserves to prepare for tonight. After sundown on the first night, my creative and clever husband thought it would be fun to use our fireplace to light the menorah. Good thing we had an extinguisher nearby—he nearly lit the entire family room on fire! Tonight marked the seventh night of the holiday. And it worked out well because each child was able to light their own candle. As they did, we asked that he or she shared the charity of their choice and why they chose it. We lowered the overhead lights before we began the prayer.

"*Baruch, atah adonai. Eloheinu melech ha'olam.*" This was my favorite holiday. As the candles flickered, they cast tall shadows on the painted backsplash of the bar, mirroring the generations who gathered around the hanukkiah. Natalia sneezed right onto the shamash when it was my turn. I withdrew another match, watching the tiny, white wick ignite.

Andre rubbed my neck, and I rested the back of my head on his chest. *She's missing another holiday, another first without her.* I excused myself to use the restroom, splashed freezing water on my face, then walked into the kitchen.

"I forgot about one topping—I'm in the pantry!" I yelled, responding to Carmen's question. I examined each shelf, pondering what could be an appropriate addition to Andre's already plentiful buffet. Pickles? Ew. Olives. Yuck. Black beans? Gross. I moved the cans that my hubby had arranged like a line of Rockettes. Ah! I finally found an unopened tube of vanilla icing and ambled to the basement.

Sprinkles were scattered all over the tablecloth, syrup dripped down the side of the bar, and I heard Andre swear under his breath. I quickly moved closer, reminding him that little ones were nearby.

"Shit, you heard me?" he muttered, raising an eyebrow.

"Yup. Maybe we should've put carpet down here. It would absorb the sound better," I replied.

"But then it would be harder to clean after parties." He gripped the horizontal handle of the wine opener and twisted it. We loved collecting and opening bottles for special occasions. I joked it'd be helpful to read the corks we saved to spark our memories if we were all senile one day.

Andre and his brothers preferred beer or cider, both of which we usually had in the house from local distilleries. Andre also had an affinity for Whistle Pig whiskey and Barr Hill gin. Our bar was fully stocked, always. He finally uncorked the Cabernet Sauvignon. Andre took out two glasses, the handblown ones from Simon Pearce, and placed them next to the ceramic sink. He tilted the bottle and liquid grapes landed onto the countertop instead of in the goblet.

Though the lights were dim, I saw Andre's face flush with frustration. I touched his arm, and he withdrew it as if I'd zapped him.

"Let go of me!" he barked. *What the hell?* His shaky hand smacked the goblet and glass shattered to the floor.

Carlos briskly strode toward us, our eyes meeting.

"Are you both okay?" he asked, squatting to pick up shards.

"Yes. Go back to your grandkids—I've got this," Andre said as he continued to sweep the broken pieces into a metal dustpan.

Carlos didn't believe it, clearly. His bushy, salt-and-pepper brows drew closer as though they were having a concerned conversation. He also knew that his eldest son was proud and stubborn as hell. So, my father-in-law walked away.

I didn't back down.

"Andre, what is going on?" I stared up at him, not blinking until he responded.

"Nothing, Joy. It was an accident. As if you've never dropped a glass before. Let it go. Please." He grunted.

I'd zip it, for now.

———

I heard the kids giggling behind me. I spun on my heels to face them, amused by their innocence and enthusiasm. And I wondered what prompted the peals of laughter.

Natalia's chin was covered in milk chocolate. Pablo held a handful of maple leaf candies he'd pilfered from the heart-shaped dish on the end table. Joseph caught me gaping at him and smirked. Joseph and Tamara stood close together, the teenagers, and they exchanged sheepish glances as I edged closer.

My mouth nearly dislocated when I saw what Joseph held in his hands.

"Ummmm, you two," I started, trying to regain my composure. I bit the inside of my cheeks and remembered how my mom would get quiet, which encouraged my brother and me to confess.

Joseph coughed. Natalia blushed. I stood there staring at them.

"Don't be mad at us, Auntie Joy!" Natalia began, her words rushing out of her mouth like rapids over rocks.

"It's not our fault," Joseph added. He tried to tuck the item under his oversized sweatshirt.

"Where did you find it?" I wiped the moisture on my upper lip. I heard hilarity on the other side of the room, a clear indicator that the parents were plastered.

"In the closet," they shrilled in unison before breaking into a fit of laughter. Were they messing with their Auntie?

I took a deep, calming breath.

"Let me have it please," I uttered, hoping my staccato speech sounded confident. "What on earth—" My eyes widened, and I tilted my head.

Natalia brought her dainty finger to her lips. I started to sweat profusely.

"Great Aunt Allegra must've been wild back in the day," Natalia rambled. I rubbed my hands on my jeans, trying to be patient.

Joseph nodded as his cousin continued.

"Joey was looking for paper towels to clean up a spill. He tripped over this box—" said Natalia, covering her face to stifle a laugh.

"Good thing I have fast reflexes—I grabbed it before Pablo or Tammy could open it." Joseph cracked his knuckles and smirked. I gave him a thumbs-up and mouthed "crisis averted." Then I turned around, opened the box, and suppressed a smile.

Scrawled on a tiny piece of unlined paper was an inscription:

Happy Hanukkah to the woman who lights up my life and all of me.

Let's play this tonight!

Love you forever,
Benito

Well, well, well Mom. A dirty dreidel game? And that note from Dad!

Maybe it wasn't the worst thing that parenting wouldn't be in my future.

CHAPTER 11

love when two light-filled holidays overlap; today was Chrismukkah. I'd even convinced Andre to get a Hanukkah bush. We had put it away for the party because Carmen and Carlos would have been horrified. I decorated the tree with tinsel, blue ornaments, and topped it off with a Star of David. I turned on the tiny lights that we'd strung around the room, and we headed out for night skiing at Bolton Valley.

Andre, my ever-romantic hubby, brought hot chocolate, mini marshmallows, and caramel popcorn. He surprised me with gorgeous new gloves and the Canada Goose ski jacket I'd wanted but was too frugal to get for myself. I thought about our one-year date-a-versary—when we'd skied a double black together; his first and my last. I preferred to stick to blues now, especially in the dark.

We snagged the last spot in the parking lot. I'd purchased the ski lift tickets in advance, which allowed us to avoid the long lines of college students. I started to wonder if we were too old for this adventure.

As if reading my thoughts, Andre asked, "Is it just me or does it feel like we're the chaperones?"

"Totally. Sometimes I forget our age!" I snorted and playfully swatted at his *tuchus*. He intercepted my hand and brought it to his lips, kissing each frozen fingertip.

"*Cuidado* mi amor," he teased.

"Oh, I'll be careful—you know I'm a cautious skier."

His smile widened and he winked.

"You know that's not what I mean." Even years later, Andre evoked tingly sensations in me in all the right places. My mind started to drift somewhere else, and I almost missed the chairlift. Andre's arm linked into mine as he guided me toward the seat.

"We're not even up the mountain and you almost landed on your ass!" he said, laughing.

"Well stop with your suave, sexy innuendos, mister!" I retorted as the bar lowered, and I grabbed it with my gloved hands. As we ascended, our legs swung in sync like two kids on a playground swing. Twinkly, festive lights illuminated the top of the mountain. A jovial Santa Claus sped by on a sled. We passed a group of twenty-something girls who looked like pledges; they all wore their hair in braids and the same magenta scarves with matching dove-colored coats. University of Vermont was nearby, but I didn't think they had a big sorority scene. I mentioned it to Andre, who enlightened me.

"I don't think they're pledges—it's the end of the semester," he said. "But it is interesting that they look like sextuplets!" And with that, we took off down the mountain, leaning left and right, digging our skis into the icy moguls. I was grateful we did four runs in an hour. We'd downloaded an app that provided updates so we could maximize our time on the slopes. I loved my new jacket and thanked Andre again.

"Honey, I'm starting to lose steam. I think this'll be my last one." I sighed, not wanting to disappoint my husband. Hosting the family party had depleted me. "I thought that two-hour nap would keep me going."

Andre wrapped his arm around my waist and pulled me close to his side.

"No worries. I understand. This mountain isn't going anywhere," he replied. I still couldn't decipher natural snow from the manufactured kind. The serious skiers spoke about "powder" versus the other stuff. For me, it was all the same.

We made arcs, going back and forth, a synchronized duo. Suddenly, Andre's ski got stuck, and he tumbled forward, somersaulting downhill, and he couldn't stop the fall. I dug my poles into the ice, propelling myself faster.

I swung around to face Andre, reaching out my hand to help hoist him up. He ignored me and struggled to take off his skies.

"Please, let me help you," I pleaded. The group of college girls we'd seen earlier zoomed past us and snow blanketed Andre's face like baby powder. I couldn't see his expression but heard him huff.

"I've been skiing forever. I've got it," he said curtly. *You do not, actually.* I wondered how long he'll torture himself. Not one to give up easily, Andre kept fussing with the steel lock until the ski released. Without a word, he shoved the skis under his arm and stomped toward the resort. We ordered two decaf coffees to go.

We didn't speak on the ride home. I pressed my lips tightly together and closed my eyes, claiming I was exhausted. After luxuriating in a steamy shower and lathering my legs with lotion, I buried myself in our bed and pretended to fall asleep. Andre was snoring within minutes.

The baseboard heating banged like an MRI machine. After hours of tossing and turning, I threw off the covers. I changed into a T-shirt and sweats, then I tiptoed to Andre's office. I cursed his latest find: a unique but useless antique, bronze lamp. I couldn't understand how he created in this space with such dim lighting. After pushing the button on the computer, I pulled back the double-lined curtains. The moon beamed behind me, casting a glow across the room.

Then I did the absolute worst thing—I consulted with Dr. Internet. Not exactly a cure for insomnia. I brightened the screen and increased the font size, rubbing my eyes that were perpetually dry this time of year. As the sun eclipsed the moon, rising and reaching over the mountain, I quivered and closed the computer with more questions instead of answers.

"*¿Dónde está?*" Andre boomed from the bedroom.

"I couldn't sleep, sweetie. I'm making breakfast!" I replied, hoping my puffy eyelids would deflate before he joined me. I downed two shots of espresso while whisking the eggs in a metal bowl. I'd told Andre we should get our own chickens; I'd just heard about a place that rented them. Only in Vermont and one of the gazillion reasons I loved living here. Laughing to myself, I took the multigrain slices of bread out of the toaster.

Andre sauntered toward me, stretching his long, lean arms while yawning audibly.

"Don't even tell me you're tired," I grimaced. "I've been up for hours. I can't believe it's 9:30. You feeling okay?"

Andre nodded. "I was stunned when I looked at the clock! Thanks for whipping up this delicious meal." His thick hair, usually smoothed with gel he ordered from Italy, splayed in all directions.

Our Jewish friends, the few who were observant, spent Saturdays off of electronics and refrained from work. I joked that our Sunday mornings were our own version of an abbreviated Shabbat. We'd lounge in our jammies and catch up on the news—our own and the world.

I typically started with *The New York Times* and then moved to local papers. Though I'd scan headlines on my phone each night, nothing could replace the smell and feel of holding a newspaper in my hands. My favorite section in the Sunday *NYT* was the Arts and Leisure, and I also did the crossword puzzle, often asking Andre for input. Even when we collaborated, he'd give up readily. Me? No chance. I'd also heard from a friend, whose mom has Alzheimer's, that it's important to challenge the brain in various ways.

Andre cleared the table, and I drizzled dark maple syrup into my coffee, stirring it into the hot liquid and licking the remainder off the spoon. Mel gifted me this unique mug for Hanukkah; I appreciated that she and Jake celebrated with us even though they were not Jewish. When I opened the present, I wondered why the wide cup didn't have a handle. Mel explained that her friend, who she'd met at the farmer's market, believed it created a streamlined look. There were ridges on the side, which I realized fit my small fingers perfectly. It had quickly become my favorite, and I swear my coffee tasted better in it.

I joined Andre at the sink and squirted dish soap into the mug. Then I watered the seven succulents on the windowsill. Next, the bamboo plants in the family room. Tolerant and resilient, they somehow survived even when I neglected them. My mom had a green thumb; orchids and bromeliads bloomed year-round in the backyard of my childhood home. I didn't inherit that gene, apparently. Grateful that in the springtime, flowers bloomed here in Burlington without much cajoling.

After refilling the glass watering pitcher, I sat on the sofa and opened the main section of the *Burlington Free Press*.

"Honey. Listen to this police blotter: 'A bear and her two cubs explored Charlotte yesterday afternoon. Residents reported they spotted the trio on the doorstep of a few homes. Stop feeding the animals human food. They're getting braver!'"

We cracked up, constantly entertained by the thankfully low level of crime in the area. I licked my index finger and turned the page. Sunlight shimmered between the blinds and onto the page. I savored these moments of brightness, especially in January. My chest tightened as the reality of moving forward without my mom struck me.

The translucent seashell chimes that hung above the succulents clinked like champagne glasses. My mom bought these for me during spring break when I was a junior in college. We'd spent a Saturday afternoon at Fairchild Tropical Gardens in Miami; I snapped photos of bougainvillea, orchids, palms, and species of flowers I couldn't remember.

I wished I'd taken more pictures of her. And of us. On the way out, in a strategically placed gift shop, my mom had squealed with delight when she saw these chimes.

"I'm getting these for you, Joy. Wouldn't they be great for your apartment? And look at the colors—they represent the chakras," she said to me with her wide smile.

Meditating since Mom died had been harder than ever. I tried clearing my throat again and again. But that indomitable pebble persistently made its presence known. I touched the tiny concave part of my neck, the dip just above my collarbone, and moved my fingers up and down, wishing the sensation would wane.

I put down the newspaper and massaged the back of my shoulder. Looking at a photo of snowboarders, I saw a crescent of indigo, orange, and yellow just below the image. Was I hallucinating?

I peered at the paragraph, reading and rereading the words.

"For sale by owner. Camp Von Glad, a fifty-year-old summer camp where every child matters and every voice is heard.…"

"Joy?"

Andre's voice sounded quieter than usual. I read the words again as the rainbow faded.

"What's up?" I replied, not moving from the chair.

"You made a weird noise."

He's going to check me into an institution if I tell him.

"Oh, I did? How funny!" I bluffed, still staring at the advertisement. The camp had baby goats, sheep, a vegetable garden, and more. I grabbed my phone and took a picture. I planned to send an email first thing tomorrow morning. But I needed to do something else first.

CHAPTER 12

Dear Mom,

I know you always believed in signs. Dad and Uncle Jack used to tease you all the time about how you'd find meaning in little moments like ladybugs landing on your lap or when certain songs came on the radio. Even the clients that came your way—you always told us that nothing is random.

I'm starting to think you were right. Either that or I am officially going crazy. Maybe a bit of both? Tali and I sat on the sand at our cousin hangout for your celebration of life. I'll never ever forget the rainbow that suddenly appeared within seconds of us talking about you. The biggest, brightest, most beautiful one I've ever seen!

So back to my idea about buying a camp, inspired by your diary entry. I promised Andre I'd only pursue it if it made sense. You know for him that boils down to numbers, blah, blah. For me, it's about feeling fulfilled. Especially now that I know kids are out of the question, which really sucks. Work doesn't excite me like it used to, Mom. Some days the things that used to make me happy don't anymore. I feel guilty that at the end of a photo shoot with an about-to-pop pregnant mom, all dewy and glowing with anticipation, I wish I were the one with the burgeoning belly.

And I wish you were here. I need you. Your wisdom, your kisses on my forehead, reassuring me everything will work out, as you always said, "the way and when it's supposed to, sweetie."

Speaking of rainbows, I cannot believe what happened a little while ago! We were having breakfast—you know our Sunday routine—and I flipped through the local paper. Suddenly, a teeny crescent-shaped image appeared on an advertisement. I wasn't wearing my solitaire or wedding band; I used to love how you'd move your hands in the light to make little rainbows on airplane rides. I don't even know how this prism projected onto the page. But there it was.

A freaking sleepaway camp for sale. And literally an hour from our house! With a baby animal farm, veggie garden, oh so Vermont! It's on a lake! I rubbed my eyes and read the words over and over. The rainbow faded as soon as Andre started talking.

Is this how you'll visit me, Mom? Is this a coincidence or is it you? I gotta tell Mel—she'll get it. Woo-woo and all.

I already emailed the owner, Vivienne Von Glad. Her name gives me movie star vibes. I am envisioning her with a massive, emerald-cut diamond on her left ring finger, layers of pearls on the daily, and flammable hair. I did research already (of course), and this camp has been around for decades. Oh, Mom, I haven't felt this jazzed in months. Seriously. I hope these feelings aren't fleeting—everything else seems to be these days. January feels like it's been the longest month ever—these are the times I feel like such a native Floridian. You'd be proud of me. I finally scheduled an appointment with a therapist that Mel recommended.

I miss you. So. Fucking. Much.

(Andre's not a fan of my f bombs and other frequent swearing. Fuck him.)

I could fill all these pages with those words. Will I ever feel like myself again, Mom?

CHAPTER 13

She picked up on the first ring.

"Ms. Von Glad's office. How may I assist you?" A high-pitched, nasally voice chimed.

I took a sip of green tea and cleared my throat.

"I read the advertisement about the sale of Camp Von Glad. I'd like to get more information, please." I fanned my face with an envelope and remembered I needed to pay the electric bill.

"Oh yes, splendid! Who may I say is calling?" she shrilled with a London-esque lilt. I pictured her with opaque stockings, patent pumps, and a frosted bouffant.

"My name is Joy Stern." I tried to keep my voice steady.

"One moment, please. Let me see if Ms. Von Glad is available," she replied.

I tapped my ballpoint pen to the beat of the dreadful on-hold music. After what seemed like a century, an alto voice crooned "hello" from the other end of the line. Then I heard her briefly hack. I added long, skinny cigarettes to Ms. Von Glad's ensemble.

"Tabitha! What is this woman's name?" Ms. Von Glad demanded. I held the receiver away from my ear while she yelled. "Joy? Thank you, dear."

Was this a mistake? I twirled a strand of hair and knotted it.

"Good morning, Ms. Von Glad. I'd like to speak with you about your camp," I began, biting my lower lip and relieved this was a phone call rather than Zoom.

"I assume you saw that asinine advertisement my assistant designed? She insisted it was necessary. I thought we could send a mass mailing to my affluent friends, and it'd be off my hands by

"

now," she said haughtily. I imagined a faint swirl of smoke floating in little "o" shapes from burgundy-stained lips.

"Yes, I did. And I have so many questions. Is now a good time for you?" I asked. This was not what I expected. I foolishly assumed that a camp owner would be nurturing and kindhearted.

"Darling, I don't have all day. I have a luncheon at Bergdorf's, and my driver will be here shortly. Perhaps we can schedule a proper meeting for next week?" she replied.

"That would be amazing! What day and time works best for you?" I asked eagerly.

"Tabitha, dear! Please schedule Ms. Stern. Block out at least thirty minutes—she has questions." *Does she realize I'm still on the phone?* I stifled a laugh.

"Lovely to make your acquaintance. I must go now. We'll discuss this further on our next call," Ms. Von Glad said.

Tabitha took over from there. I didn't think I'd sleep much until I had answers. I'd never negotiated a deal before—this seemed too good to be true. Today the high was thirty-six degrees, a rarity in late January. Needing to clear my head, I threw on a base layer, thick sweatshirt, fleece leggings, and hiking boots. Andre was at the office, and I didn't have any clients. On the way out the door, I felt cautiously optimistic as I dialed Mel's number. I heard a whirring sound when she answered.

"One sec, Joy. I need to finish soldering this piece," Mel shouted. If I picked up the phone with any sharp objects nearby, I'd detach a digit and end up in the emergency room.

"You amaze me, my friend. Your multitasking skills are something to behold," I said.

"Ha! It's a byproduct of parenting, I suppose!" Mel snorted. "I only have a small window to work and need to make the most of every minute before the stinkers get home from school."

"Maybe," I responded. "But you'd blast music while studying for chemistry and somehow ace all your tests. I needed total silence and double the amount of time yet still the highest grade I'd ever get was a 'B'."

Mel giggled. "That's not the only time you got high!"

Fair point. I reminded her that only happened during our freshman year. I didn't like the lack of control. Mel, on the other hand, could open a dispensary if the jewelry business ever folded.

"Are you out for a walk? I hear the snowplow," Mel said. "And why're you calling me midday—something is up."

"Damn straight, chica! *Wait* until you hear about the last twenty-four hours!" I squealed.

"I haven't heard you like this in ages. Whatever it is, tell me everything. What are you doing for lunch? Want me to order in and you can come to the shop? I'd also love your opinion on a new design I'm working on," she said.

I had to upload some images for a client but that could wait.

"Such a fun idea. I feel like we're skipping school—I'll be there as soon as I can. I may smell, though. Getting a bit sweaty. Maybe I will go home and change before—"

"Don't be ridiculous. I'll order us salads and sweet potato fries. Good?" I knew she was already online before I could even respond.

"That sounds delish—thank you! Can't wait to see you soon."

When I arrived, Mel didn't notice me peering into the window. Condensation from the inside heat mixed with the outside temps, making the oblong window semi-opaque. I loved watching Mel immersed in her work and marveled at her talent. I wished she'd use her full name, Melody, because it absolutely suited her.

I tapped on the door. She looked up and removed her plastic goggles. I chuckled seeing the deep mark they left around her upper face.

"Hello there, raccoon!"

Mel tilted her head.

"Take a look in the mirror," I said and hugged her. "This is such a treat; thanks for suggesting I come here."

She sniffed near my armpit.

"You weren't joking earlier. Have you heard of real deodorant? I mean, I know we're in Vermont, but still. Sometimes chemicals are necessary," Mel said.

I lifted my arm and affirmed her assessment.

"I told you I should've showered first!"

"I'm just kidding, Joy. You smell like a bouquet of roses!" She chuckled.

I rolled my eyes.

"I am ravenous—my appetite is finally returning. It's probably the overthinking more than my workout," I joked. Mel handed me a deep bowl with a bamboo fork and knife. She often worked through lunch.

"This is absolute perfection," I said after my third bite of tofu mixed with arugula and spinach. "Fork over those fries. They get mushy in minutes!"

"What else is up?" Mel studied me with her cornflower blue eyes.

"I'm distracted, not sleeping well, and now I have this idea that's swimming around." I sighed, not wanting to discuss my husband's restless legs with my best friend. The real reason I couldn't sleep lately.

She rested her chin on her hand. "Sooo. Tell me more!"

"Remember my mom's camp journal that I found?" I began.

Mel nodded vigorously, her two braids swinging like jump ropes in tandem.

"Yes! And that one entry—something about camp, right?" She leaned forward and munched on a crispy fry.

"Exactly! I couldn't let it go. I hate to admit but lately, I've felt kinda uninspired with my work. I guess it's not just between the covers and—"

She interrupted enthusiastically.

"That is the worst. I hear you. Like you feel suffocated because the creative faucet is clogged." Mel scratched behind her tiny ear and repositioned the dangly earring in it.

"You nailed it. That is the perfect description." I shoveled another forkful of greens into my mouth. Something in my back molar felt gritty; it was likely dirt, which I used to find gross but now saw as proof of how fresh the food was in Vermont.

"Whatcha going to do about this fabulous idea? This is wonderful, Joy. I can already envision—"

I couldn't let her finish. It felt good to hear her excitement and encouragement. I started telling her the story about Camp Von Glad.

"After a brief call with the owner, Vivienne, and her assistant, Tabitha, I scheduled a Zoom for next week!" I sipped spring water through the paper straw. It nearly disintegrated between my lips, so I took it out and tossed it into the recycling bin.

"Holy shit! That is freaking amaaaaazing! Can we discuss those names?" Mel retied her green bandana and cackled. "Were they born in this century?"

I told her how thankful I was that the first call wasn't in person. We bantered about the possibility that these two women were likely living antiques. Feeling suddenly downtrodden, I thought about how my mom wouldn't experience old age.

"Tell me about this new design—I'd love to see it," I said, not wanting to hijack our time together. That's another shitty thing about grief. It shoved its way front and center into my life, even when I didn't want to go there.

Mel tilted her head. "You okay?"

Damn, I hated that question, a short sentence that steamrolled over me. I'll never be able to answer it honestly. I shared this in my first session with the grief therapist. She suggested that I practice a few lines like, "I'm struggling and can't put it into words yet," and "It helps to know you're here." Even memorizing some canned replies felt overwhelming right now.

"I'm fine, thanks. Now where is the sketch or casting mold?"

Grateful for the pivot, we cleaned up and made our way to the back of Mel's studio. She offered to take me home before going to her kids' school. But I decided to walk back, needing some time to myself. I wondered if exercise would ease the pain or fill the emptiness I felt.

CHAPTER 14

Mercury was in retrograde. How'd I know? My computer kept crashing. Emails vanished from my inbox. Then a circuit breaker tripped. As if that weren't enough, Andre and I had a bit of a tiff before he left for a meeting.

And my Zoom with Vivienne Von Glad was scheduled for this afternoon.

I didn't buy into this mercurial, astrological nonsense. But too much conflict and wonkiness prompted me to look it up. Yup, we were smack in the middle of it. I rewound and revisited the discussion with my husband, if you could call it that, from earlier this morning. It didn't end well.

"Andre, I'm a little worried about you," I began. He ignored me and crunched on the avocado toast.

I tried again.

"Sweetie, can you please listen?"

His deep blue eyes bored into me like a steel drill bit.

"What are you concerned about?" His words were clipped and dropping at the end of the question.

I inhaled deeply and moved closer to him.

"Did you hear that? How your voice trails off at the end of a sentence?"

He shook his head and rolled his eyes.

"What's the big deal? I'm tired and trying to finish my breakfast," he retorted, picking up the sports section of the newspaper.

I gnawed at my lower lip.

"Andre."

"Joy."

"Hilarious, honey. Now that we've established that we remember each other's names, I need you to not just hear me but also listen. Please." I clasped my hands tightly in my lap. "I want you to see an ear, nose, and throat doctor. Something doesn't seem right."

Andre's thumb vibrated as he tried three times to turn the page of the newspaper.

"I hate doctors," he grunted. "Maybe I'm getting a cold—it's not urgent."

I'd been delaying this discussion for weeks. And had anticipated pushback from my hubby.

"I made an appointment. It won't interfere with work; it's at 12:30. And I cleared my afternoon, so I'll be with you." I braced myself for what he'd say next.

Shockingly, he agreed without much resistance. I already knew he was available because his assistant had confirmed; I also knew he needed control, so I asked her to wait until I told him before putting it in his calendar. He looked up from his phone.

"I'll go because I know once you get something in your head, you won't relent. But after this, mi amor, no more appointments. Deal?"

I didn't answer. How could I make a promise I wasn't sure I could keep?

———

After checking that my laptop was fully charged, I straightened my hair with a flatiron. A wiry, willful piece of my curtain bangs took on a life of its own. It wouldn't lie flat until I tamed it with gel. Then I applied mauve, matte lipstick, a few coats of mascara, and a bit of blush. I stared at my reflection in the beveled mirror, thankful I'd kept this nineteenth-century vanity from my mom. It was worth the wait (and cost) to ship it here from Miami.

I changed my outfit three times. Who knew what to wear when negotiating the purchase of a camp? Overalls? Pajamas? A swimsuit? I mean, why'd I even obsess about the shades of makeup? I contemplated scrubbing off the mascara then checked my watch. I needed to get online in a few minutes.

I'd settled on a crisp, white cotton button-down and cultured pearl studs. Andre surprised me with the earrings for our first anniversary. I needed to remind myself not to stand up while on camera—the jitters made me sweat, even though I'd lowered the heat—so I wore shorts instead of slacks. Just thinking about that potential faux pas, imagining an appalled look on Vivienne's face, cracked me up.

Adjusting the angle of the screen, I straightened my back and wiggled into the mesh office chair. And hoped that I appeared more assured than I felt as I waited for the meeting to begin.

Two squares popped onto the screen. Wait, what? I thought the only person with whom I was meeting was Vivienne. The moisture at the base of my neck crept up my scalp. So much for straightening my hair. I dabbed lavender-eucalyptus oil onto my wrists.

"Hello, dear!" A rosy-cheeked, plump woman appeared on the screen. "Ms. Glad is a bit delayed. She will join us in a few minutes," Tabitha crooned. She delicately wiped her nose with a linen handkerchief. Just as I'd pictured, Tabitha resembled a fusion of Mrs. Doubtfire and Mary Poppins.

"It's lovely to meet you," I said, stifling a smile. *Oh boy, I couldn't wait to see the esteemed Ms. Gladstone.*

As if on cue, she entered the online room. I nearly dislocated my jaw—my imagination had conjured a caricature—yet remarkably accurate. The flammable, coiffed hair. The three opulent strands of pearls, resting perfectly on her pale neck. She must have a fabulous plastic surgeon. When she opened her mouth, her skin could barely stretch. And zero crow's feet—the woman must've started Botox in her twenties. I silently reprimanded myself for the judgmental thoughts.

"Joy, you are rather young!" She began and then hacked. *Yup— definitely a smoker.*

I wasn't sure how to respond, so I said, "Thank you for making the time to meet today, Ms. Glad."

"You are doing me a favor, doll. Don't you know the story about Camp Von Glad?" She fluffed her already poofy hair with her long, thin fingers. There it was—the glittery rock set in platinum, not emerald cut like I'd pictured. Pear shaped and, goodness, it must've been at least seven carats. The diamonds in her ears weren't much smaller.

"Yes, I read about the camp and such a beautiful story behind it. Your husband sounds like a generous man and—"

"My late husband. He dropped dead two years ago. Heart attack. Told him to quit eating porterhouse steaks but the obstinate man wouldn't listen to me." She raised the collar on her black, long-sleeved blouse. "I've been in charge of his lovely *project* (she said with air quotes) ever since." I glanced quickly at Tabitha, who was taking notes and not at all flustered.

"I am so sorry! My mother passed away recently—" I removed my glasses and rubbed my eyes. Shit. What a way to show strength.

"Never mind, darling. Who has time for tears, right? Onward. What are your questions?" She reapplied her already saturated lipstick. Then blotted her lips on a tissue.

I wondered if robots really existed. It seemed like this woman's emotional wiring was disconnected—how could she speak so callously about her late husband? I swallowed hard and took a few sips of tea before answering.

"Tabitha shared that you have a jam-packed day, so I'll get right to it. I'd like to purchase the camp." I looked at the chartreuse Post-it notes just below my laptop; I'd jotted bullet points on them. "What is the cost? Do you have staff who've already committed to working this summer? What about equipment and supplies? I read that staff and counselor training typically begins in early June. Given that it's already late January—"

She held up her hand, adorned with impeccably manicured fingernails. The mother-of-pearl and gold clover bracelets—Van Cleef and Arpels bracelets—slid down her freckled forearm.

"Yes to all. I see you've done your research." She offered a half-smile, revealing chalk white veneers. No evidence of what I guessed had been decades of inhaling cigarettes. She must have an extraordinary dentist, too. And I bet she sipped coffee through a straw.

"I'd love to hear more about the story of the camp!" I piped, trying to temper my exhilaration. *Cool it, chica.* This woman is savvy and shrewd.

While applying presumably overpriced hand cream, Vivienne talked about her billionaire husband, Bernard, who made his money as a real estate mogul. A native New Yorker, he'd always wanted kids but decided it just wouldn't suit his—and their—lavish, demanding lifestyle.

"So, he got this hare-brained idea to start a summer camp. A percentage of the kids are offered full scholarships. The property is one that foreclosed, and he figured it was a fitting ambiance due to the landscape and lake." She paused and fiddled with the pearls. "We also have a family foundation, and our focus is on children's causes."

I brushed beneath my eye with the back of my hand. Tabitha mouthed something I couldn't discern.

"I suppose I should tell you Bernard's brother died of leukemia," she continued, flippantly, as if talking about having a cold.

Speaking of which, this woman's heart must be made of ice. Maybe Bernard was afraid to have kids? Maybe he thought losing someone he loved would be too great a risk? I wish I could've met this man.

"Joy? Are you still there, dear?" Tabitha said. I tried to maintain a neutral expression.

"Yes, yes. Just listening and thinking about Bernard. He sounded like such a generous, kindhearted person," I managed, doodling on a yellow legal pad and gathering my composure. "Do you have written material regarding specifics about the maintenance, staffing, funding, programming? I'd like to consider moving forward. We also need to discuss the cost because—"

Vivienne moved closer to the screen, her powdered face filling the entire space.

"I don't want to deal with this camp or any of it. There've been other offers, but they didn't seem like a good fit. I rarely do what I'm told; but Bernard specified in his will how important it was that Camp Von Glad continued to thrive. He'd adore you—I have no doubt," she said, her pitch dropping as she took a wheezy breath.

"I don't need the money. And our camp director, Dave, has been with us for over twenty years. He runs the whole operation; he promised he'd stay on. The goats, sheep, kayaks, art supplies—my husband thought ahead. He established a trust that will support most of the camp's operational costs in perpetuity." I scribbled notes between the infinity symbols I'd drawn all over the page.

I was so stunned I didn't move for a few moments. Tabitha pushed her tortoiseshell glasses higher on the bridge of her nose.

"You remind me of my daughter, dear. She's much more American than I could ever be—you know, expressing her emotions and all of that. She tells me about 'processing' or some other psychology term. Ms. Glad, perhaps Joy needs a bit of time to contemplate all that you shared?"

I wanted to leap through the screen and hug Tabitha. Mel always joked that what my mouth didn't say my face always did. But I'd never felt so certain of something in my entire life.

"Thank you both so much. I need to talk about this with my husband. I also need to read and review a contract with all of the details we discussed," I began, pressing my palms into my thighs. "I already know this is meant to be—the story, the timing, the generosity of spirit." Vivienne squinted her eyes and started to hack again. I realized I was about to dive into woo-woo waters. Vivienne seemed to be shutting down.

She fluttered her fingers as if playing an invisible piano in the air.

"Well then, it's settled! Tabitha, please send Joy the documents no later than Monday morning so she will have the week to review it," Vivienne exclaimed, more animated than I'd seen during our entire meeting. "This is such a relief to finally have this burden lifted. I did consider keeping the camp; it's certainly beneficial, especially for optics. People just love kids."

I pursed my lips together, picturing glue that would prevent me from saying what hammered in my head. Then I chewed on an ice cube before speaking.

"I'm truly speechless, Ms. Glad. I love animals; actually, when I was in college, that was my focus in addition to nature photography. And I don't think I shared that the camp is near my home," I rambled.

"Please call me Vivienne. And though our advertisement said the price is negotiable, I've decided to lower it much further than I initially intended. Well, I need to consult with my attorneys..."

Now I was definitely hallucinating. I could swear she winked with her left eyelid. It was barely perceptible because her skin hardly moved.

We said goodbye, and I thanked them again. I closed the laptop, stood up, and stretched my arms over my head. The earlier dampness had progressed to a pool of sweat. I didn't even notice until now.

CHAPTER 15

I decided I'd prepare Andre's favorite meal for Shabbat the next night. We both had jam-packed Fridays, and I needed him fully present. On my way to the grocery store, I texted Mel—I just had to tell someone.

Hi! Got a sec?
Is it important?
Mmmmmm. I guess it can wait until later.

My phone buzzed. Oh, how I loved her.

"Everything okay?" Mel asked breathlessly.

Oy, I'd worried my friend.

"Oh yes! Gosh, I didn't mean to worry you. You sure you're not Jewish?" I laughed. "It's how our family answers nearly every call."

We cackled in unison.

"That's a freaking riot!" Mel shrieked. "Give me all the deets."

"How much time do you have?"

"Girl, c'mon, you're wasting it. Lemme hear what's up!" she replied. I squeezed my truck into a parking space, turned off the engine, and put the AirPods in my ears. I meandered down the aisles, surveying the squash, and headed to the butcher as I told Mel about the meeting with Vivienne.

"Hello? Hello?"

"I can't hear you!"

Ugh, damn dairy section. I nearly dropped a block of Cabot cheddar cheese on a customer next to me.

"Sorry!" I squeaked.

The connection returned while I was placing my items on the black, sticky conveyor belt. I tried to avoid the streak of amber syrup on it.

"Hey! What's the last thing you heard, Mel?" I handed the cashier my two reusable cloth bags. "Let me call you from the car—I'm being rude."

On the drive home, I relayed the rest of the story. She was shocked and thrilled for me.

"Have you told Andre? Ha! And he doubted my girl!" Mel snarked.

"Not yet. I don't blame him, though you know I was pissed. Who ever thought it would be this easy? I'm really starting to wonder if my mom was right. She said after souls transition, they can show up in ways we could never predict," I mused, rubbing my damp cheek on my shoulder.

"It's like bashert—meant to be—right?" I said as I pulled the car into the garage.

Mel murmured in agreement and suggested I wear a negligee while cooking dinner. I laughed, telling her to get her head out of the gutter. And promised I'd update her soon.

"Hi sweetie, I'm home!" I yelled from the laundry room. "Need some help, please."

"Whoa, are we having a party?" Andre chuckled, taking the heavy bags and placing them on the granite countertops.

"Sort of, but just us." I stood on my tippy toes and planted a long kiss on his mouth. "And I'm making your favorite meal—*bandeja paisa*, minus the pork, of course. And I also got ingredients for empanadas! Thought that'd be fun to make tomorrow."

"What a wonderful surprise—thank you!" His voice sounded breathy. I reminded him that we had the doctor appointment in a week. He nodded and said he'd be right back. I knew his schtick: shoes off, wash hands, then off to our bedroom to change into some version of a T-shirt and flannel drawstring pants.

He sauntered toward me about ten minutes later and I smiled. Yup. In his loungewear. Somehow, he'd snuck a quick shower in there. I held the sharp knife away from me as he kissed my neck. Andre breathed into my ear, murmuring.

"Honey, I love you and—"

"You were saying?" Andre said as he untied my apron, gently took the knife from my hand, and turned me to face him. Then he lifted me onto the countertop and parted my legs, still clad in dark blue jeans. My nipples hardened against my thin shirt as Andre cupped my bottom, pulling me closer to him. My eyes traveled to the chiseled area below his waist.

"Oh, oh Andre," I managed. "I want you, and as much as you know I love eating dessert first, let's wait."

He sighed and started to boil the water.

"I am hungry." His dimple deepened as he flashed me that irresistible, sexy smile.

"Funny. I am, too. You are delicious, my love," I winked. "But I need to talk to you about something super exciting tonight." I lowered the heat on the gas stove and took the rice and bean concoction (my attempt at Colombian cuisine) out of the oven. Andre commented on the table setting.

"You took out our wedding crystal? This must be major. And the candlesticks we bought from that trip, too. My mom would be so happy; let's call her real quick," Andre said as he picked up the phone.

He put Carmen on speaker.

"*Hola mis hijos.* Shabbat Shalom! I was just thinking about you two!" Carmen said in a singsong voice.

"I owe you a call—so sorry—it's been busy," I said, feeling guilty because I usually spoke to my mother-in-law once a week.

"It's okay, Joy," she said. "You don't usually call together—do you have news? *Un momento*—wait—let me get Carlos," she squealed.

"Hello, you two! I hear you have something big—"

Carmen interrupted. "Ohhhhhh. Are you finally pregnant?"

Andre and I locked gazes. My stomach cramped and that damn pebble lodged itself in my throat.

"No, Mami. Joy set such a stunning table tonight, and we thought of you because we're lighting the candles soon, using those hand-painted candlesticks from Bogotá," he said. I turned away.

He continued. "She also made your favorite recipe, the one you gave Joy at her bridal shower." Andre knew just what to say. The receiver shook slightly in his hand.

"Anyway, Shabbat shalom *y te amamos*!" he said and I spoke the same words from a distance. I needed to reignite the spark I'd felt just an hour ago. Nothing could or would extinguish it, I'd decided. The seashell chimes jingled, a tiny percussive interlude as if echoing my thoughts. I looked up, wishing my mom were here to hear what I was about to tell my husband.

Andre plated the food. I watched him straighten the silverware until satisfied with the alignment. Then he decanted a bottle of Cabernet that we'd bought during a trip to Napa Valley. Before I asked, he set aside the cork, knowing I'd want to add this one to our growing collection. His handwriting had gotten smaller and harder to read; I'd make sure to find a fine point pen (instead of our usual Sharpie) for him to write the date on it.

"This is amazing!" Andre said between bites. I touched his warm hand.

"Pour me a glass, please. And before you give me the whole spiel about it 'opening up' or 'airing out' or whatever—"

Andre laughed. "You know me well! Maybe just give it five more minutes?"

"Pardon my reach," I said, chuckling. I wasn't waiting. Not for the wine. And not any longer about sharing my news.

"Well, alrighty then! What's up?" Andre asked.

As I watched the ruby liquid swish in the goblet, I started to tell him about the meeting.

His eyes widened and he said, "Dios mio! Tell me more!"

I couldn't gauge if his countenance was one of disbelief, awe, shock, or perhaps all three. Lately his facial movements were slightly diminished, the range of expressions not as varied. It didn't matter. I kept talking. He roared when I described Vivienne.

"Wow, I don't even know what to say." Andre took a generous gulp of wine.

"I know, right? I was nervous and never, ever expected such an easy conversation," I gushed. "I was a hot, sweaty mess. Thank G-d it was on Zoom. This woman seemed straight out of a film from the 1940s. What an ice queen, too. I couldn't believe how she spoke about her husband and the camp—it's seriously unreal." I rubbed the back of my neck.

"What are the next steps?" Andre asked quietly.

"I told Vivienne that I needed a contract and the details to review with you. And if it is all she's promised, I am ready to move forward." I paused to let him process.

"Joy, you're serious about this?" Andre probed. *What the fuck— was he still doubting me?*

"Yes, Andre. Is it scary to try something new? Sure. But this feels divinely guided—kismet. Like us," I added, inching closer toward him. We locked eyes. I didn't blink.

"I am stunned and so proud of you," he said, taking my hands in his. "I'll call our attorney tomorrow—I know it's Saturday but let's have him on standby. I hear the urgency, and we need to be mindful of the timing, *sí*?"

That's all I needed to hear. I crawled into his lap and curled into him like a satisfied kitten. I may've purred, too. Then we finished what we'd started earlier in the evening. And that night, again, I couldn't sleep. I felt hopeful and a flicker of happiness.

As promised, the agreement arrived in my inbox at 8 a.m. Monday morning. I immediately sent it to our lawyer, Bill. Contracts were his specialty; he'd worked on tons over the years for Andre. He emailed that it seemed straightforward, and he'd get back with me by end of day with comments/questions.

Kismet. The word and emotions it evoked reverberated like a whisper, a loving nudge. What if I renamed the camp? Yes. That would be nonnegotiable.

I printed the agreement. I put away my pens, photo paper, pencils, and any other visual distractions. Then I spread each sheet vertically, lined up like rows of corn, to peruse each word. I looked up some legal jargon. At least to me, this seemed to be exactly as Vivienne had described it.

I'd started to research camp associations and found one with a plethora of resources. The American Camp Association offered both online and in-person sessions; it also hosted an annual conference. There was a forum where camp owners could ask questions or post information. As I scanned the topics ranging from marketing to registration to recruitment, I became overwhelmed with how much I needed to learn. I figured I should probably stop with the obsessive information seeking until I knew this was a done deal.

Tabitha had also sent a detailed description of not only the camp property, but maps, surveys, (Andre would love this part!) and abundant information regarding the bunks, equipment, previous programs, and more. One paragraph surprised me—a photo lab.

Oh my gosh! Vivienne hadn't mentioned this or the arts and crafts hut. I ran my index finger over the words, feeling that tranquil sensation I couldn't quite yet describe.

Mom, is that you?

A calendar reminder pinged on my laptop about Andre's doctor appointment. As if I could forget. The volume of his voice diminished, especially in the afternoon and evenings. I even noticed it crack occasionally. He'd never smoked and after years of soccer and other sports, he had the breath control of an opera singer.

Back to the camp. I needed to sign this contract before I chickened out. I saw another notification in the right upper corner of my computer screen. I clicked on the message from Bill.

Hi Joy,

I reviewed the agreement. As I suspected, it's rather straightforward. And this Ms. Von Glad is being extremely generous. We need to discuss it, of course, but if you feel confident this is what you'd like to pursue, it appears to be feasible. You'll need to confirm what property and liability insurance she has used in the past.

When can you talk?

My heart thumped, and I bounced in my chair like Tigger from *Winnie the Pooh*. Holy shit, this was happening. I replied right away, and we planned a call for the next morning.

Bill marked up the agreement, providing additional language to clarify some ambiguous areas. He wrote notes in the margins and explained his reasons why. Bill also suggested I set up an LLC or S corporation to protect my personal assets. I could see why his students loved him at the community college where he taught;

Bill's passion and patience were a rare mix, and it bolstered my confidence.

"I can't thank you enough, Bill. Please charge me extra hours. I know how busy you are and this must've totally disrupted your schedule," I said, feeling guilty and simultaneously grateful.

"It's my pleasure, Joy; it's wonderful to hear you so excited. It is quite extraordinary how Vivienne's husband, Bernard, thought of every detail. Your biggest risk is fire or injury, as I see it, versus financial. And it seems like a well-oiled machine," he added.

"Do you have a few more minutes?" I asked, suddenly wanting to tell him what sparked this idea.

"Sure. I have a hard stop at one o'clock, though," he said.

I spoke without taking a breath, telling him about my mom's camp diary and the possible name change.

"Oh, that's meaningful!" Bill said. I could envision him running the tips of his stubby fingers through his salt-and-pepper beard. "Let me add language about changing the name to Kismet. I don't see any issue there, but maybe you should reach out to Vivienne first? You know best. Trust yourself."

Two wise words that also scared the hell out of me.

How could I move forward without trust?

CHAPTER 16

He was never late. Why wasn't Andre home yet?

I did laps around our living room. I picked at the hangnail on my ring finger. I watered the succulents and bamboo plants. It was 11:55 and we needed to leave the house soon. Just as I was about to text him, I heard the back door creak.

"Can you grab me a kombucha and banana? I didn't have time to eat," Andre said. "I'll wait in the car."

Terrific. We're almost late and now he's hypoglycemic. Andre was always mindful of eating every few hours, likely a healthy habit from his days as an athlete. We were out of bananas, so I tossed an apple, some almonds, and a granola bar into a worn lunch tote.

The car skidded as Andre turned toward the highway. I dug what was left of my nails into the plush leather seat.

"Honey, please be careful," I muttered through clenched teeth. I was already a bit anxious, and his lead foot on the gas pedal wasn't helping. The office assistant wanted us there early to fill out paperwork. I'd completed what I could online.

We found a spot in the parking garage. We zipped up our jackets and rewrapped our scarves. As we walked toward the brick building, I thought about how what we see isn't always truth. The clear azure sky. The sun glimmering on Lake Champlain. If not for college students bundled in hoodies and heavy outerwear, the frigid temperature would be jarring.

"Give me a sec," I uttered, stopping at the step in front of the doctor's office. I nearly tripped on the long shoelaces of my mid-calf boots. After tightening and retying them, I walked through the door Andre held open for me. Then I exhaled with relief, noting that there were only two other people in the waiting room.

A softspoken woman at the front desk asked for Andre's license and insurance card. Then she handed him a form on a clipboard.

"Please fill this out, and we'll be right with you," she said. "Dr. Goldman is on time today." *Was my concern that apparent?*

True to her word, we were quickly called back to a room. I sat on a dingy, aluminum seat while Andre eased into the black, pleather exam chair. I saw his thumb twitching and looked around the room, not wanting him to notice that I did. The photo behind Andre was a serene image of a waterfall that looked like the one in Quechee, Vermont. A landscape portrait of an old farmhouse painted against a fall landscape with a herd of brown-spotted cattle hung on the other wall. To the left of the sink, near instruments I tried to ignore, was a poster detailing the anatomy of the ear, nose, and throat. A simple office that felt sterile but not scary. Someone knocked on the door, snapping me out of my surveillance.

"May I come in?" Dr. Goldman entered the room and extended his hand toward Andre. Then he walked to the sink, scrubbed his palms, wiped the water around the area, and turned toward us. I liked that he was meticulous. I smiled at Andre. He noticed it, too.

"My husband's voice is—" I started to speak.

"I am here because my wife wouldn't stop worrying unless I agreed to see you," Andre snarked, shooting me a grin. "I keep telling her nothing is wrong."

Of course his voice sounds loud and strong today. What's that old adage? When you bring a car to the shop and it's not broken?

I twisted my wedding band and popped a piece of peppermint gum into my mouth.

"I reviewed your medical history and findings from your most recent visit to your primary care physician. Everything looked good;

she did note a slight tremor in one hand," Dr. Goldman said, ruffling through the papers front of him. "She also mentioned 'stiff movement when walking and to possibly follow up with a neurologist.' All of your basic labs and vitals were normal." He closed the folder.

Why didn't Andre tell me about what the PCP observed? That visit was over a year ago.

"What are you concerned about, Mrs. Stern? I am glad you're here with Andre; it's not uncommon for a family member to notice subtle changes in a loved one," Dr. Goldman said while withdrawing a penlight from his lab coat pocket.

I chose my words carefully, not wanting to sound like an alarmist even though I sensed something was wrong with my husband.

"Andre's always had a strong, even booming, voice. We've been together since college. In recent months, maybe even longer, I don't know exactly, it sounds different. Like he can't quite speak on a full breath. Sometimes it's softer and—"

"That's completely normal, I'm sure," Andre interjected. "After all, I speak to clients all day and now that I'm in my forties, fatigue can be anywhere in the body, right?"

I gritted my teeth, aggravated that I'd barely gotten a few sentences out. Dr. Goldman uncrossed his legs and looked at Andre.

"I'd like to examine you before offering my opinion," he said. Andre nodded and I chewed on the inside of my cheek.

After peering in his ears and assessing all areas from the neck upward, Dr. Goldman suggested an endoscopy. Andre's breathing became shallow.

"A what? That doesn't sound fun," Andre muttered.

"It is a bit uncomfortable but painless. I'll spray a numbing liquid into your nose. Then I put a tiny tube into one nostril—it has a camera at the end of it. It's the best way to thoroughly assess the inside of your throat," Dr. Goldman explained.

Andre opened the top button of his shirt as if he couldn't breathe. I stood and lightly put my hand on his shoulder.

"Honey, I think it's important. Unless you want to come back?" I said. He shook his head and pitched forward.

"Let's get this over with while you have me in this chair," Andre grumbled. I was intrigued by the tiny camera that was about to be inserted in my husband's nose. Did it take photos? Were there different lenses?

"Yuck! What's that nasty taste?" Andre's head jerked backward as the doctor sprayed the anesthetic into his nose. Maybe that's another reason exam chairs had a cushy surface.

I squinted at the doctor and wondered if this was normal. I spaced out, curious about the apparatus that snaked into my husband's nostril.

Dr. Goldman patted Andre's fisted palm. "That's the lidocaine, which numbs the area. If I could invent a way to make it chocolate flavored, I'd be a millionaire."

Andre's eyes crinkled in the corners. I laughed and studied the small screen. Fascinated by the hi-def, I stood transfixed as the doctor continued the exam.

"No vocal nodules. The throat looks healthy. And I didn't see any nasal polyps. All good!" Dr. Goldman said as he slowly withdrew the narrow, tiny tube from Andre's nose. He gagged a bit then coughed. I smoothed the back of his hair with my hand.

"Glad that's over with! Will my wife stop ruminating now?" Andre asked, turning his head toward me.

"I am not that type of physician, though otolaryngology does include the head, too! But no promises," Dr. Goldman joked. Thank goodness this man had a sense of humor.

"What is wrong with his voice? Why does it get softer at times and more frequently in recent months?" I asked. Questions spun in my mind like a record stuck on one track.

"We've ruled out most physical causes. I reviewed the notes your primary care physician faxed over and there is nothing clinically significant, other than the concerns she had about your gait and shaky hand. I would like to order a scan of the brain," Dr. Goldman said, writing on a prescription pad.

The pebble reappeared in my throat, feeling more like a rock, as if it had doubled in size. Andre shrugged his shoulders and seemed content with the doctor's answer.

"Although it's inconsistent, I did hear your voice fade in and out during our visit. Have you thought about seeing a neurologist?"

Andre looked at me then at the doctor, and back again, as if watching a ping-pong game. I hoped my face didn't project the paralyzing fear I felt. Before my husband had a chance to argue, I asked Dr. Goldman for the name and contact information.

Something wasn't right. We needed to know the cause. I needed to know. No warning with my mom. Only the headache.

I couldn't lose Andre, too.

CHAPTER 17

We never ran out of topics to discuss. Except for today. Thoughts reverberated in my head so loudly that I wondered if Andre could hear them. I figured we'd leave this doctor's appointment with clarity—not more questions. I pulled on my upper lip, already anticipating pushback from Andre about seeing the neurologist Dr. Goldman had recommended. He did agree to the brain scan, though.

Snow wasn't forecasted for today, yet the white dusting on our street proved otherwise. The low, leaden clouds further tanked my mood. It seemed that I'd better get accustomed to the unpredictable. Andre reached up and pressed the garage clicker. His index finger and thumb twitched after he turned off the car. I briefly thought about how much easier pushing a flat button was versus turning a metal key. It wasn't yet five o'clock but an old-fashioned, or something stronger, sounded appealing right now.

"You up for a cocktail, mi amor?" Andre called as he walked to his office.

I laughed. "Are you living in my head? Hell yes! You're heading in the wrong direction, sweetie. Unless you have a secret stash in that new desk."

My mom would've chided us for this occasional coping mechanism. She'd tell me to go to a sauna. Or listen to a meditation. Attend a yoga class. I yearned for a hug, her small, strong arms that would smooth my hair while I put my head on her shoulder. We usually had an "only on the weekends" drink rule—one of many that Andre suggested—in addition to other healthy lifestyle changes we'd made when we moved to Vermont.

Who cared that today was Wednesday? I snickered to myself, remembering a shirt I'd seen once when we were in Stowe skiing with a group of friends. "A drinking town with a ski problem." Funny and a bit true. Like other jokes, there's often some truth in even the silliest statements. I heard ice crackling in a tumbler and cabinets closing. As I approached the minibar in the family room, I inhaled deeply and tried to ground myself. The word *neurologist* echoed in my mind, and I shuddered.

We had a drink, and then another, numbing our collective fears with tawny liquid. The whiskey slid down my throat and burned into my chest. Though I preferred wine, I welcomed the warmth and intensity as a distraction from my terrifying thoughts. *He's in his early forties. He runs marathons. Intellectually brilliant and a keen memory.* With each sip, I tried to rationalize the fear that threatened to engulf my heart.

Neither of us had an appetite. Instead of a proper dinner, we snacked on chevre from a local farm. We drizzled balsamic vinegar on shredded kale. And I had a few slices of organic Vermont turkey pepperoni. We both conked out quickly—my sleep interrupted by strange images of a massive X-ray machine, then a pharmacy filled with perfectly organized pill bottles, and Dr. Goldman, I think, popped into my dreams, too. Though I didn't feel rested, I awoke before the sun, and I didn't need coffee today. The unknown can cause jitters, apparently.

I joined Andre at the hammered copper sink. He set a timer while brushing his teeth to ensure a thorough cleaning. Between sudsy spits of Crest, I figured that now might be a good time to broach the subject.

"Please let me know if mornings or afternoons are better for you," I said, swishing my mouth with water.

"Mi amor, you know the answer." Andre's eyes moved from my mouth to my bare breasts.

"Oh my gosh. That is not what I'm referencing." I picked up the hand towel and flung it at him. He looked down at the growing bulge in his boxers.

"You know stress makes me horny!" he said.

Clearly, I thought. I took a deep breath and exhaled.

"We may need to find another outlet for that today," I replied with a wink. I followed him into his closet, surveying the tops and perfectly pressed slacks. Each item on identical hangers, evenly spaced apart and straight. Andre pulled open a drawer, looking for socks to match his forest green sweater.

"I was trying to ask you about the appointment. We need to schedule it."

Andre fixated on folding and refolding his shirts. He didn't turn around.

"I did what you asked. Now we are done," he said curtly. Then he moved to his color-coordinated tie collection.

I tapped his broad, bronzed shoulder.

"Honey, I know neither of us expected Dr. Goldman to make the referral that he did." I chose my words carefully. Not just for Andre, but perhaps for myself. Any word with "—ologist" at the end of it made me quiver.

His upper back tensed and the tips of his ears reddened. He slammed the drawer shut.

"We had a deal. I did what you asked. I am not going to another doctor!" he bellowed. "You hear me, right? Do I sound like I can't shout? Nothing is wrong with me!" Andre turned on his heels and stormed out of the closet. I followed him.

Maybe I should let it go.

But how could I?

"Andre. Wait. Please."

He looked up while buttoning his long, wool coat. Andre's bright blue eyes had darkened to midnight.

"You heard what I said," he spat through his clamped jaw.

"I don't want you driving like this—all angry and agitated." I took the keys from his hand.

He begrudgingly leaned against the washing machine and folded his arms over his chest. I pressed my palms together, trying to ground myself.

"I'm scared, too. But we can't ignore what Dr. Goldman said. You trusted him, right?"

Andre nodded then looked away, studying the intricate crown molding that I still thought was a total waste of money. Who puts that in a laundry room?

"Do this for me. It can't hurt to get checked out. You're so healthy otherwise; this doesn't make sense. I'm not the only one who's noticed that—"

I went too far. He looked at his watch and his thick brows furrowed.

"Are we done? I need to go," Andre muttered.

"Yes, just give me dates."

"Like the one we're going on this weekend—remember it's Valentine's Day." His lips brushed my cheek.

"I'm looking forward to whatever you planned. But we're not going anywhere until this is on the calendar," I replied boldly. Perspiration pooled under my armpits.

Andre huffed and said he'd text me a few options. I knew I'd broken through his obstinance like a lumberjack chopping wood. Between reviewing the camp agreement, speaking with our attorney Bill, and now this squabble, I needed a nap.

The rest of the week crawled by, and I only had one photo shoot scheduled of a high school senior's last snowboarding tournament. But the icy conditions prompted cancellations, which was rare because I'm convinced that Vermonters are the most resilient people on the planet. When we first built our home, a seventy-year-old man climbed on the roof to inspect it. I couldn't believe his agility and fearlessness. I'd shouted nervously, "Be careful, it's windy up there!"

He'd replied, "Ma'am, this is nothing. I'm a sixth generation Vermonter; I've got this. Don't worry about me!" I'd had visions of the compact man, clad in boots, barely laced and caked with mud, tumbling rapidly and becoming a paraplegic. He worked until after dusk. I heard recently that his sons had joined the company.

A colleague let me rent her studio for a few hours. The teen and his parents were gracious; I told them I'd still take pictures of him snowboarding when the weather improved.

I felt like I had earned a master's degree in resilience. But the lessons and tests weren't over yet. If getting vertical every morning and making it through each day counted for credits, I'd passed these life classes with high scores. And I hoped I wouldn't fail the final exam. Or pop quizzes along the way. Though I loved to learn, these weren't lessons I wanted.

A persistent honk startled me. I waved my hand and mouthed an apology; I hadn't realized the light had turned green. I was on my way to the salon to darken the tufts of silvery sprouts on my head. Maybe I'd dye my hair blonde, which is technically my natural color. That would be a surprise for Valentine's Day—Andre would be shocked.

I mentioned this idea to my stylist, Taylor, who tilted her head and grinned. "Oh no, Joy. You need to really give that thought—

it's a commitment. Let's cover those roots and what about a trim instead?" she wisely suggested.

Taylor was right. As I flipped through magazines mindlessly while the chestnut brown dye saturated my hair, I was starting to understand why women make standing appointments. I savored the fingertips that massaged my head, the shampoo suds bubbling on my scalp, the warm water during the rinse. The best part was the neck massage. I raised my chin, leaning back further, and asked for a hand towel to wipe the water that dripped into my ear.

My mom always said self-care wasn't only what we eat and how we move. A quick polish change or making time to have tea with a friend were important for overall health. She also told me it took her years to treat herself the way she'd advise her patients. Her first facial, she'd said, was when my brother and I were in high school.

As I opened another magazine, yearning dripped onto the page, blurring words and smearing images. I guess accepting I'd never be a mother would take longer than I thought.

"I'm ready for you, Joy!" Taylor chirped, retrieving me from the quicksand of gloom.

I left the magazine open, hoping the vent that blew hot air above me would dry the pages.

"Wow, your hair has gotten so long! And I haven't seen you since—"

I cut her off and changed the subject.

"Great snow on the mountain. How many runs have you done?" I watched in the mirror as Taylor divided my hair into even sections. Then she wrapped the first wide piece over a round brush, going over it from top to bottom with her Dyson dryer. I marveled at Taylor's patience and ability to tame my frizzy, thick hair into a smooth work of art.

"Funny you ask. Not as many as normal; the kids are more into snowboarding than skiing these days. But I told my partner we need to go this weekend, even if it's just us," she said, spraying heat protectant into the ends of my hair.

"How're you doing? Andre?"

I twisted my wedding ring and unsnapped the top of the rayon cape. The one journalism class I'd taken in college came back to me, something specific the professor had shared. She'd said that the best sources were hairdressers and bartenders. For many people, it's almost like informal therapy. I didn't tend to talk about personal stuff here. Mel and other friends came to this salon, too; they yapped about their sex lives, children, perimenopause with literally no filter.

I'd known Taylor since we first moved to Vermont. And, clearly, she knew me well. I released air slowly from my mouth.

"It's been hard. I miss my mom more than I can put into words," I started. "It's so kind of you to ask. Yet when people do, I know they are being caring and compassionate, but it sometimes makes me feel worse. Does that make sense?"

Taylor turned off the blow dryer and plugged in the flatiron. Then she placed her steady hands on my elevated shoulders. Our eyes met in the reflection.

"I totally get it. I know it's not the same, but my grandmother was like a mother to me, more than my own ever was. She died in her sleep. No pain. No suffering. Lived to an old-ish age. Still hurts even though I'm told I should be grateful I had her in my life for so long," Taylor prattled. She handed me a box of tissues.

"Did I say too much? Shit, I never know when to shut up," she said, running a comb down the middle of my head and parting my hair.

I wiped my nose and lifted the corners of my mouth.

"Oh Taylor, not at all. I appreciate you understanding, getting it, getting me. Honestly, it helps to hear. I wish the tightness in my chest would soften; I've never had asthma, but this must be how it feels," I said, sighing and clasping my shaky hands in my lap.

"Let's talk about something else. What spicy plans do you have with your hot Valentine this weekend?" Taylor winked and continued to press my hair between the scorching steel plates.

"I made him a photo album and tried to capture our two decades in milestone images. Our tenth anniversary. Walking down the aisle. The first time we went snowshoeing," I shared.

Taylor beamed. "Of course you did. Creative, thoughtful, unique. Gurl, you make the rest of us look lame. I got my boyfriend Lake Champlain truffles, and he can have me for dessert. Scored a deal on slutty jammies and got us a new toy that—"

I held up my palm, not wanting to hear the details.

"Taylor, save that for him, please." I wrinkled my nose. "Oh. *Oh!* I didn't tell you. I have freaking huge news!"

She dropped the thin, plastic comb. As she squatted to pick it up, I saw a sliver of a rainbow on the shiny tile. When she stood, it was gone.

"Oooooooo, Joy! I knew it. You're finally pregnant, right?" Taylor shrieked. I've never been so thankful for a room full of chatter and blow dryers, which muted her embarrassingly loud (and false) guess.

I looked down at my taupe, lambskin boots, noticing a scratch and swearing under my breath. I'd recently purchased them.

Taylor shimmied her upper body and puckered her lips like she was in on a secret. I ripped off the cape, suddenly feeling nauseated and needing the bathroom.

"I'll be right back." I stood and bolted to the back of the salon. Splashing icy water on my face, I dabbed my forehead and cheeks with the recycled paper towels. Though I appreciate environmental conservation, the rough materials (like the crepey toilet paper) weren't absorbent. I needed to use extra, which of course canceled, at least in my opinion, the whole intention of saving trees.

A firm knock on the door jarred me.

"Almost done!" I lied, seeing that I'd dampened a few strands of hair near my temples.

I sank back into the soft, vinyl chair.

"So? Was I right?" she asked. Taylor didn't relent.

"No. But there's something else I can't wait to tell you about!" She handed me a mug, and steam rose from the top of it. "You're the best. How'd you know I needed a cup of ginger tea?"

She grinned and tightened the strap on her corduroy overalls.

"I am listening. I hate to rush you, but my next client will be arriving soon. She's rarely late. Start talking while I finish straightening your gorgeous locks," Taylor said. "And tell me all the deets!"

I rambled about the rainbow, the ad in the newspaper, and that I was about to sign the contract. As I shared more about the camp, it started to feel real. I was proud of myself for navigating and negotiating this deal all on my own. I'd driven by the property, which was about an hour from our house, but Andre hadn't seen it yet. I told him that's all I wanted for Valentine's Day—time together that included a visit to Camp Von Glad.

———

Andre had booked a reservation at Shelburne Chalet, a quaint restaurant with all local fare. He also brought a bottle of Cabernet, showing me the vintage: it was the same year we'd gotten married. Hints of blackberry and cherry lingered on my lips. The wine perfectly paired with our cuisine. Pickled cauliflower and carrots accompanied rosemary, roasted chicken from the nearby Misty

Knolls farm. We also ordered a cheese sampler—all my faves—goat cheese, aged cheddar, and sheep feta served with fresh fig jam and crispy flatbread crackers.

We both promised not to talk about work. As I savored the homemade pistachio gelato, I thought about how being present and focusing on us had never been challenging for me. Yet now, all I could think about was my upcoming meeting with the camp director, Dave, who I'd heard was like a puppeteer maneuvering marionettes. His knowledge and the ease with which he ran the camp was the main reason for its longevity and success, Vivienne had told me.

Counselors were loyal to him as well, which accounted for the low turnover rate with staff. I'd researched comparable camps nationwide, and the camper-to-counselor ratio was one of the lowest in the region. This mattered to me. I wanted all children to receive the attention and nurturing they deserved. Kids that returned became junior counselors; there was a thoughtful system in place to foster a multigenerational community. In fact, Dave was a camper back in the 1990s.

"Mi amor. Where'd you go?" Andre asked softly, his voice trailing off at the end of the question. His hand shook after he finished signing the check.

I'd totally zoned out and didn't realize we'd finished our dinner.

"I'm right here!" I joked, hoping he wouldn't probe further.

He sighed and raised an eyebrow.

"Hilarious. Let's get going—the blizzard is supposed to start soon. Though you know what they say here. Wait five minutes and the weather will change," he said. Andre stood and held my coat as I slipped my arms into the sleeves.

I directed him down a gravel road, not far from the restaurant. He squinted and I handed him his glasses.

"Damn, it's dark outside," Andre remarked. "And these rocks better not put dings in my car; I got it detailed last week."

My heartbeat quickened as we got closer. Maybe coming here at night wasn't the most brilliant idea. I squirmed in the leather seat like a toddler who needed the potty. Andre looked at me sideways.

"Here it is! Put on your brights so you can see it better!" I shrieked. And I thought telling Taylor about the camp made it real. Seeing it as the soon-to-be official owner through this lens, no longer in the distance, but zoomed in, overwhelmed me. Doubt seeped into my heart, threatening to dampen my exhilaration. I chewed the bottom of my lip as we approached the entrance.

"Joy?"

"Yes?"

"Is this the camp?" Andre asked, seeming puzzled and mildly disappointed.

"It sure is, sweetie." My pitch shot up an octave. I twisted my hair into a low bun, totally ruining Taylor's artistry.

"Now I'm thinking that taking you here for the first time in the dark—"

Andre put the car in park and pressed an olive finger to my lips. Then he unbuckled his seatbelt, reached across the console, and kissed me until I was breathless. He started to move his hand under my cashmere sweater—I squeezed it and pushed it away.

"What? Can't a guy who's got the hots for a gal get to second base?" Andre laughed.

"As much as that sounds enticing, I'm about to own this place. Not a good look for me to make out with you here," I giggled, planting another kiss on Andre's full lips. "C'mon. I brought flashlights. I want to show you the camp."

I walked Andre around some of the property, bummed that he couldn't see the lakefront or the garden. I'd also brought a lantern, which illuminated the flagpole area. I snuck him into one of the cabins; he couldn't believe kids survived for weeks in such a rustic environment. And the thought of a bunch of campers sharing two toilets was incomprehensible to my husband.

"Do you smell that?" I asked excitedly.

"I'm not sure," Andre said quizzically.

He never left home. None of them did. Carmen kept her babies close to the nest.

"The pine needles, firewood, damp dirt—it smells like camp!" I shrieked. Andre squeezed my hand and looked at me. It was tough to tell what he was thinking.

The wind picked up, and we dashed back to the car. Vivienne told me I could stop by camp anytime; the renderings and copious information Tabitha sent were accurate. But seeing drawings and reading data paled in comparison to being there on this beautiful campus. Dave, the camp director, had offered to meet us here. I'd already visited during the day, yet now I felt like a teen trespassing on a locked property, but we didn't have to scale the fence. Visualizing that image made me laugh.

"Are you sure all the structures are solid? Some of those bunks looked like they'd collapse with a heavy rainstorm. And the roof on the health clinic—" Andre started picking apart the architectural aspects on our way home. I'd been ready for this possibility.

"I hear you. The camp just passed reaccreditation, which gives us enhanced exposure and credibility. There are extra inspections scheduled for early spring; I've been assured that there's a specific and comprehensive checklist. After that's completed, I'd love for you to take another look; you always notice what others do not," I blathered on in one breath. Andre smiled and I unwound my hair, which curled at the ends and skimmed my shoulders.

Flurries danced in front of the headlights, blowing sideways and downward as the storm started. When we pulled into the driveway, the snowflakes got larger and snow fell faster. I was glad I'd stocked up on food in case we lost power. Childhood training in hurricane preparedness never leaves a native Floridian.

After hanging up my coat in the mudroom closet, I rummaged through the pantry. I had a hankering for hot cocoa. I boiled water in the teapot on our gas stove. Then popped some mini marshmallows in my mouth, each one dissolving into sugary velvet on my tongue. I reached for the phone and began to dial my mom's number.

The tea kettle sang, signaling the water was ready, and jolting me as I became aware of what I was doing. Pouring the piping water over the powdered chocolate, I stood there, mesmerized, and couldn't believe it'd been five months since I'd heard my mother's voice. The crater in my chest widened.

"Joy! ¡*Te necesito ahora mismo*!" Andre shouted, though not as loudly as he would've a year ago. My husband only spoke full sentences in Spanish when he was upset. I patted my eyes with the dark gray dishtowel and bounded down the steps to the basement.

"What's up?"

"I need towels. ¡*Es urgente*!"

"Why?"

"A pipe burst. Stop asking questions and get the towels," Andre grumbled.

"But didn't we put the heat up before we left? I don't understand," I said.

He was on all fours, a wrench in one hand while his other wrapped around the copper pipe. I looked down and saw his knees sitting in about two inches of water.

"Ohhhh. I'll be right back!"

I joined him on the cement floor in the boiler room and cleaned up the water. Something dripped on my ear.

"Is it still leaking?" I looked up and saw Andre's pursed lips.

"Almost fixed it," he said as the wrench clanged to the floor. "This is annoying."

I picked it up. His hand trembled where it rested on his leg.

There's no way he hasn't noticed this time. We've got to see that specialist Dr. Goldman recommended.

"All done! Whew! I thought I might have had to call the plumber," Andre said, wiping his forehead with the sleeve of his sweater. "These weren't the pipes I hoped would blow tonight." I laughed, grateful for the distraction.

"I'm exhausted and you look tired, too. Mind if we wind down?" Andre said sheepishly. The pressure from society to produce Hallmark-worthy celebrations on stupid holidays like this one irritated me. His forehead scrunched like an accordion.

"It is fine. Tonight was as it was meant to be—thanks for trudging out in this glacial weather to see the camp," I murmured, resting my forehead on his firm chest. "Clearly I need to take you back during the day; I should've brought headlamps!"

As we headed back upstairs, Andre wriggled his nose and sniffed the air like a bunny rabbit.

"Do I smell hot chocolate?"

"You sure do. Except it's likely now more of a milkshake. I'll reheat it," I said. We lit a fire and snuggled on the couch, sipping from oversized mugs while listening to the logs crackle. I polished off the rest of the mini marshmallows before we got ready for bed. And I brushed my teeth mindfully, longer than Andre for once.

CHAPTER 18

Several inches of snow accumulated overnight. Our backyard looked like a gingerbread house; a thick, white layer of snowflakes covered the deck. Pompoms of frosty fluffs adorned pine needles and low bushes. I threw off the down comforter, slid my feet into slippers, and padded to the family room. I had a sudden urge to make a snowman.

I looked out the narrow windows that flanked our front door. The pathway to our house must've had at least a foot of snow. We'd need to plow it later; the streets would be cleared by our association management company. Days like these I was extra thankful for whoever invented the garage.

"Andre! Have you been outside yet?" I shrieked as I skipped to his office.

He held up a finger and pointed to the computer. *What the heck was he doing on a Zoom call on a Sunday?* I mouthed, "Who're you meeting with?"

Scribbling on a ripped sheet of paper, he handed me a note.

"I'll be off in five minutes. Promise. Get dressed. Someone's stopping by soon," he wrote.

Now I was totally perplexed.

I threw on a scarlet hoodie, soft sweatpants, and met my husband in the kitchen.

"I made us omelets and Belgian waffles." He handed me a plate. The dish shook a bit, which was concerning because it wasn't the heavy ceramic one. He'd arranged the food on light bamboo, reusable plates.

"Thank you, sweetie." I took a bite and savored the kale, mushrooms, and broccoli. Then I drizzled dark maple syrup in each square of the waffle, remembering when my mom would do that when I was a kid. Julian and I would say it was like tic-tac-toe.

I wiped a crumb from the corner of Andre's mouth. He gently pushed my hand away, embarrassed it seemed.

"You are welcome," he said in what sounded like a whisper. He cleared his throat, then spoke again. "Your Valentine's gift should be here soon."

I told him no presents this year. The camp and all it would entail was enough for a lifetime. I tilted my head.

"I know you have questions—always." Andre chortled. "Nothing to answer other than the doorbell."

As if on cue, the chime rang and my heart pounded—excitement mixed with anxiety. Though I usually loved surprises, lately they made me nervous. Too many unknowns this year. Too much out of my control. I wiped my palms on my thighs before unlocking the door.

A woman with silvery hair pulled back in a long, thick braid stood in front of me. I'd never seen her before.

"Hello dear, I'm Peggy. It's nice to meet you!" she said with a southern drawl. "Is your sweet husband around? He's such a doll."

Who on earth was this fairy-like person?

"May I help you with something?" Maybe she was lost?

Andre joined me in the doorway, embracing this woman as if they were long-lost cousins.

"Peggy! It's lovely to meet you in person. Thanks for trekking here—I hope the ride wasn't too terrible," he said, inviting her into our home. I looked up at my husband and back down at Peggy.

"Would you kindly open the garage? I forgot something in my car. And I don't want to mess up this stunning home," she said, her sapphire eyes twinkling.

Andre always told me way ahead of time if we were having visitors. This was getting more bizarre by the minute. Before I could interrogate him, Andre pivoted and asked me to come with him. What greeted us wasn't a human visitor. The cutest, honey-colored puppy wriggled in Peggy's arms.

"Happy Valentine's Day!" she said, carefully placing the pup on the ground and handing me a short leash. I was so shocked I didn't even blink. Or, possibly, breathe.

Peggy laughed as Andre looped the end of the leash over his wrist.

"Welcome home, little one. Let's show you the mudroom," he said. The puppy's round, toffee eyes gazed at my husband.

"Let me leave you with your new baby for a bit. I have the food, chew toys, vaccine records, and crate in my trunk. It's best if you sit on the floor and let her explore her surroundings," Peggy called over her shoulder.

Was this a joke? What the hell was happening?

"Ummm. I. Don't. Know. What. To. Say," I said, the staccato words escaping between my pursed lips.

"I thought this would cheer you up. You've always said that you miss having a dog, and since we're not having kids, I figured we could raise a puppy!" He picked up the pup, who nuzzled her tiny, wet nose into Andre's neck.

Is he fucking serious? Did my husband dare to insinuate that a dog could replace having a baby? The pebble in my throat widened, and I couldn't swallow.

Absorbed in canine cuteness, Andre didn't notice my reaction. Then he pulled on my hand, dragging me downward to join him. Sweat beaded on my upper lip. I felt queasy.

He handed me the squirmy animal, placing her in the middle of my lap. She licked my fingers, tickling my hands with her teeny, pink tongue. My anger began to thaw, though not totally defrosted. The puppy was admittedly adorable.

The dog burrowed her downy head into the space where I'd crisscrossed my legs. I swear I heard her sigh contentedly. I rubbed behind her floppy ears, refusing to meet Andre's eyes.

Peggy bopped back into the room, and Andre stood to help her bring in the crate. What a smart woman; she had put everything in it that we would need.

"Is it okay to bring her into the kitchen yet? That's where we'll probably have her sleep and eat," Andre said. I almost snarked, "Oh this is a twofer—the pup and Peggy are moving in?" But I stayed quiet, grappling with intense irritation and a wave of sadness.

I'd never seen Andre so exuberant about an animal. I *kvelled* when we saw ducklings or even others' dogs on hikes. He couldn't care less. I felt the puppy's heartbeat against my calf. Her eyes were closed, and I heard the sweetest sound resembling a snore.

"Mi amor, are you coming?" Andre asked. I wiggled my toes and the bottom of my feet tingled as I tried to wake them up without disturbing the pup's sleep.

"I don't want to wake her," I stage-whispered to Andre. The puppy stirred, turned her head, then rested it back on her paws. Andre padded toward me, squatting and scooping her up in his arms.

"Let's go inside, little one. We also need to name you!" he said into the fluffy fur.

He doesn't ask if I'm okay with this and assumes we're keeping the animal. Had Andre officially lost his mind?

"It's good you asked for me to bring her now rather than at ten weeks old; she's learned how to go on the training pads, and she's also doing super well in the crate," Peggy said to us, gazing at the pup like a proud grandma. "She can make it at least five hours at night now!"

My pursed lips parted, and a gazillion questions pinged in my head like a group text. Andre saw my expression.

"I've got all the night walks. I've been watching dog training videos for a few weeks. I'll help with teaching her commands, too." He kissed my blazing cheek.

I'd taken off my socks and left them in the laundry room. I felt a creature nibbling at my big toe and, despite my irritation, I chuckled. Then the pup tinkled right there next to my foot; I couldn't even get angry. She seemed thoughtful and brilliant, clearly. At fourteen weeks old, she already knew that piddling on the wood was a better idea than peeing on a person.

"If y'all don't have any questions, I need to get going. You have my cell phone number and email; we can FaceTime if you ever need help," Peggy said as she floated toward the front door.

I cleared my throat loudly. "I have many questions but just one for you," I said, glaring at my husband. "Where is she from, this cutie pie?"

"Your hubby did a darn good job. Boy, does he love you. We're the top Goldendoodle breeder in the nation—our place is in northern Florida," she replied. "And this sweetie is an F1B, so she won't shed. Small-medium because the mister mentioned that y'all travel a ton—she's portable."

My eyes darted around the area. I was already looking for potential choking hazards and any other spaces we'd need to puppy proof. Andre locked the door and stuck out his chest.

"So?" The cleft in his chin deepened.

"I am totally stunned," I began. "I'm not sure what to say."

I tore the last paper towel off the roll, wiping the pup's third little liquid gift in an hour. Interestingly, Andre didn't seem to mind. Yet he'd flip if there was even one crumb on the countertop. I watched the puppy explore our family room and couldn't suppress a small smile.

"Admit it—she's adorable, right? I searched for the perfect breeder and temperament. I literally interviewed nine different people. Then I asked them for videos, the genetic testing on each parent, and—"

I swallowed hard, my breathing returning to normal. I thanked the pebble for leaving, at least for now.

"This is so thoughtful and kind. I am overwhelmed with many emotions that I cannot explain. I need to process this all—it's going to change our lives in epic ways. You do understand that?" I asked, twirling a strand of hair into a knot. My mom used to tell me this habit would cause split ends.

"I know it's shocking, but you've talked about wanting a dog for years. And I really thought it would bring back some of your joy. You've always said puppies and babies are a balm for the soul," Andre said quoting me. I guess he did listen and remember.

I nodded and hugged him.

"I just need time," I said and dropped my arms by my waist. "Please, leave me alone for a few hours."

"That's why I asked Peggy to bring her today; I planned to take care of the puppy all week so we can get adjusted. I also paid for six weeks of training," Andre said, looking a bit dejected.

I heard the pup's little feet pitter-patter on the wood like raindrops falling into a pond. Andre said, "Sit" and she did right away. Then the pup gobbled up the treat that Andre gave her as a reward.

"She's such a good listener already!" He handed her a doggie rattle to chew on. I had to admit that it was both impressive and encouraging.

I told Andre I'd be in our bedroom for a bit, smirking as he spoke to the pup in Spanish.

"You also want our puppy to be bilingual?" I snorted, walking away and shaking my head. It'd been a while since I'd written in my journal. I had an intense longing to talk to my mom. I couldn't fill my lungs with enough air. And the damn pebble reappeared.

CHAPTER 19

Dear Mom,

Will this ever get easier? I wish I could speak to you right this second. I wake up with a jolt as if my heart has been electrocuted. Also, I think Andre's insane. Like in a great way and I want to wring his fucking neck. You won't believe what he did. I know you'd never see a family member, but seriously, Mom. He may need a psych eval.

I'm picturing your face right now doing that squishy thing you'd do with your lips when mulling over something. A freaking dog, Mom. A live, little animal. He surprised me for Valentine's Day with a puppy. Well, I was shocked, that's for sure! Yeah, she's annoyingly adorable and has these soulful eyes that look like melted Milk Duds. Her paws I already want to photograph—I can see a series in black and white. And that tiny blush tongue. Shit. Am I becoming smitten with this creature who'll cause total upheaval in my life?

Here's the crazy thing: The animal peed like at least three times in the middle of the kitchen. In like ninety minutes. Anal-retentive Andre didn't make a peep. In fact, he cleaned up the mess the first time! At least the dog didn't pish directly on my feet; she had the decency to do her business right next to me. It seems Andre thought of everything. He supposedly did a ton of research regarding the most well-respected breeder and obtained a comprehensive genetic profile on the pup, too.

So why am I livid? Scared? I don't even know exactly how to explain what I'm feeling. One thing my darling husband said made me furious. He implied that since we're not having kids, a puppy would be a good idea. Then he hinted at my mood since you've been gone (I can't bring myself to write the "d" word) as if this dog will be a serotonin or dopamine replacement. My doctor already prescribed Zoloft—acupuncture, meditation, and supplements weren't enough—so that's been helping me feel a bit more balanced. I remember you'd tell your patients how healing it was to be in nature and with animals. My therapist also suggested that I make time every day to draw my feelings or take photos just for me, rather than only when I'm working.

But don't you think he should've asked me first? I sure as hell do. I mean, can you imagine if I brought home a puppy without consulting with Andre? You know he'd flip out. Totally lose his shit. Though lately he can't consistently raise his voice. Even when he's upset and takes a big breath first, Andre's volume goes in and out like a radio that's running out of batteries. I'm worried about him. Something isn't right.

We went to see an ENT, who examined everything from the neck and northward. No nodules, no polyps, absolutely nothing. The doc also ordered a brain scan; something about ruling out a mass that could impact his voice. It took coaxing (understatement) to get him to the appointment. And our deal was one doctor visit and that's it.

But the ENT, clearly not convinced despite the extensive exam, recommended that Andre see a neurologist. Gave us a name, a buddy of his from med school who happens to be the chair of the neurology department at UVM. After more convincing, chiding, nearly begging, Andre finally agreed to go. As I write to you, it's a painful reminder of how much can and does happen in such a short time.

OMG, I just realized I haven't written about the camp. I did it, Mom. All by myself. Reached out to the owner—what a self-absorbed, haughty woman—and her assistant. You would've cracked up if you saw her ridiculously long, pointy nails and strands of pearls. I swear if I lit a match near her coiffed hair, it'd ignite and become a bonfire!

Since we last spoke (here I am again trying to fool myself as if writing one-way letters can be a substitute for you being alive), I am now the owner of Camp Von Glad. Writing this here makes it real. Also, that you're gone. And that I took a leap of faith, despite Andre doubting me, and I'm going to foster this community.

Every single child matters. You taught me that. You showed me that. You lived by that in every word and action. I've been thinking about that time in fourth grade when I was bullied. Then again in middle school. You're the one who encouraged me to take swimming lessons and pick up a camera in high school. I learned how to express myself in quiet yet strong ways.

I want to empower these children. I want them to know that even if they're shy or insecure, they've got to use their voices. After finding your camp diary, which I am starting to wonder if you made that happen, I feel hopeful for the first time in what feels like forever.

I've been incessantly researching every aspect of running a camp. The more I read, the more I realize there's so much I need to know. I missed a national conference but I'm grateful that the American Camp Association offers specific and thoughtful online seminars. I've already taken twelve of them and filled two notebooks with information!

The community of camp owners and directors has been kind; I've connected with people nationally and also in the New England area. Though Camp Von Glad has a long-standing history, I am understanding how important marketing is— even more so since the Covid pandemic. Speaking of which, mental health and well-being for kids—younger than I'd ever expect—has declined. I'm considering hiring a full-time thera-pist to support both our campers and staff. I can't believe what these kids endure! The teasing for being shy when I was a child was awful. But at least we didn't have social media. And when I got home from school, you and Dad were there. I'd get a break from the bullying at night. These children have no relief.

I'm changing the name because I am now convinced you are sending love from somewhere above. I saw this ad for the camp, and it's only about an hour away! Then a tiny rainbow appeared right in the center of the name, right there on the newspaper. I went for it. It's like kismet.

So, I'm renaming the place either Camp Kismet or Camp Keshet, which my rabbi told me means "rainbow" in Hebrew. It won't be a Jewish camp. I want this to be a place where all feel welcome regardless of race, religion, gender, the whole gamut. Now that I think about it, it's like the spectrum of colors in a rainbow. Distinct, vivid, individualistic. In its entirety, as a whole entity, it's an arc of harmony and beauty.

Send me a sign, Mom. You did with that journal entry. You did with the rainbows, especially the fleeting yet vibrant one that appeared on the advertisement for the camp.

Please, Mom, keep showing up. I need you. Even on the darkest days—and not only the unpredictable weather—these visits, these rainbows, light up my world. Signing off for now. I love you more. Never thought I'd add to our daily calls—I guess now letters—"I'll miss you forever."

CHAPTER 20

I put the cap back on the purple pen, remembering that it was Mom's favorite color, and decided to keep it in the drawer. From now on, I'd always write to her with it. I closed the journal, sitting quietly, bringing it to my chest. Then I heard my cell phone ding.

Hey there. You okay or do you need more time alone? Andre texted. Usually, he'd holler from wherever he was in the house.

Thanks. I'll be there in a bit. I wrote back. My neck tensed and my hands felt sweaty. I grabbed my brush in a futile attempt to tame my curls.

My bedroom lights were on, so I was surprised when I stepped into the foyer and saw the sun setting through the round window at the end of the hallway. The pup dashed toward me, and I crouched down to meet her. Immersed in writing to my mom, I'd temporarily forgotten that we were a party of three. She rolled over and her ears flopped to the side. I rubbed her soft belly as she gazed at me with those human-esque eyes.

Andre planted his tanned, flat feet in front of us. I looked up and he grinned broadly.

"Let's take her outside! I didn't want to do that without you. Peggy taught her to go on those potty pads, which are great, but we still need to walk her for exercise and training," Andre said, holding out a hand to pull me up.

"I could use some fresh air, actually." I wiped the remaining mascara from under my right eye.

"Here, hold her for a second, and I'll grab our coats," he replied.

Andre also said he'd learned that routine is important for dogs. I laughed and told him he already knew that because he loved his structured days. My husband rarely had white space in his calendar, planning nearly every minute as if his waking hours required an architectural sketch. He suggested teaching the pup that walks will always begin when we open the garage door.

Her little tail wagged as we tottered down our driveway. Icicles hung from the edge of the roof like hand-blown glass. I marveled at the snow-speckled hydrangea, periwinkle in the springtime and dormant in the winter. Why did this plant survive all seasons while others withered away?

Close to succumbing to these thoughts, the pup barked for the first time, snapping me back to her and reality. She walked ahead eagerly, pulling me as if I were the one wearing the leash. I wondered if she was cold, being from Florida and now here.

Andre and I looked at each other and chuckled.

"Wasn't that the sweetest sound?" he cooed, his voice trailing off at the end.

"Oh, look at her! Remember what we heard about not eating the yellow snow?" Like proud parents, we praised our pup for going in the proper place. She looked up at us, panting and pulling us forward.

The pup tripped on a slender stick that'd fallen from the tree above her. Then she explored it with her mouth; I thought about tossing it to see if dogs innately know how to fetch. Or is that a learned skill? Instead, I swiped it from her jaws, afraid she might choke. Andre yapped about us being in charge; he explained that dogs are pack animals and will behave better if they understand who's the boss. I tuned him out after ten minutes; she was so precious.

"I wish I'd brought my camera," I said, captivated while watching the pup leave paw prints in the snow. Then she stuck her entire face in a heaping pile right in front of her! I withdrew my cell phone from the pocket of my puffer coat. I plopped next to her, snapping pics from every angle.

"We need to give her a name," I said to Andre, still annoyed with him. He joined me on the ground—another rare moment because he didn't like to get his clothes dirty.

"I didn't want to push because you seemed pissed off enough," he said cautiously. *He had noticed.* "I'm thrilled to hear you've fallen in love with her, too."

I held up a gloved hand. "Let's not get carried away. And just to be clear, you *do* understand that you'll need to be involved—and I mean like daily—with caring for this creature. Camp planning revs up soon, and my schedule won't be as flexible. Are you sure this is what you want?" I pulled the hood over my head; the wool beanie wasn't enough.

"Yes. Honestly, I had this idea before you purchased the camp. Will it be a bit more challenging? Absolutely. But I promise to do my part. And I'll do the early walks—I know you prefer leisurely mornings," Andre reassured me. I wasn't totally convinced.

"What about during the day? Who will walk her if we're not home? What if we're out late at a dinner? Or on a trip? And how will we—"

The puppy discovered a pinecone that was buried in the snow. She held it in her mouth as she bounded toward me and dropped it into my lap. I couldn't help myself—I cracked up. We stood and brushed the smattering of snow off our backsides. We strode past our neighbor's house, waving at the two girls and their younger brother who were sledding down a hill. I told them they could play with our puppy as soon as we had a name for her. Then Andre tripped, and I grabbed his arm right before he face planted. He'd been clumsy in recent weeks, which was odd for a man who was usually so coordinated.

Though it was freezing, the back of my neck was slick with moisture when I thought about what the neurologist could say. Andre took care of everything—our finances, mortgage, cooking. I wasn't a kept woman. I knew he liked the control, especially since I'd launched my photography company. I welcomed him balancing the books and managing other house stuff. Pushing, prodding, and what felt like perseverating about getting answers made me uneasy, to say the least. My in-laws never went to doctors. Not only was Andre stubborn, but my nagging conflicted with how our relationship usually worked.

This wasn't us. I hated being in this position. I detested the nudging; it was depleting. I loved our carefree life.

As if my mom dying wasn't enough. I was starting to wonder if G-d had a sick sense of humor.

CHAPTER 21

I pried open one eye and my joints ached as if my whole body was recovering from a tetanus shot. I'd started to recognize these creaky sensations as grief. It seemed, or so I heard about it from podcasts I'd listened to, that what we don't release consciously may show up in a physical form.

I tossed and turned all night. My entire body was inflamed. I took Andre's poufy pillow and smushed it over my face. I'd dreamt about the camp—panicked that no counselors showed up on opening day. I'd seen images of my mom's funeral—my dad sobbing, her best friend hyperventilating, the casket being lowered into the ground. I wished my psyche would stop producing these harrowing images like a nocturnal horror film. If only I could find the button to erase it all. I threw the pillow on the floor, rolled to my side, and reluctantly propped myself into an upright position.

Andre's appointment with the neurologist was in an hour. As I flossed my teeth, I looked in the mirror, distressed at my matted hair and the dark circles under my eyes. I rarely wore makeup other than mascara and tinted lip balm. Maybe I needed to start. Carmen or my cousin, Tali, would love to give me a tutorial. I laughed, spewing water all over the mirror, envisioning their reactions if I asked. Those two had a full face—foundation, lipstick, eyeliner, the works—even when they played tennis. That fast-paced, externally focused lifestyle is one of many reasons Andre and I moved away from Miami. That's what we'd told our family and friends there, anyway.

After a quick shower, I rubbed moisturizer onto my arms, legs, and neck. Then I pulled a merino wool sweater over my head and buttoned my corduroy pants. I didn't need to ask if my husband was ready. I walked briskly toward the kitchen, startled by the sound of the puppy yelping. Andre was downing the last sip of his café con leche, unbothered. He was reading the business section of the newspaper, each hair on his head gelled and arranged perfectly. Did I now need to worry about his hearing, too?

"I know it's late, but it seemed you needed the rest," Andre said, looking above his wire-rimmed glasses. "I made you an egg and spinach wrap. Figured you could eat it in the car." Then licked his finger and turned the page. "The market is up today!"

The dog whimpered, her literal puppy dog eyes pleading with me through the slats of the black, wire crate.

"You do know there's an animal in the corner of our family room," I snapped, tapping my foot impatiently. He didn't look up and kept reading.

"Andre!"

"Babe, chill please. I'm training her. It's normal for her to resist. Everything I read and watched says the calmer we are, the faster she'll acclimate to her home," he said condescendingly. The fork shook slightly when he lifted to his lips.

I could barely deal with my own emotions. I related to the dog—I felt caged and wanted to escape.

"This feels cruel. How is it kind to keep her trapped in that tight space?" I turned on my heels and headed toward the crate.

"NO! Do not open it!" Andre yelled. Huh. I guess when he was pissed off, he could summon enough air to shout at me. Jackass. I briefly wondered if we should cancel the appointment. Speaking of which, we had to leave now.

"Who made you the dog whisperer?" I retorted, bending down, about to unlock the door. The puppy began to bark, her little voice getting louder. A clattering sound distracted me.

"What the—"

I looked over my shoulder and saw Andre picking up broken ceramic pieces. He'd dropped the mug. Andre started to clean everything up and was ready to go. I still wanted to release the animal from captivity—then I fretted that our fur baby might cut her tender paws on a fragment he might've missed. My husband must've seen my worried expression.

"She is fine. I walked her, fed her, gave her water. They don't poop or pee where they live. Let's go," he muttered.

Thankfully, we lived close to the University of Vermont campus. We drove past the entrance to UVM, and I watched students scurry like mice as they rushed to their classes. Some had headphones on. Others had their heads down, likely texting a friend. What happened to old-fashioned chatting? Gossiping about a party or complaining about an annoying roommate?

It felt like ages since I'd been in college. The sturdy, brick buildings flanked sprawling spaces where kids would throw frisbees and swing in hammocks during the warmer months. Now a light dusting of snow covered the green areas. I couldn't wait for spring to arrive.

I glanced sideways at Andre, who stared straight ahead. His hands firmly gripped the wheel; I bet he'd previewed the directions because he seemed to know where we were headed. Though it was a quick drive, I enjoyed the silence and tried to employ the calming techniques my mother had taught her patients. Lavender essential oil would be a dead giveaway—I had to be calm for me, for us. I reached into my canvas messenger bag, grasping the shiny hematite stone that I'd tucked into the inside pocket. And wished I could hold my mother's hand instead.

As we pulled into the last parking spot, right in front of the medical building, my stomach tightened. Perspiration pooled under my arms.

"Ready to meet Dr. Garcia?" I piped, sounding like I'd inhaled helium.

"Never been more psyched about an appointment!" Andre snorted, raising an eyebrow at me and taking my hand. "We just made it in time."

If you hadn't dropped the cup, then we would've been early. It occurred to me that I should share my observation about Andre's trembly fingers and clumsiness with the doctor.

We walked up the four, chunky granite steps. Andre held open the narrow door. A woman with strawberry blonde hair, cut in a short bob, sat behind the reception desk. She asked us for the insurance card and handed us paperwork to complete.

"I already filled it out online," Andre said. I looked up at him, astonished because he'd been dreading this appointment. "I appreciate the efficiency and environmentally mindful approach." Charmed by his wide grin, the woman thanked him for the feedback and smiled coquettishly.

"I wish all of our patients followed the directions on our website," she said. "Please sign this HIPPA privacy form. Dr. Garcia will be right with you. He's a stickler for punctuality."

I tucked my hair behind my ears. This man sounded like the perfect fit for my finicky husband. There was only one other person in the waiting room, a woman who looked like she was about twenty-five years old. My mind drifted like snow falling from a rooftop. I wondered why someone so young would be seeing a neurologist.

The paper fluttered in Andre's hand as he gave it back to the kind woman. She exuded a grounded, peaceful energy that I needed right now. Her face an unmarred canvas with minimal lines and a smattering of freckles. She was probably older than she appeared, with her dewy skin and a muscular frame. I bet she skied all winter and biked during the summer. And ate whatever she wanted. All in moderation, of course.

Summer. Camp. Garden. Oh! I needed to add that to my growing list of questions for Dave, the esteemed director. We'd spoken several times on the phone, and as Vivienne promised, he knew literally everything about the camp.

"Mi amor?" Andre said, draping his arm over my shoulders, pulling me out of my musing.

"Yes? Oh! You must be Dr. Garcia," I said sheepishly. "Dr. Goldman raved about you—so grateful you got us in." Tall and tan like my husband. I was starting to wonder if Andre had more relatives than he knew about.

"It's wonderful to meet you both. Come in," he said, guiding us down a short hallway. Vibrant photographs of Mount Mansfield, covered bridges, and cornfields hung on the buttercup yellow walls. It was a gallery of seasons, a picturesque portrayal of the Green Mountain state. When we entered the small office, I saw a few more wood-framed photos. These were a series of sunflowers, and they were stunning. I had to ask.

"I have a question," I said to Dr. Garcia.

"We haven't even sat down yet and already you're going to interrogate him?" Andre teased.

"It's not about you." I rolled my eyes. Dr. Garcia moved his head back and forth, seemingly amused by our banter. "These images are magnificent! The depth, clarity, and composition—all of it. Is the photographer a local?"

Dr. Garcia scrubbed his hands and then dried them thoroughly. Excellent. The man was methodical. Then he sat on his stool and spun around to look at us. He cleared his throat.

"My wife suggested I decorate this room—you both know how dismal winter can be. She thought drawings of the brain weren't particularly uplifting. Of course, I find them fascinating!" He laughed and rolled the stool closer to Andre. "Photography is one of my hobbies."

Mom, did you send this doctor? Dr. Garcia's face blurred, and I felt woozy.

"Joy?" Dr. Garcia lightly touched the inside of my wrist. "Pulse is strong. Let's get you a glass of water before we begin." He pushed a button, and a nurse seemed to teleport into the room. She handed me a cup of cold water along with an ice pack.

"This is hilarious. I'm not the patient!" I said sarcastically.

Andre felt my forehead with the back of his palm as everything became clearer. The stainless-steel faucet, box of green gloves, bottle of soap, the reflex hammer Dr. Garcia held in his hand.

"Your color looks better," the doctor said. "Andre, please sit on the exam table."

I pulled my hair into a loose ponytail at the nape of my neck. Then I opened the tin of Altoids and popped one into my mouth. When I was anxious as a kid, my mom gave me mints or gum; I found it still helped soothe my nerves. As I silenced my phone, I saw a text from Mel.

You've got this and you've got me.
You are not alone.

XO,
M

My shoulders relaxed a bit. I took out a spiral notepad and a blue ballpoint pen.

"Seriously? This isn't a college course," Andre said.

I laughed and blamed it on my muddled midlife memory.

"I don't want to forget anything," I replied, quickly flipping the page. I'd been documenting what I had observed. Andre didn't need to see my worries on the pages.

The doctor began asking about Andre's family history. Nobody had dementia. No relatives had any diagnosed degenerative diseases or movement disorders. Andre shared about his great uncle, and he vaguely remembered some siblings calling him Shakey Uncle Saul. Dr. Garcia asked about pesticides and chemical use. Andre said he'd never been a farmer or termite inspector. We all chuckled.

"It's great that you two have a sense of humor. It's refreshing and much needed!" Dr. Garcia's bushy brows united while he typed on his laptop. Then he proceeded with a detailed physical exam. He peered into Andre's eyes with a penlight. Tested his arm strength. Rapped each knee with the hammer tool.

He told Andre to sit and stand a few times without using his arms. Then he had him walk up and down the hallway. Dr. Garcia asked Andre to tap his index finger and thumb together repeatedly and as fast as he could. Oddly, he inquired about my husband's bowels.

"Actually, I've been constipated often the past five years. Coffee and smoothies don't seem to help anymore," he said sheepishly. *What else don't I know?*

I studied Dr. Garcia's face, searching for a signal like a new driver in traffic, but the man had mastered a neutral expression. I dreaded what he'd say. And yet I needed to know. My heart pounded as Dr. Garcia crossed his legs and put the cap back on his pen. Then he asked Andre to sit next to me on the other curved, plastic chair.

"I'm glad Dr. Goldman referred you. Andre, may I have your permission to be fully transparent?"

My husband nodded, his face paling from olive to beige. I took his hand and squeezed it gently.

"Let me begin with your strengths, and there are many. Our bodies have muscle memory. Those years you played soccer, the weight training, skiing, and regular physical activity are beneficial; I'm sure you know that, Andre."

Come on, doc. Tell us already. I pushed my feet into my boots, trying to steady myself.

Dr. Garcia rubbed under his eyes and continued.

"The information you gathered and shared, Joy, is also tremendously helpful," he said. "Based on my assessment, Dr. Goldman's exam, the MRI results (the radiology report stated no masses), we need to do more testing to rule out other possibilities." Dr. Garcia pitched forward slightly and paused.

My heart knew the answer before my head could process it. The pebble in my throat felt like a boulder. I glanced at Andre, hoping I still seemed calm. His mouth hung open, and he stared at the doctor, speechless. I put my other hand over his, pressing it between my clammy palms.

Say something, Joy. Shit.

"You seem to know what's wrong," I said.

"Is this serious? Will I be able to work? Am I going to die?" Andre said, his right finger shaking in his lap.

Dr. Garcia uncrossed his legs and raked a hand through his hair.

I rested my head on Andre's shoulder, worried that the man who'd anchored me our entire relationship must be shaken to the core. I popped my head back up and scooched to the edge of the seat, sitting taller.

"Why won't you tell us?" I asked quietly. "Dr. Goldman said you're the best neurologist in all of New England."

Andre didn't blink or budge. I downed the last sip of water and inhaled deeply, suddenly feeling like a full-fledged grown up.

"Dr. Garcia, what happens next?" I whispered, willing my pulse to slow down.

He moved the stool closer to us and cupped his knees with his hands.

"Those are all excellent questions, and in the coming weeks, I anticipate you will have more," he said softly. "Let's start by answering the first one, okay?"

We both nodded. Dr. Garcia started to explain the next steps. I jotted notes, flipping the pages furiously and hoping I didn't miss anything. Genetic testing. Brain scans. Medication for the tremors. I wish the doc would write me script for a sedative, I thought.

"I hesitate responding to these questions without further testing; we need to rule out other possibilities," he began. "The results of the brain MRI are unremarkable, and Dr. Goldman's findings are helpful but not enough for a definitive diagnosis," Dr. Garcia continued.

No no no. I'm not leaving this office without an answer.

"Please. We need to know what we might be dealing with." I choked on my words.

Dr. Garcia rested his hand on his chin, looking at the wall beyond us, pensive as we waited.

"What I'll say is that practicing medicine, in my opinion, is part art and part science. I've also found during my thirty years as a neurologist that bloodwork and scans don't tell the whole story." Dr. Garcia's earnest, hazel eyes darted from my face to Andre's.

"My research has focused primarily on neurodegenerative disorders, Parkinson's and Alzheimer's disease. I feel fairly confident that Andre, you may have Early-Onset Parkinson's Disease. I can't confirm this until we have all of the test results. And I'll be here for you both along this journey," he said.

"Andre, *yo sé que estás muy preocupado*. It's understandable. All the feelings and none at all are normal."

I didn't think it was possible to stun my husband further. Boy, was I wrong! Now I wanted DNA testing. Maybe these two were long-lost cousins.

My husband's jaw relaxed, he cracked his knuckles, and color returned to his face.

"*¡Tú hablas español! ¿De dónde eres?*" Andre exclaimed.

"*Soy de Colombia*," Dr. Garcia replied.

No fucking way.

The corners of Andre's mouth lifted as his cleft deepened.

"*Yo también*. Bogotá?"

"*¡Sí!*"

I think these two were on the way to a beautiful bromance. I started to chuckle. Four eyeballs fixed themselves on me. I burst into a fit of giggles.

"What's so funny, mi amor?" Andre asked, perplexed.

"I mean seriously. This is unreal—there aren't many Latinos in Burlington. What are the chances? Oh, Dr. Garcia, you're going to make a religious woman out of me," I quipped. "Lately I haven't had much faith in anything, to be honest." I took a crumpled tissue out of my pocket. Gross. It was used, but whatever. I blew my nose as Dr. Garcia handed me an entire box.

He led us toward the checkout desk.

"Hope will schedule you for those scans. I already sent the lab scripts electronically; please make an appointment. Let's meet again next month to review the results," Dr. Garcia said, shaking my outstretched hand. He gave Andre a quasi-bro hug, patting him on the back like he'd scored a touchdown. At least he didn't grab his ass.

They exchanged more pleasantries in Spanish; this time I didn't understand all of it. My proficiency in the language didn't exceed that of a ten-year-old. But their body language looked harmonious, well, as much as that was possible after receiving a potentially devastating diagnosis.

"One more thing, doctor. If you know what it is, why all the testing?"

He took off his glasses, slipping them into the pocket of his lab coat. Then he motioned for us to move into an empty exam room.

"In recent years, we've sometimes been able to target treatment and clarify the prognosis with these tests," Dr. Garcia replied. "Let's take it one day at a time. For now, continue with consistent exercise and a balanced diet. I'd also like to start you on a low dose of Levodopa for the tremors. How you respond to the medication will give us additional information," he said.

We left the office as the wind whipped and flakes floated from the sky. I couldn't believe tomorrow was March first. I pulled my turtleneck over my chin and didn't know if I quivered from the cold or what lay ahead. I knew Andre needed to be alone. Frankly, so did I.

I promised him I wouldn't tell anyone—not even Mel—about what the doctor said. Now I regretted committing to keeping this a secret. I needed support. I got it that some people preferred processing their emotions in silence. Not me.

As dusk turned to nightfall, my mood plummeted while the sun sank behind the mountains. I was desperate to go for a jog but sadly I couldn't. It was ten degrees and the weather app indicated that with the windchill, it felt like negative fifteen. I flipped through my notes, unable to read some of my own words. Then I checked my calendar, as I always do before bedtime, and forgot I had that in-person meeting in a few days with Dave, the camp director.

Camp.

I owned it.

How could I be there for those kids and my husband?

I had to make a call.

Screw the promise I'd made hours earlier.

He picked up on the second ring.

"Joy? Everything okay? You never call at night," Bill asked. "Hold on a sec, let me go to the other room."

I was sitting on the floor of my tiny office in a fuzzy, fleece robe. And not only thankful Bill had answered the phone but also relieved that Andre had passed out unusually early. He'd sleep off his emotions like oil burning in a frying pan. I ruminated out loud until things started to somewhat make sense. Since my mom's death, I'd started to understand that not everything could be rationalized. Still, I clearly hadn't accepted this fact.

"Before I say another word, will you promise me this stays between us?"

"Of course. Attorney-client privilege. Always," Bill reassured me.

I rolled up my sleeves and dabbed lavender essential oil on my collarbone. Then I had a flashback, remembering my mom doing this when she first taught me yoga. We'd lie side by side on our mats.

"Andre would be absolutely livid if he knew I'd called you." I tugged on my upper lip. In all the years we'd been together, I never went behind my husband's back. I cringed as I opened my mouth then clamped it shut. Bill sighed audibly as I nearly lost my nerve.

"I can't give you all of the details; I promised my husband not to share anything yet. We're still in shock and—"

"Is he terminal?" Bill yelped.

"Oh goodness, nothing like that, but it's rocked our world," I answered, trying to keep my voice steady.

"I'm calling because I've got to find a way out of this contract. After what we heard, I don't know how I can be there for Andre and manage a new business. I've always said family comes first, as you well know." My chest heaved and I started to sob.

"Now you have me worried," Bill said, his nurturing tone making the tears fall faster. "I don't want to pry but it seems this is serious."

"It is, and I need out of this agreement. Like now," I said, while choking on the last word. "Tell me it's possible."

Bill didn't answer.

"Are you still there?"

I heard ice clang in a glass. It must've been scotch-o-clock.

"Yes. Trying to find a gentle way to tell you this—"

"Ummmm. What?" I interrupted Bill, my heart clenching along with my teeth.

"There's no way out."

"How is that possible?"

"Let me rephrase that, Joy. It would require exorbitant fees and probably months to break the contract. May I offer you my advice—professional and personal?" he countered.

"I have a hunch you're about to do so regardless of my answer," I retorted.

Bill's bass laughter boomed from the speaker on my cell phone.

"You're damn right. Listen to me. With your brilliant brain and that huge heart of yours, too. I'll never forget when you called about finding the camp. Then your elation, the connection to your mom's childhood journal. In all the years I've known you, even with the photography business, I've never heard you so enthusiastic. As your attorney and as your friend, I cannot, in good conscience, support this decision. Not to mention it would cost a fucking fortune," Bill said. I heard him inhale. He was sneaking a cigarette—I thought he'd quit months ago.

"Tell me how you really feel!" I snorted. "I am a wreck. I can't share more right now. Let's just say we received life-altering news." I trembled as the words left my mouth. "Camp starts in three months," I whispered.

"You've got this. Friends who adore you. And Andre's family who'd fly here in a heartbeat. Don't give up on this dream—it's yours and also as you said before—continuing your mom's legacy. It truly is kismet," Bill said. "I need to go; my wife is starting to wonder where I went."

I thanked him for the pep talk. My head and heart had an emergency committee meeting. So many unknowns. Everything had changed in an instant. First my mom left us without warning. Now I might be a young caregiver.

What I did know for sure is I'd need to amplify my voice as Andre lost his.

What other choice did I have?

—⁓—

I must've fallen asleep on the braided, blue rug in my office. I turned onto my stomach, my fingers exploring the area in the dark. I finally found my phone near the leg of the desk and had no idea how it landed so many feet away from me. Holy crap, it was 3 a.m. Andre would be up soon for his workout.

I scrambled to my feet and tiptoed into my bedroom, hoping the puppy wouldn't bark. Andre murmured something unintelligible, turned over, and breathed heavily. I lay flat on my back staring at the ceiling, wishing I could erase the doctor's words that echoed again and again. I turned my head toward Andre, my virile, agile, and gorgeous soulmate. My eyes scanned each groove of his sculpted arms. Like a camera lens, I zoomed in on his calf muscle after he threw the covers off. I admired his six pack, dusted with a bit of hair like moss in the forest.

His syncopated snoring didn't irritate me tonight. It was a symphonic reminder of his aliveness, his strength, his existence.

I didn't know what would come next. I knew when I'd vowed for better or worse, in sickness and in health, I was here for the long haul. I wasn't giving up on him or on us. But how much more could my heart endure?

CHAPTER 22

Murky puddles pooled at the end of driveways as the snow melted. Mud season had officially arrived. Speckled with dirt like ground coffee beans, streams of brown-tinged water seeped into the street. I welcomed the warmer temperatures yet yearned for sunnier skies and drier terrain.

I'd hiked alone yesterday and almost wiped out in the woods. A couple and their young kids had asked if I was okay. Physically, yes. Emotionally? Not so much. Then I kept trekking down the trail, a bit more apprehensive than usual. Toward the end of the path, two feisty labs dashed toward me. Dogs, like their owners, often roamed freely here. I heard a man call for his pups; I squatted to greet them, chuckling as the bigger one put her paws on my chest.

Vermonters get the concept of community. It's not uncommon for strangers to reach out on the road, offering help whether it's a flat tire or that one time I got stuck in a ditch. It's funny how I had to learn to trust their intentions. Growing up in Miami, I'd rarely roll down my window. Here, I get out of my car and often end up engaging in a conversation.

When I looked at the calendar on my fridge a few days ago, I couldn't believe it was March. Mel teased me that I still used a paper one, in addition to putting dates on my phone. This one had inspirational quotes with floral images. Another lie I told myself—a pretty calendar would make moving on a bit more bearable. With every passing day, week, month, the canyon in my chest widened; I felt my mom's absence as time passed without her. It was unfair that the world still spun on its axis while mine had screeched to a halt.

As I read and researched obsessively about running a camp, my photography biz shrunk. I didn't seek new clients—I only had one shoot this week. Tomorrow I'd meet with Dave. I wrote an agenda of what we needed to review. I also prepared a list of questions and some new ideas. Connecting with camp owners from across the country had been helpful. But using the knowledge I'd gained from my self-imposed crash course filled me with a blizzard of fear.

On my drive to Camp Von Glad, which soon would officially be Camp Kismet, fog smothered my vehicle and I drove cautiously. This didn't feel like an auspicious beginning. I gripped my hands on the steering wheel, glancing at my sparkly wedding band. It's the March morning mist, I chided myself, trying to shift my mood like the gears in my truck.

My mind meandered as I neared the camp, again questioning how I'd be a young caregiver while embarking on this new endeavor. I turned onto the gravel road, lined with maple and pine trees, and the sky morphed from a listless gray to a serene, pale blue.

The rustic, rectangular sign emerged as I parked next to a Ford F150, a shiny, ketchup-red pickup truck. It must be Dave's—exactly what I'd pictured. I pointed the key fob at my car, and after hearing it beep twice, headed toward the camp office. Opening the rusty, screen door, I looked up behind me while making a note to replace the hinges. A radiant rainbow reached across the sky; I quickly took out my phone, snapped a few photos, and stepped inside. Then I watched it disappear.

"Joy! Is that you?" A baritone voice bellowed.

"Yep! It sure is," I replied.

Whoa. Our FaceTime and phone chats didn't represent the human being who stood in front of me. I hoped my countenance wasn't streaming the subtitles that needed to stay buried in my brain. Dressed in a navy and white flannel and baggy, worn jeans,

Dave clearly spent time outdoors. His rolled-up shirt revealed tan, tawny forearms with a dusting of golden hair. Lanky and lean, he had a close-cut beard that framed thin lips. Clunky hiking boots clad his gigantic feet.

I stepped forward and stuck out my sweaty hand. Dave opened his arms, a wide wingspan like a hawk, and gave me a quick hug. His relaxed demeanor put me at ease right away. I pulled back and looked into the greenest eyes I'd ever seen. Then I shook my head, envisioning an Etch A Sketch, trying to erase the images my mind conjured. *What was wrong with me?*

"Glad you're here. I can't wait to show you around; I know you've visited lots of times but we gotta get into the nitty-gritty now. Summer's just around the corner," Dave said. I noticed a tiny chip in his front tooth. "I have a detailed list of what I've already fixed and what needs to be tended to."

Vivienne had really nailed it—this man embodied the camp in every way. Our first stop was the dining hall. I peppered Dave with questions, and he somehow had answers for every single one. He'd fixed the circuit breaker, so all the lights now worked. He did an inventory of utensils, trays, and cups, and based on the current camper list, food orders. Dave explained this would likely change; we continued to work on outreach via emails and social media. He'd also arranged a meeting today with the head of food service who, like Dave, had been a camper. During the year, the woman taught high school nutrition in a nearby town. I introduced myself and quickly felt confident in her knowledge and ability. She, too, was affable and welcoming.

Then we moved on to the activities hut, which rested on top of a hill in the distance. Lanyards in yellows, reds, blues, violets, oranges, and greens hung on little metal hooks. Long benches accompanied rustic tables in the center of the square room. Faded splatters of paint streaked across the planks of wood—a visual story of the camp's history.

"Come with me. I have a feeling this'll be your favorite space!" Dave said, pointing toward the right back corner.

I don't remember a room being here before, I thought. As we neared the area, I saw a narrow, pine door.

"Go ahead and open it," he said eagerly, like a kid excited about show-and-tell. "I hope it's okay that I didn't ask first. Bernard gave me full reign here. And after I heard that you—"

"Holy shit! I'm sorry for the profanity," I said, covering my mouth.

Dave tossed his head back and howled.

"Are you kidding me? Wait until you hear the counselors on their days off. And the teens, too. We try our best to keep camp at a PG level, but with social media it's tough. Damn good thing the parents are still cool with our no-phone policy."

I stepped into the middle of the tiny room—the pungent smell of darkroom chemicals bathed me in nostalgia. White trays and stacks of photo paper brightened the space.

"You did this by yourself? I don't know what to say," I began.

He shoved his hands in his pockets. Then he stroked his beard and fiddled with the tongs near the water basin.

"Are you upset? Crap, I totally should've asked you first," Dave said, looking at the floor.

"Not at all—quite the opposite! When I stopped by here before, I found a few old cameras, a box of film, other stuff in the camp office. And I wondered how we could integrate it into the offerings. This is mind-blowing—I haven't been in a darkroom since college," I gushed, feeling unprofessional and trying to chill out. I was his boss, after all.

Dave cleared his throat and relaxed his shoulders.

"Guess Ms. Von Glad didn't tell ya that I'm an amateur photographer. In recent years, the parents and caregivers expect daily photos of their darlins; I fill in when the staff members are off. Back in the eighties and nineties, Bernard had a darkroom for kids to learn how to develop and process film. It got destroyed in a storm. When I heard what you do, I figured I'd rebuild it!" Dave bent over to tie his laces.

A warm, buzzy feeling spread through my body. *Mom, is that you?* I nearly said aloud. I'd started to recognize what I hoped, in addition to the rainbows, were her visits. I needed to be more consistent with writing it down. Maybe there was a pattern?

Those emerald, fiery eyes bore into mine. *Did Dave read minds, too?* I popped a piece of spearmint gum into my mouth and offered one to him. Then I glanced at my phone, seeing the three texts from Andre.

"Please give me a moment—I'll meet you at the junior bunks," I said, walking away from Dave. I'd totally lost track of time. As I strode toward the cabins, I decided to call my husband instead of replying.

"*¿Qué pasa?*" Andre answered, his voice laced with concern. "Did you get my texts?"

"I just did—so sorry! I'm not sure if the cell reception is consistent. Going to add that to my list for today's meeting," I replied, wiping the sweat off my neck.

"So proud of our girl. She mastered 'leave it.' When are you home? You've been gone for longer than I expected." His words trailed off at the end. I could barely hear him even with my headphones in my ears.

"I should be home by six. I'll let you know if anything changes," I said.

"Should? Dios mio, that's a long day," he responded gruffly. "Whatever. I'll make dinner. Call when you're on your way."

Dave took long strides and nodded toward the health center, which was nestled between tall pine trees.

"I need to go. Love you!" I tucked the phone into my back pocket. The effervescent energy I'd felt earlier fizzled. I didn't like the curt tone I'd heard in my husband's voice. Folding the papers in my hands, I knocked on the window of the clinic.

The lump in my throat had taken a vacation today. Until right now. Scanning the area, I saw that the clinic seemed sufficiently stocked. Q-tip swabs filled a tall glass container, probably for strep throat testing. When I was a camper, we'd have to drive an hour to a bigger town. Packets of alcohol wipes, bags of honey lemon cough drops, and packets of generic ibuprofen filled woven baskets. On another shelf, I saw metal combs and gloves, presumably for lice checks. I scratched the top of my scalp, not realizing how aggressively I'd done it until feeling moisture under my nails.

Straightening his mesh trucker cap, Dave chuckled and raised a golden eyebrow.

"Funny how even thinking about tiny critters latching onto kids' strands of hair can make you feel like—"

"Stop. Please. Yuck!" I interjected, tightening my ponytail. I continued to scan the room, surprised to see a stethoscope and other high-level items. The pebble occupied more of my throat, making it harder to breathe.

"You okay? I know some people get weird around medical stuff," Dave said, tilting his head.

No, I'm a fucking mess, actually. Being in this space suddenly felt suffocating, though all the windows were open. I'd temporarily forgotten about the visit with Dr. Garcia. I'd consciously forced myself to be present, trying to absorb all that Dave shared with me.

The exam table, which looked more like a stretcher, triggered a jolt of fear that nearly knocked me over.

How could I do this? What the hell kind of wife am I to run a new business and take care of my husband?

"Joy?"

I stared at the walls, pretending to be fascinated by the knots in the wood. Then I molded my dry lips into some semblance of a smile, turned around, and told Dave we should move on to the rest of the tour. I checked my watch, noting the time, and said we needed to go over other questions I had. He shrugged his shoulders and led the way, clearly not convinced. I shouldn't be surprised that a fellow photographer was also a keen observer. Dave assured me all was under control; still, I wanted to understand every aspect of the operations. And now with Andre's likely diagnosis, it would take extra concentration to navigate whatever arose. I guess my husband wasn't the only control freak.

Taking an admittedly longer route home, I tried to synthesize the tsunami of information I'd heard today. I kneaded the bumps in the back of my neck. At a traffic light, one of the few, I dialed Mel's number. Before she answered, I scribbled "don't tell her about PD" on the back of a receipt. I'd rarely kept anything from my bestie.

"Hey there, chiquita!" I said, hoping my upbeat tone would be convincing.

I heard a grinding sound. She must've been at the shop, though it was unusually late for her to be there.

"One sec, I need to finish cleaning this stone," Mel shouted. I continued driving, the road winding and my ears popping as I descended toward Burlington. I loved this time of day, an intermission before dusk as the light lingered, molten and glowing across the lush mountain tops.

"I've been waiting for this call, guuuurl. Spill. Tell me everything!" Mel chirped. I gave her a play-by-play of the meetings and told her about the activities center and how cool it would be to offer a jewelry-making class. She loved the idea, and the stream of others that cascaded from my mouth, but she cautioned me to ease into it.

"Whoa, my friend. I'm super psyched to hear you jazzed—I haven't heard you so upbeat since, well, you know." Mel caught herself. "Why don't you stick with what's worked for decades? Maybe next year incorporate these brilliant additions? It's gonna be a big learning curve." I sighed resignedly. Adrenaline had fueled my neurons, apparently.

"This is a switch!" I chuckled. "Since when are you the rational one?"

"You know I'm right. And don't you think Andre would agree?" An animal appeared in the road a few feet ahead of me. I swerved so I wouldn't hit it.

"What was that noise? Joy?"

"Oh, just me avoiding an animal homicide," I snarked.

"Deer? Bear? Raccoon?" Mel asked.

"Nope. Fox! What a beauty, too. I haven't seen one in ages," I said as I watched it edge toward the thicket of bushes.

"OOOO! This may be a sign—lemme go grab my spirit animal book," she shrieked. The phone clanked in my ear, as if she'd dropped it on the slate floor in her studio. "Okay! I'm back. Ah-ha. I knew it—listen to this!"

"Here comes your woo-woo wisdom. Hurry up, my friend. I'll be home in about five minutes; Andre's already less than thrilled that I've been gone all day," I said, lowering the heat in my car.

"I'll be quick. A fox symbolizes being clever, trickery, and things not always being what they seem. That's the gist of it."

"What else does it mean?" I jiggled my keys.

"It indicates a life shift and to be discerning in all decisions. There's more but I know you need to go. I'll snap a pic and text it to you," Mel said. "Kinda interesting, eh?" I bit the inside of my cheek.

I pushed the button on the garage clicker. "It sounds like you're home. Can't wait to hear more soon—love you tons!" Mel said.

Stepping into the mudroom, I pulled off my shoes and hung up my jacket. I heard the puppy scratching the other side of the door. It reminded me that we still hadn't given her a name.

"Hi sweetie!" She piddled right at my feet. "Thanks for the glee pee—I missed you, too." I laughed, grabbing a nearby towel to wipe it up.

"I am so proud of our girl. Wait until I show you what she learned—she's a genius. C'mon, Maple! Let's show Mommy," Andre said zealously.

Wait. What? Did he name her without asking me? Sweat beaded on my upper lip, and I yanked the rubber band out of my hair.

"Ummm. Really?"

He ignored me, consumed with tossing the ball and clapping when the puppy caught it in her mouth.

"Andre."

"Isn't she brilliant? I taught her this earlier, and she's mastered it already. *Maplecita*, such a good girl." He sat on the floor and cooed.

He not only gave our pup a name. The dog he didn't ask if I'd want inhabiting our clean, quiet home. Now he's using an affectionate version of it? I bit off the remaining part of my pinky nail.

"Would you look at me?"

Andre turned his head.

"Did something go wrong at camp? Why are you upset?"

Not until I came home.

"Well, a few things. How could you name our fur baby without me? That's not right and it's hurtful. I had an amazing, fulfilling, somewhat overwhelming day that I wanted to share with you. Silly me, assuming you'd ask." The staccato words shot out of my mouth.

"Ohhhhhh."

"Seriously? That's all you have to say?" I said as I stood unflinchingly. The pup—Maple—yelped and yipped. She must've sensed the tension.

Andre tripped on a squeaky toy as he stood up. For a second, I felt bad, like I shouldn't shout at a man who may have a neurodegenerative disease. I heard my mom's faint whisper, not quite her voice, yet, from when I was bullied as a kid. "Remember you are worthy. You matter."

I stood straighter, lifted my chin, and planted my legs farther apart.

"*Lo siento,* mi amor. You're right; I should've asked," Andre apologized and leaned in to kiss me. I pulled away after our lips barely touched.

I didn't have the energy to continue this conversation—at least he had owned it. Damn that sexy smile. It got me every time.

"I'm ravenous. I guess I like the name. It suits her," I uttered, sitting at the table and unfolding a napkin. "Thanks for making dinner—I'm a lucky gal that my guy likes to cook."

I twirled linguini on my fork, mesmerized by the circular patterns in the homemade marinara sauce. Grass-fed ground beef, bits of bliss between the strands of pasta, blended like a kaleidoscope of cuisine. After a few bites, my blood sugar stabilized, and I began to speak. I'd learned that flooding Andre with information never ended well. He'd tune me out after a few sentences, and we'd both feel frustrated.

He bombarded me with questions about structural concerns and outdated design. About to get defensive, I instead heaped a second serving of steamed spinach onto my plate. Then I sprinkled freshly shaved parmesan over it, watching it melt before responding.

"I hear you, sweetie. All excellent points and I'll write everything down later," I began. "I'm feeling more confident than I did this morning—the camp director has it all under control. He's thought of things I didn't find in my research." I took a generous sip of Pinot Noir.

Andre studied my face as if revising an architectural plan. *Why did it make me uncomfortable?*

"Are you saving this for later?" He chuckled, wiping a smidgen of sauce off my chin with his index finger. His other hand shook in his lap, which reminded me to ask about those follow-up appointments.

"Speaking of sanguine stuff, did you schedule the bloodwork?" he nodded and sighed. "I know it's a lot and I want to be there. Camp prep is revving up—I need to get those appointments on my calendar."

"Actually, I'm getting the labs done tomorrow. I know you're worried about my voice. But the shaking impacts my work the most. I've been reading the material Dr. Garcia suggested and meds can really help."

Wow, he is listening. Interesting that he also noticed the shaking. First time he's admitted it. How long has he known?

"Sweetie that's fantastic. Please give me the dates before we forget," I replied, keeping the questions in my head. I'd recently discovered that shoveling food in my mouth was like shoving a mute in a trumpet, except it's delicious. I placed my palm over Andre's hand, the one that didn't seem to shake. He turned it over, brought it to his soft mouth, and kissed each finger tenderly.

My pulse quickened and my insides quivered. Satiated by food but now starved with desire, I inched closer and ran my fingers through Andre's thick hair. I stacked the plates, pushed them away, and positioned myself face forward on my husband's lap. As he unbuttoned his shirt, I thought briefly that one day Andre might not be able to do this by himself.

Instead of succumbing to fear, I surrendered to my arousal, stroking him as his body responded. Words weren't necessary. Or high decibels. I pressed myself into him as he moaned in my ear. We never made it to the bedroom. Who knew my husband's follow-through on a doctor's appointment could be an aphrodisiac?

CHAPTER 23

awoke the next morning, upbeat instead of despondent for the first time in months. Andre had already left for work; I reached to the right side of the bed and pulled open the drawer. I propped the journal on my bent knees and took the cap off the pen. It'd been a while since I'd written to my mom. So much to share.

Dear Mom,

I spotted a daffodil sprouting between two rocks, its tiny yellow blossom about to open. It made me think of you—I'm about to enter yet another season without you here. When will the ache cease? I've read grief from losing a loved one never goes away; you learn to live with it. And the stages are bullshit. I can't even imagine experiencing the anger phase. Denial would be lovely cause it would anesthetize some of the pain.

You taught me to deal with life stuff head-on, though having my head up my ass would certainly be easier. Like my husband. He can compartmentalize his emotions, even detach from them. I know, I know. Not healthy, yet lately I kinda wish I could.

Speaking of Andre, I have news. No, we're not pregnant nor will we ever be, sadly. (Honestly, I'm not sure that yearning will ever disappear, either.) Remember I told you (shit, wrote) about my worries? This is one thing I wish I were wrong about. We saw that neurologist. His name is Dr. Garcia. Kind, patient, and though I want to hate him for rocking our world,

I'm also grateful the ENT doctor referred us to him. He's also nearby at the University of Vermont.

Mommy. My Andre may have Parkinson's Disease. Writing that in your favorite color, this purple marker, scares me. I want to rewrite it in pencil. I wish I could erase these words, unhear everything the doctor said to us.

I am terrified. And tormented by conflict, too. I mean it is frickin March, Mommy. (Why does regressing to this juvenile term make me feel better? Weird. Nothing is normal anymore.) Camp planning is about to kick into high gear.

My healthy husband, my bashert, my everything. He's always been thoughtful, level-headed, and lately, he's irritable. I honestly don't know how I'll manage it all. SO much to learn as a camp owner. Liability, programming, staffing, the health and well-being of the counselors, kids, entire community.

I've been interviewing mental health professionals, and I'm close to hiring someone. So many applicants, which I suppose is a good problem to have! Her name is Jenny—she's caring, compassionate, and relatable. She has experience with kids and adults. Without this upsetting news, it was still going to be hard. I mean, obviously. Now? Is it even possible?

I called our lawyer, Bill, and didn't ask or tell Andre. I preempted our chat with the promise he'd keep all I shared confidential; client/attorney privilege or whatever. I didn't give him details. I did panic, asking how I could get out of the camp contract. (Same guy who helped me sort out your estate—thank you again for planning ahead.) I can't imagine even getting out of bed if you hadn't been so thoughtful and organized. As you know, Julian's so far away; thank G-d for email and Zoom!

Bill didn't budge. He said I can't break the agreement because it would cost a fortune. But even more than that, he said purchasing and planning for camp has uplifted me. And Bill added that it was your dream, the journal entry you wrote, that inspired this crazy-ass idea. What was I thinking?

Anyway, Andre is insisting we keep his diagnosis a secret. Can't tell Mel. Or even his parents! First his infertility. Now this disease. It's going to kill me. Since you've been gone, I've already felt as if I have adult-onset asthma. You always encouraged me to talk it out. Trying to do that on the page. As I write, I feel a tiny bit better. Will this feeling last? Ugh. I think I know the answer. And I'll respect his wishes about the PD. Until I can't.

I have tons to share about this director, Dave. You'd like him. He's such a Vermonter—chill, grounded, and, of course, he has a beard. More than that, he's super knowledgeable about all things camp. I know there'll be bumps and detours. But it calmed my nerves to meet with him in person, knowing he's been there for a few decades. And most of the unit heads, nurses, cafeteria staff, and even some counselors have been there for a long time.

We set up frequent meetings that start in April. Then in May, we'll meet daily with different departments. Dave's updating me every morning with what's needed; I'm calling myself the CCO—Chief Camp Officer. OH! Officially changed the name to Camp Kismet. I'm going to redesign the logo and the website. I also hired an accountant who specializes in summer *camps. How cool is that? (You know numbers have never been my forte.)*

One more thing—can you believe Andre had the nerve to name our puppy without checking with me? I wanted to wring his freaking neck. I must admit I like what he chose so we're going with it. Maple is her name. And she's readily responding to it—it suits her. Like a proud papa, he's crate trained her and taught her five commands. It's honestly super impressive. She's adorable with the sweetest eyes. And empathic as well; she senses when our energy shifts. (I sound like you!) Charming like my husband, except he doesn't nibble on the furniture.

Sounds all peachy, right? Damn, I wish that were true. I need support. I need you. How can I be there for Andre and the campers—the entire community? I don't think I'll ever sleep again.

CHAPTER 24

aple had discovered her voice. Once a timid soprano, she'd expanded her range to alto and, occasionally, a tenor. Back when Andre and I tried to conceive, I'd read (obsessively) about child development and how babies have certain cries that communicate their needs. It seems that dogs do as well. I'd figured out the hunger bark and the "I need to go potty" whine. Andre trained Maple to ring this ridiculous bell he'd hung from the doorknob near the garage. When she nudged it with her nose, I knew she needed to empty her bladder.

The bitter apple spray we spritzed on furniture deterred her from gnawing. Unfortunately, she loved my bras and underwear. Clean, dirty, crumpled, she didn't care. The other day, I heard Andre yell louder than he had in a while. I bolted outside to see what on earth was going on.

Mud covered Maple's paws as if thick, asymmetrical boots had been molded to her little feet. She shook her head, splattering dirty water onto my fleece leggings, which were already headed for the wash after my morning run.

"Don't tell me you're mad at her for playing and acting like, well, an animal?" I said, staring up at my exasperated husband.

"That is annoying, for sure. But this is worse," Andre said, holding a piece of fabric between his trembling thumb and index finger. "She was doing her business, skooching across the pavement and looking uncomfortable. I pulled this from her rear!"

I studied the material he dangled in front of me.

"What the hell is that?"

"I have no clue, but it sure looks like something of yours," he snapped accusingly.

"You've got to be kidding me. You're blaming me for the puppy's dietary indiscretions? Also, not to mention, you are the chef and self-proclaimed dog trainer. Andre, really," I huffed, putting my hands on my hips. "Do I need to remind you whose brilliant idea it was to bring an animal into our pristine home?"

He held the wet item in front of him as if expecting me to take it. *No chance.*

"She could've had a bowel obstruction!" *Now he thinks he's a veterinarian, too?*

I sighed silently, watching steam swirl from my breath. It was freezing again.

"Well, what the fuck is it anyway?" I grumbled.

"It. Is. Your. Favorite. Underwear," Andre sputtered.

I couldn't help myself. Laughter bubbled from my belly as my lips refused to stay together. Maple chased her tail, her tongue hanging out of the side of her mouth. I made high-pitched kissy noises, and she dashed toward me.

"Sweet girl, you act so human. Sometimes I wonder if you are. You've got Daddy all frenetic; we have enough to deal with, Maple. Would you please stop stealing my clothes?" She wagged her tail, and I could swear she smiled.

Andre rolled his eyes and grunted.

"This isn't funny," he muttered, stomping in his black boots toward our driveway.

"Your daddy is like a crotchety, cranky old man lately," I whispered in Maple's ear. She jumped on me, her paw prints making a pattern on my T-shirt like an Impressionist painting on canvas.

I scooped her up in my arms, and she rested her soft head on my shoulder. I had the sudden urge to rock her like a baby. As if she sensed it, Maple tickled my earlobe with the sweetest puppy kisses. After dousing her in the laundry room basin, I towel dried her, hoping she wouldn't dry the rest of her body all over our family room rug. Andre murmured "thanks" as I put Maple down on the wood floor.

"We need to get going. Let's give her a treat and put her in the crate," I said, worried we'd be late for the follow-up appointment with Dr. Garcia. I was eager to hear what he'd say about Andre's lab results and scans.

"Just waiting for you, mi amor."

He had some nerve, my husband. His hair was immaculate, every piece lacquered with gel. Lately, he'd started wearing pullovers, a change from his typical button-up shirts. I bristled but kept my mouth shut, which had been tougher in recent weeks. I'd rarely argued with Andre until my mom passed—our squabbling felt foreign to me.

I wondered why. Maybe I'd always acquiesced to his needs in the past. Maybe our idyllic life made dealing with conflict uncomfortable. We didn't have much experience with bickering. Mel, Jake, and our other friends often joked we had the perfect marriage.

Grabbing my stretchy jeans off the hanger, I slid into them while pulling a jade, cable-knit sweater over my head.

"Let's take my truck, Andre." I said, my stomach roiling. I thought about the bag I kept in the glove compartment. When I had started my photography business, I'd had an experience early on that prompted me to put together a "in case of emergency" pouch. I was in the middle of a photo session with a young expectant couple. Nature demanded my attention, urgently. We'd arrived at a stream that in summertime would become rushing water. That day it was framed with icicles like the Waterford crystal glasses we'd received as a wedding gift from my parents.

Suddenly, my stomach cramped, and I needed to find a restroom. We weren't near the entrance of the trails. Shit. Like literally—I was about do so right there in my pants. Thankfully, I somehow held it in for another hour. And the photos were some of the best I'd ever taken.

As Andre drove to UVM, I unzipped the plastic pouch, taking out the Tums and deodorant. I also kept a pack of tissues, Band-Aids, alcohol wipes, tea tree oil, Advil, and bug spray in there.

"What if someone sees you? Lower your shirt," Andre said, his words clipped.

"Well, lucky them!" I applied the lavender Tom's deodorant in the crease of my armpits, ignoring my husband. "I refuse to go anywhere au naturel, though I know nobody would care." I popped a mint in my mouth, dabbed balm on my cracked lips, and put the bag back into the glove compartment.

Andre took a sharp turn, and I dug my fingernails into my palms. There were lots of spaces in the parking garage today; I was glad he'd booked the first appointment. Less waiting resulted in a better mood when it came to Andre. He valued efficiency over anything else. Speaking of moods, I jotted a note to ask the doctor about my husband's mercurial mood shifts.

We only waited about ten minutes. I wished *my* doctors were this punctual! Dr. Garcia shook our hands and led us to a different room than last time. The pebble lodged itself in my throat. It hadn't been present for a record-breaking week.

"Why are we in here today?" Andre asked as he sank into the oversized, camel leather chair in Dr Garcia's personal office. I twisted my wedding band, waiting nervously for the doctor's reply.

"I like to review test results in here. It's quieter and cozier," Dr. Garcia replied. My eyes darted from his desk to the walls, admiring his impressive diplomas and awards. Then I glanced behind him at a narrow console that displayed a collage of black and white photos—two adorable boys and a stunning woman.

"What a beautiful family," I remarked, pointing over Dr. Garcia's left shoulder. "And those other photos—I love the baby goats and dairy cows. Is that nearby?" The corners of his mouth lifted.

"Ah, my twins and the love of my life," he said. "Thank you for the kind words. Yes, that's Shelburne Farm where my kids love to visit. It was a monthly outing when they were little; it is tougher now with sports and study commitments."

Andre's leg bounced up and down. He cleared his throat and shot me a look. Message received. Dr. Garcia opened the file folder that sat on his desk. Then he shifted in his mesh, armless chair.

"Let's start with the good news! The medication I started you on—tell me, have you noticed any decrease in the tremors?"

Andre nodded. I didn't see a significant improvement, though I waited while the doctor continued talking.

"That's great to hear! As I shared in our first appointment, I'll reevaluate and adjust the treatments based on symptoms. You tested positive for a LRRK2 gene mutation, which is more common among people of Ashkenazi Jewish heritage with Parkinson's disease. It's a bit unusual because your family is Sephardic, yes?" He paused.

"Actually, my dad's family is originally from Poland. I wonder if my brothers should get tested?"

I lightly touched Andre's forearm, and he turned toward me.

"Sweetie, let's focus on you right now," I said. "I do think we need to tell your parents."

Andre planted his hands on his thighs, steadying the tremor that seemed to worsen with intense emotions.

"No. I don't want to worry them," he said emphatically.

Dr. Garcia took off his glasses and rubbed his eyelids.

"Can we go over the rest of the results? And then, if you'd like, let's talk about the extended family." We both nodded reluctantly. "The decreased dopamine signal on the dopamine scan—the DAT scan—further support my impression. And your responsiveness to medication makes your having something else very unlikely."

I cautiously glanced at Andre, the color draining from his chiseled face. My heartbeat tripled as I rubbed the inside of his palm with my thumb and uncrossed my legs. Questions flew around in my brain like bats in a cave. Dr. Garcia rested his chin on his clasped hands and looked at us.

"Andre, Joy, I am here for you both. And your whole family. Do you have children you'd like to bring in next time? We have a social worker who can—"

Words squeaked out of me as if a field mouse had hijacked my larynx.

"No. We don't and won't," I said woefully. Andre's breath hitched and he yanked his hand away from mine. *Maybe we couldn't get pregnant because of the Parkinson's?* I wondered if Andre's infertility was an early sign of the disease. Then my chest tightened as I thought about never having kids, feeling barren and broken, again. *Who would help me when Andre got worse?*

"Oh, I see. You mentioned siblings, Andre. Do they live here?"

Andre shook his head, telling Dr. Garcia that everyone, including his parents, still resided in Florida.

"*¿Y tú mama está preocupada, sí?*" Dr. Garcia asked, his gaze compassionate.

My shoulders lowered, and I jumped in before Andre could answer.

"I'm glad you brought this up. It's been hard lying to the family, and especially Andre's parents. The brothers, all younger with bustling, kid-filled lives, are a bit easier. But I don't feel right about—"

"Enough, please. ¡*Cállate la boca*!" Andre snapped. Even if I didn't understand the phrase "shut your mouth," his tone and expression would be sufficient.

"I know this is upsetting. But do not speak to me like that," I said unsteadily, heat flushing my face. "This reminds me, actually, to ask the doctor something." I glanced at Dr. Garcia. He mouthed "go ahead."

"Is there a connection between Parkinson's and moods that shift rapidly?" I inhaled deeply through my nose. I stared straight ahead, ignoring Andre's agitated visage in my peripheral vision.

Dr. Garcia put down his pen and rested his elbows on his legs.

"Yes, there is and it can be modulated with medicine. Andre, do you feel differently? And how is your sleep?"

"Oh, that too! I had that on my list to ask you about as well," I blurted. "He thrashes around a lot, especially his legs, and lots of shouting. I can't understand what he's saying." Andre blew air audibly from his lips.

"Anyone mind if I answer?" Andre snipped, the tops of his ears reddening. I looked down at the canvas messenger bag on the floor.

"Of course, please share. And I apologize if you didn't feel heard," Dr. Garcia said calmly.

"Nothing's wrong with me. Yes, I know the hand is shaking. Even my finger has taken on a life of its own, twitching when I'm not even moving it. Yes, sometimes my voice gets soft at the end of sentences. But what the hell regarding my mood? I am who I am and always will be." Andre pounded a fist on Dr. Garcia's desk.

"*Mantén la calma.*" The doctor stood up and walked to his cabinet in the corner. "It's common, Andre, for loved ones to notice before the patient does. I understand all of this is overwhelming—it's a lot to process," Dr. Garcia said, reaching for a box on the top shelf. Then he sat back down and took out his prescription pad.

"Hell no, doc. I don't need anxiety meds or whatever you're scribbling on that paper," Andre said emphatically. *I could use a double dose of mine right about now*, I thought.

Dr. Garcia continued, explaining that changes in neurochemistry could occur faster in some people and slower in others. The type of Parkinson's Andre had could present different challenges than if the symptoms appeared when he was older.

"Take a few days. Go on a hike. Get some air and spend time together. I strongly encourage you to start the medication next week. We can have phone check-ins to monitor how you feel. Sometimes, like with grief or depression, our awareness is clouded. It doesn't make you weak, Andre. You're still the same man who just needs some support. Would you refuse insulin if you were diabetic?" Dr. Garcia waited.

Bless this angel in human form. He was brilliant, empathetic, and figured out how to reach my headstrong (and understandably petrified) husband. The men talked and I took some deep breaths. I, too, was scared about our future. My phone vibrated—it was a text from Dave, saying we needed to meet sooner than later. A few hiccups, not much to worry about, but he needed my approval on some things.

I rubbed my temples, trying to assuage the headache that threatened to become a full-blown migraine. I didn't have time for it right now. My husband was hurting, and he needed me. We stood and I linked my arm in his as we walked toward the car in silence. I loosened my seat belt, already feeling stifled, and I pressed my cheek into the cold glass, hoping Andre didn't notice the tears drizzling down my face.

CHAPTER 25

After picking up Andre's prescriptions at the pharmacy, I drove to camp, welcoming the brisk breeze blowing through my hair. The scent of evergreens mixed with fir trees invigorated me. Dave had scheduled meetings with the unit directors and head counselors for each division. Normally I'd blast music from my favorite playlists. Today I craved quiet, mulling over April's arrival. I fiddled with the keys after turning off the car and strolled to the camp office.

I heard a repetitive noise and spotted a baby woodpecker persistently pecking its beak into the trunk of a tree. Its black feathers and red crest a striking contrast to the textured brown bark. Leaves formed tiny tents at the ends of branches, not quite ready to sprout. I stepped into a dip in the ground and mud splattered all over my jeans. Taking off my oversized cardigan, I wrapped it around my waist and attempted to camouflage the splotches of dirt.

Dave opened the door, took one look at me, and chuckled.

"Rough morning?" he chortled. "It's camp—you're supposed to get dirty! Wipe that mortified look off your face instead of focusing on your pants."

I grinned and stood straighter, pretending to be more confident than I felt. Conversations with Dave were comfortable and low pressure. But running my first meeting with the leadership staff was another story. *What if they didn't like me? What if they judged me for not having children? What if they asked questions I couldn't answer?*

My stomach rumbled loudly, reminding me that I had forgotten to eat breakfast. The thought of food had made me queasy earlier. Twenty eyeballs examined me as if I were a specimen under a microscope. I felt like the teenager who'd been teased for being shy. Wiping my sweaty hands on my thighs, I'd forgotten about the mud, which had dried and crumbled to the floor. *So much for first impressions*, I thought. I silently begged the pebble in my throat to take a hike, fearing I wouldn't be able to speak authoritatively (or however a camp owner is supposed to sound).

Sensing my discomfort, Dave stepped in front of me, and I exhaled.

"Everyone, this is Joy, our new owner. Let's give her our Camp Von Glad warm welcome," he boomed. The crew sang the camp song, snapping in unison at the end. Then I realized they'd arranged the chairs in a semicircle, reminding me of my preschool days. I almost said, *It's story time, kids!*

"Thank you for the introduction. It's wonderful to meet you all in person." I made a mental note to thank Dave for making name tags for the staff. I decided to leave the agenda in my bag. On a whim, I asked each staff member to share a bit about themselves: number of years on staff, their favorite activities, and one thing they'd like to improve or change this summer.

Person after person expressed gratitude for my willingness and openness. Throughout the day, I heard stories about Bernard, whom they adored and revered. Nobody mentioned his wife, Vivienne. The younger staff members, a menagerie of millennials and Gen Zers, had some ideas that were creative and cost effective. The high school division director was the only person who appeared a bit resistant.

I figured I'd wait to tell him, and the others, about the name change. I'd been ideating different designs for the new logo and overall look. And I planned to finalize it by mid-April. At first, I thought a traditional rainbow would be best. But now I saw fusing the past with the present, honoring traditions while cultivating new ones, should be represented in the graphics.

Dave thought of everything. He'd ordered pizzas—plain, meat, and vegetarian—along with garlic rolls and cider. After the meeting, we sat by the placid lake—I loved listening to the water lap the narrow shoreline. I leaned back, resting my elbows on the weathered planks of the picnic table, and realized I hadn't felt this relaxed in months.

I pulled out my phone, wiping the little lens with the sleeve of my sweater. I wanted to capture this moment, my first meeting, the camaraderie, and most of all, the harmonious vibe. After snapping a few photos of counselors skipping rocks on the water, messages popped up on my screen.

Why aren't you answering me?
When will you be home?
Did you pick up my medicine?

My jaw clenched and my breathing became jagged.

Andre's texts torpedoed my tranquility like a torrential downpour. I'd call him on my way out, which judging from the darkening sky, would be soon. I hurriedly swallowed the last sip of cider, packed up my stuff, and said goodbye to the staff. Dave offered to walk me to my truck, but I told him to hang with the team. He shrugged, straightened his cap, and headed to the cooler.

———

Bopping to the beat of Noah Kahan's latest album, I cranked up the volume and belted the lyrics. I'd started to enjoy these rides to and from camp. I'd rarely driven alone, and certainly not this frequently.

Maybe it was the movement of the car. Or the hour to myself. Ideas started to marinate in my mind like fresh veggies in the fridge that had been saturated in sauce overnight.

I was rediscovering me. Not in relation to being Andre's wife. Separate from being a photographer. I even contemplated getting a tattoo, but I knew my dad would've disapproved. He practiced Judaism more traditionally than I did. Twiddling with my latest piercing, a cartilage stud near the top of my right ear, Andre joked that I was running out of room. I loved the constellation of mixed metals that adorned my ears. I reminded him I'd even had a nose ring at Middlebury. Flashbacks from college—those carefree and idealistic days—boosted my courage as opening day for camp approached.

An ambulance siren blared from somewhere behind me, so I lowered the music. That sound always unnerved me, even when I was a kid. I slowly turned the wheel and moved to the right lane to let it pass. Then I pushed the backing of my earring closer and turned into my neighborhood.

"Hi sweetie! I'm home," I shouted from the mudroom.

No reply. *Weird.* Andre's car was parked in the garage, perfectly straight and centered. I was convinced that my husband could maneuver any vehicle even with his eyes closed. He'd always known the time—to the second—without even checking his watch. Precision. Perfection. Punctilious. Pretty much described Andre.

Recently, I noticed that he steadied his shaky hand by pressing it into his thigh. I wondered when the meds would really kick in. I hadn't seen a huge improvement, yet. I'd read that the dosage would be dynamic, needing to be tweaked as symptoms changed or progressed.

Not in the kitchen. Not in his office. *Where was he?*

I unbuttoned my jeans as I entered the bedroom, shocked to find my husband face down. Panicking at the sight, I dashed to the bed and touched his cheek. He stirred, flipped over, and breathed heavily.

It was only 7 p.m.

"Andre, wake up. Are you okay?" I felt his forehead with the back of my hand.

He opened one eye and turned his head. I turned on the lights, speaking more loudly this time.

"Get up, my love. I'm starving! I guess we should order in?"

All I needed to do was mention food.

"What time is it? Why is it dark?" Andre pushed his body upright, the tan skin on his biceps creasing between his muscles. I pointed to the clock on the nightstand.

"Holy shit! Must be those meds I started a few days ago," he grumbled, grabbing a T-shirt and pulling it over his head.

I ran my fingers through his disheveled hair and put a hand on my hip.

"Which ones are you referring to?"

"The light blue pills."

"Viagra?"

"Ha, no, we don't need those. Though I read we may one day," Andre said as he grimaced.

"Oh, the meds for mood." I chose my words carefully. The word *antidepressants* seemed to upset him.

"I talked to Dr. Garcia and he asked. Figured it was worth a try," Andre said, splashing water on his face.

"I'm so glad you started. It may take—"

"I know, I know. Four to six weeks to feel any improvement, though I think my mood is fine," Andre uttered. He called over his shoulder to tell me he would order sushi. Then he wanted to open a bottle of organic Spanish wine. I told him maybe he shouldn't drink until our next doc appointment; what if alcohol interacted with the medications? He didn't object, and I suggested we jump on a Zoom call with his parents as we did most Sundays.

Carmen's face filled the screen first. She gesticulated enthusiastically; I kept pointing to my ears, trying to signal that we couldn't hear her. Then Carlos joined her, his grounding presence palpable even miles away. He turned on the audio and smiled.

"Hola! So happy to see you both. *¿Cómo están?*" Carmen sang on one breath.

"What were you saying earlier? We couldn't hear you. Looked like good news!" Andre began.

"*¡Sí!*"

"In English please," he laughed. I squeezed his knee.

"Guess who's going to be an *abuela y abuelo* again? Your baby brother and his wife are finally pregnant!"

I whispered a weak "Mazel Tov." Then I looked away, claiming that I needed the bathroom. I lowered the lid of the toilet seat, sitting on it and studying my reflection in the mirror, wondering if I'd ever feel whole.

As I walked back into Andre's office, I heard him start to say "We have news, too. I'm so proud of Joy because—"

I quickened my pace and slid back into the seat next to my husband. Carlos made a circular movement with his index finger in the air like "hurry up." Impatient like his son yet calmer somehow. Maybe he'd chilled out over the years?

Andre brought the glass of water to his lips. His other hand trembled slightly. Now I was convinced strong emotions of any kind increased his tremors.

"My amazing wife purchased a sleepaway camp. Isn't that incredible? And it starts in June," Andre said, wrapping his arm around my shoulders and pulling me toward him. "She's a rockstar."

Carlos leaned back in his chair. Carmen fanned her face with a folded sheet of paper, and her gold bangles jingled. Maple, who'd been napping at the edge of my feet, leapt onto my lap.

Then the interrogation began.

"When did this happen? Why did you do this? What will happen with your photography business?" Carmen's questions hit my heart like darts on a dartboard. Each one closer to the bullseye.

Thank goodness Carlos interjected. He looked at his wife, then back at us.

"That's quite a big venture, Joy. We'd love to hear more about it. We've got time," he said gently.

At that moment, the Uber Eats driver arrived, and I excused myself. Maple followed me to the front door, wagging her feathery tail. After tipping the college kid, I took the sushi out of the containers and put the rolls on bamboo plates. Then I poured soy sauce into small, square dishes. Andre got up to help me just as I was about to drop everything.

"*¿Dónde estás?* Where are you going?" Carmen asked.

He held up his wooden chopsticks, showing his parents a tuna and avocado roll wrapped in cucumber.

"How you enjoy eating raw fish and seaweed will forever be a mystery to me," Carlos said, scrunching his nose. Carmen nodded in agreement.

While Andre snarfed down the roll and slurped his miso soup, I told my in-laws about Camp Kismet and what inspired my (insane) idea. Carmen blew her nose in a tissue, which had splotches of her coral lipstick on it. She crumpled it up and clutched a clean one to wipe her wet cheeks.

I decided this would be the apropos time to stuff my own cheeks with salad like a squirrel hoarding acorns.

"Mami, why are you crying?" Andre asked. *Did you really need to go there*, I thought, trying to ignore the strand of seaweed that was wedged between my two back molars.

Carmen sniffed dramatically. Carlos rubbed her upper back. You'd think I'd dropped the news that I had a terminal illness. Maybe Andre was wise to keep the PD diagnosis a secret, for now.

"My son. My eldest. The one who made me a mother," she said, unbuttoning the top button of her taupe silk blouse. "How will you take care of my boy if you're working so hard, Joy? Dios mio." She fanned her face again.

I gnawed at my lower lip and twisted my wedding band.

"We don't live in the 1950s. And you know I love to cook. This is amazing—I'm so happy for Joy," he said, rolling his chair closer so our legs touched. I'd finished the salad and had moved onto the vegetable roll. I dipped it into the soy sauce, watching it drip off the asparagus spear before dabbing it onto the plate and then into my mouth.

Then I mustered the strength to continue speaking.

"I understand your concern. I hear you. But I'm excited about this new chapter. And it's another way to be creative in a more impactful way. I can't wait to meet the campers," I said. "Plus, it feels like in some small way I'm carrying on my mother's legacy— this was her childhood dream, and now it's become my own." My breath hitched. Andre placed his hand over mine and squeezed it.

Carmen didn't look convinced. Carlos relaxed his shoulders after hearing that the financial piece would be stable, covered by the trust that already had enough funds to keep the camp going for many years.

We chitchatted about the weather, the rest of the family, and Andre's latest project. Then Carmen rattled me with what she said next.

"We're coming to visit for Mother's Day. We already booked tickets! We'll be there for a week; and now that you'll be so busy, Joy, I'll cook Andre's favorite meals." She beamed, turning her head to look at her first born. "I'll fill up that hew fridge!"

I'd never experienced my mother-in-law as passive aggressive. This made me feel even more defective. First, I couldn't give them grandchildren (they still didn't know their son was the reason). Now I felt like a neglectful wife. A fucking week in my house? G-d give me strength. I'd need to memorize the serenity prayer. Mel said it every night. At this point, I'd try anything.

Before my face said what my mouth didn't, I fibbed and piped, "We look forward to seeing you both! I'll make sure your favorite Lake Champlain truffles are on the pillows!"

After all, we hadn't seen them since the Hanukkah party back in December. I loved my in-laws; they meant well and were such kind, loving people.

Then why did I feel like I couldn't breathe?

CHAPTER 26

Dear Mom,

How is it May already? I feel like you've been gone forever. And no matter how hard I try, I still can't hear your voice. I try, really, I do. My therapist suggested that I watch my wedding video. I can't bring myself to do that yet. I hope one day it'll make me smile. Even thinking about hearing and seeing you feels like rubbing alcohol being poured into an open wound.

I'm writing because I finally dreamt about you, Mom! It felt so real. You were wearing your favorite violet, floral maxi dress. It matched the dangly earrings you bought on a trip to the Bahamas. Anyway, we were at the beach, just us, watching the sunset sink into Biscayne Bay. It was quiet and I was taking pictures of you dipping in and out of the ocean. Now that I think about it, you were younger, like my age. How odd! I mean, clearly that doesn't make any sense—it was as if we were sisters. I vaguely remember hearing your laughter, all carefree and giddy. Then I reached out to hug you and awoke in a sea of tears.

I've been reading and researching, even learning a bit about Kabbalah (I know, who is this girl!). I am craving a way to make sense of you leaving so young. People somehow find meaning, it seems, in the most devastating situations.

I can't. It's not fair. It seriously sucks.

And now Andre. The anti-anxiety meds are kicking in. He seems more balanced, or, I guess, less anxious and irritable. Damn it, Mom. If you were here, you'd make sense of it, the emotional parts, to me and Andre. I'm supposed to "process" my grief, blah, fucking, blah. Who has time? I mean, now that I'm also responsible for an entire camp community.

Oh, and did I mention my husband has Parkinson's?

Another fun update: Carmen informed us she's coming to visit. For. An. Entire. Freaking. Week. I've been short-tempered lately, which I read can be another way grief seeps like sludge into my formerly shiny world.

I don't mean that rudely, Mom. I'm still not myself. Will I ever be me again? Who am I anyway?

And I realize Carmen is coming from a kind place, but why the hell must she visit on Mother's Day? Carmen wasn't thrilled when Andre told her and Carlos about Camp Kismet. Lemme tell you—that didn't feel good. We worked through it but I'm not up for visitors—people or judgment. And she's a colossal personality. Her energy shifts everything like right before a hurricane.

The staff campfire is happening soon. It's a Camp Von Glad— now Kismet!—tradition. I've met the directors, unit heads, and other staff leaders. But it's the first time I'm meeting the counselors. I'm worried they will compare me to Bernard. What if they don't like or respect me? What if they ask why I don't have children of my own?

I have no fucking idea what I'm doing. Thank goodness for Dave—he's handled nearly every detail. So grateful that I've also connected with other camp owners through the American Camp Association. Doing a lot of observing, a ton of listening, an obsessive amount of research. This community has been incredibly supportive.

March Madness doesn't just apply to basketball—the past six weeks have been bonkers. I've had many conversations with the most amazing camp owners, who shared that springtime is when parents generally start making decisions about where to send their children for the summer. So, I continue to update the website, and I'm looking for an intern to help with social media. Turns out I'll still be taking photos; families eagerly await daily pictures of their darlings.

Despite all of the research and networking, sometimes I still feel clueless. I've been baking nonstop. A few weeks ago, I found your recipe for those gooey caramel and marshmallow brownies—I made four dozen and froze them. Bringing that for the camp crew along with ice breakers for tomorrow night. I'll write soon, Mom. I love you forever.

CHAPTER 27

"How are you feeling?" Mel asked, raising her voice over the soundscape of her bustling family. Giggles and squeals from her children. Her dogs yapping as if having a canine conversation. Jake asking where he put his car keys.

I lowered the music that blared from the speakers in my car. I didn't know how Mel could string together a sentence—let alone the pearl bracelets she'd been creating.

"I'm not sick," I retorted, twirling a frizzy strand of hair.

"A smart ass is better than a dumb—"

"You need new material," I laughed. Mel put me on hold while yelling at her eldest to stop jumping on her bed. "Why don't you sign her up for gymnastics?"

"I did. She's practicing a back flip off her mattress. I'm now hiding in the bathroom. Answer me before they find me!" Mel whispered dramatically.

I blew a bubble with the wad of gum in my mouth.

"Honestly, I haven't been able to eat anything besides carbs this week; it's the only food that'll stay down," I began. "I'm excited, nervous, curious, and having the absolute worst case of imposter syndrome." I tugged at my upper lip and bit a hangnail off my thumb.

Mel chuckled. "Pursuing a passion takes trust—in yourself and those who are on this path with you. And you know creating comes from the heart, not the head. You've got this. And I'm cheering!"

I'd heard that Bernard always attended and, although I wasn't sure how much or little I should be around, I did want to continue certain traditions. One of which was gathering at the center of camp, making s'mores, and singing songs. That was the one thing I loved when I was a camper. Now I sprinkled mini marshmallows on hot chocolate and occasionally ate them right out of the bag.

Mel twittered about the opening campfire, which I'd talked to her about for weeks. She reminded me about my skills—like being able to light a marshmallow on fire and then blow on it at the perfect moment, leaving it burnt but not charred. And about the time we went camping over a long weekend back when we were in college.

"I grew up in Vermont. Yet you got a fire going in minutes! I still have that scrapbook you made me for graduation," Mel said lovingly. "One of my favorite photos is the one of the four of us eating maple creemees—Jake and Andre had us on their shoulders."

Loosening my grip on the gear shift, I thanked Mel for the pep talk. I hung up with her as I made the now familiar turn onto the gravel road. Rays of magenta mixed with violet and tangerine streamed through the maple leaves. I'd arrived early with my tripod, two Nikons, and extra film. As I slung my backpack onto my shoulder, I swatted a mosquito at the back of my arm. Then I pulled the overstuffed basket toward me. The goodie bags I'd made for each counselor had rolled to the back of the trunk.

I hadn't been writing in my journal consistently. Between doctor appointments for Andre and last-minute camp preparations, I often collapsed into bed at the end of the day. A cardinal flew below the wispy, cirrus clouds that streaked across the vast sky. It swooped down, and I tried to capture it on my phone but fumbled. The bird disappeared into a nearby tree.

Mom, I miss you so much. I wish you could be here. Celebrate Camp Kismet. Meet the staff. I need a hug right—

"Joy! Hey there, lemme help you with your stuff," Dave said as he lifted the plastic laundry basket out of my hands.

"How long have you been standing there?" I asked, grateful that my sunglasses masked my mortification.

"Only a few minutes. I thought you were on the phone—I heard you speaking to someone," he replied.

My eyes widened. *Was I actually talking out loud to my mom?* I pivoted my body so he couldn't see my expression.

The gum I'd been chewing hardened, so I swapped it for a few mints. I forgot until my tight jaws reminded me that I needed to break up with my wads of gum. Since the day Mom died, my mouth clamped and clenched every night. The muscle relaxers the dentist prescribed had stopped working. He was making me another mouthguard because I'd chomped right through the first one.

The counselors had prepared hilarious skits; I'd read a few of the scripts that Dave sent me. I smiled as I thought about how entertained our campers would be.

Our. Our campers. Our community.

Our collective commitment to making an impact on these kids. I hadn't met any campers, but I already felt protective of them. The responsibility to keep them safe as their parents and caregivers entrusted us to treat them as our own.

Ours. One word with such visceral impact. I didn't use it much other than related to my marriage and Maple. Photography and creating behind the lens were solitary, a quiet collaboration between what I envisioned and the subject in front of me.

I told Dave to go ahead, and I'd join everyone shortly. I wanted to triple-check we were ready for the campers' arrival. And to thank each person, again, for the hours and months of dedication. I distributed the bags filled with the delectable brownies I'd made and notes I'd handwritten on cards from a local artist. The counselors' passion inspired me, and seeing how so many of them connected calmed my nerves.

I had decaf iced coffee instead of my regular, full-octane dark roast. I was excited and energized about the night before. Even Andre was surprised to find me fully dressed after a quick jog when he'd just gotten up. He lifted my chin and kissed me deeply. Then he told me that he couldn't wait to hear all about my first official day and wished me luck.

When I entered the car, I saw an envelope on the console. I decided to wait until I got to camp, smiling as I thought about the letters my parents used to send when I was a camper. My usual parking space was occupied by an unfamiliar truck; luckily, I found a spot across the street. I turned off the engine, slathered sunscreen on my face, and opened the card. A pastel rainbow was painted on the front of it.

Dear Joy,

You've got this, mi amor. I am so proud of you! Can't wait to hear everything later.

All my love,
Andre

His handwriting had changed, uneven and smaller, the letters smushed together. Those were the words I needed to hear from the person who mattered the most. Straightening my back, I strode toward the camp office.

Swatting at the buzz near my pocket, I blew air through my pursed lips. The damn internet was down again—I had a conference call with Bill and the insurance company representative. Apparently, he'd gotten a notice that we needed to increase coverage, and we were trying to ask for a grace period.

I chewed on a piece of crisp kale from the camp garden, which I clearly didn't wash sufficiently because it tasted gritty. Dirt wouldn't hurt me. But being late for this meeting could.

"Emma! Can you please come here," I shouted from my office. "I need tech help." I sighed, exasperated. Thank goodness for Emma's computer proficiency and patience.

"So frustrating, Joy. I'll figure it out," she replied. The buzzing sensation didn't quit. A citronella candle I'd lit next to my laptop didn't do a damn thing. Why did critters, especially bees and mosquitos, find me? No perfume. Unscented lotion. Did they follow me from Florida? I didn't even wash my hair today. A total mystery and absolutely annoying.

I downed the last drop of my coffee and wiped the corners of my mouth with a napkin. This year I'd purchased small cotton squares for the campers and staff. Part of our philosophy was to reduce, reuse, and recycle. When I asked Vivienne on a recent call why the camp still used paper products, she scoffed, saying, "Who could keep up with the hippy-dippy trends?" I chuckled after I hung up.

Another tradition I decided to continue was the uniform policy. When I'd redesigned the logo, I took a deep dive into the camp archives. Bernard believed uniforms leveled the playing field; campers on scholarship blended with those who paid the full tuition.

"Fixed it—you're good to go!" Emma chirped, bringing me back to the blinking cursor.

"I don't know what I'd do without you!" I eased into the wooden chair. Another relic from the past, it wasn't comfortable, but I'd heard a story about the camper who constructed it. Madison had difficulty with fine motor tasks like handwriting and opening small containers. After three summers, she signed up for the first woodworking class ever offered and she thrived. Madison became an occupational therapist at a preschool in New Hampshire. The oak had become burnt, light brown. Chips added character to the low back and a simple, rectangular seat. Madison had etched her name on one of the wobbly legs—the block, capital letters reminiscent of a pre-teen. I clicked the mouse and started the meeting.

"Hello there! The insurance rep is running a few minutes late," Bill said as I tightened my ponytail. "Do I hear mooing?"

I chuckled. "One of our mommas birthed her calf earlier this week. The goats and chickens are ecstatic!"

"It seems Camp Kismet is helping to mend your heart," he replied, adjusting his wire glasses and smiling. The insurance rep logged on.

Struggling to sit still, I smacked another mosquito that bit my forearm. Flying insects loved to feast on my skin.

I pulled my phone from the pocket of my drawstring pants. I was so consumed with trying to fix the tech issues that I'd confused the earlier buzzing for bugs, rather than incoming messages. Texts from Andre, Carmen, Carlos. As I scrolled through each one, the pebble returned and rapidly grew to a boulder. I couldn't swallow. Taking a breath took effort. I tried to keep my composure as I scanned the messages.

> 1:05 Call me. It's important.
> 1:07 Why can't I reach you?
> 1:10 Did you get my voicemail?
> 1:11 Joy, mi hijo is in trouble.
> 1:12 ¿Dónde estás? Call us!
> 1:13 This is urgent. It's Carlos. I'm using Carmen's phone.

My chest constricted. The call, the one that nearly shattered my soul, just months ago.

I couldn't bear another loss.

I had to get home.

Now.

1:15: 911. 911. Andre said this is the code to send. He can barely speak.

I didn't recognize the number.

"I, I need to go. I'm so sorry. It's a family emergency," I said, shutting my laptop and scrambling to gather my keys, purse, and grounding. My fingers trembled as I dialed Andre's number. No answer. Campers and counselors blurred around me as I bolted to my car.

Reversing without checking the rearview mirror, a cloud of dust billowed in front me as I sped up the gravel road. Beeping sounds kept reminding me to buckle my seatbelt. Carmen answered her phone on the first ring.

"Joy! Dios mio. Finally!" she said, gasping and panicky.

"Carmen. What's going on?" I dug my fingernails into my palm. I could barely get the words out.

"My boy. It's bad. The ambulance is here—" Carmen cried, and I heard a thud.

"What?!"

"He lost his balance and hit his head," Carlos explained, his voice hoarse and low. "We walked in the house and heard a strangled sound. Andre was on the floor. In the kitchen."

I couldn't inhale fully, and my clammy hand slid from the wheel.

"Is he okay? Is he talking? What did the EMTs say? Does he need to go to the hospital?" I ran the two red lights in town, hoping there weren't any police nearby. I still had forty minutes to go.

"I dropped the phone earlier, sorry. They're still here checking his—*¿Cómo se dice?*—vitals," Carmen said, her pitch rising at the end.

The word triggered terrifying flashbacks. My mom went to her doctor. She'd gotten headaches as a kid and often around the time of her cycle. But the usual meds didn't help with this migraine. She didn't tell me, Julian, or Dad because she figured it was hormonal or sleep deprivation.

She never came home. Her doctor sent her to the emergency room, concerned about the severity of the pain. When they found the aneurysm, she went into a coma just hours later.

My chest heaved and my vision blurred.

"How much longer until you're here?" Carlos asked.

"Joy?" Carmen said.

"I'm on my way and getting there as fast as I can. I'm so sorry—" I choked on my words.

Another voice I didn't recognize spoke from far away.

"Mrs. Stern, your husband will be okay. He has a small laceration on his head, but it doesn't require stitches. We were able to stop the bleeding. He's responsive and didn't lose consciousness."

Woozy and winded, I thought I might faint. I grabbed a bottle of cold water and pressed it into the back of my neck.

"Do we know what happened? Does he have a headache? He never gets them," I managed, gnawing on my lower lip.

"No, and his pupils are normal. Vision clear, memory good. One of the medications he takes can lower blood pressure. We're thinking he may've had a sudden drop and then lost his balance," he said.

This should've reassured me. It did not. I needed to see my husband. Now. Just as my heart slowed from a marathon to a 5k, the traffic did too. What the hell? Midday on this road was typically smooth sailing.

Then the cars stopped completely. Parents with their kids lined the highway. I didn't see signs of an accident—no ambulance or firetrucks. How strange. I mean, holy shit, the timing couldn't have been worse. *Seriously?*

Shifting the gear into park, I opened the door and jumped out. I approached the truck in front of me. A burly arm rested on the edge of the open window.

"Hey there. Do you know what's going on?" I said, asking Carmen to hang tight.

"It's a moose, ma'am. Takin' her sweet old time. Guess it's that time of year with the tourists. Great for our town. Not for the roads!" he said.

This could not be happening right now. How would I explain this to my in-laws? As if the cell towers heard me, I lost service, and the call dropped.

"You okay? Ya look like ya saw a ghost. Here's a Gatorade, I have an extra." He offered me a big, blue bottle.

"Thanks so much—I guess it's that obvious, huh?" I forced a small smile. "My husband needs me, and I should've been home hours ago. Appreciate the gesture."

He took off his cap and scratched the back of his head.

"Damn, that stinks. When these creatures get cozy, they don't move quick. Doesn't help with all the folks taking pictures. Whaddaya gonna do?" He shrugged, taking a bite of an apple.

Maybe focusing on this majestic creature would calm me the fuck down. I dialed my mother-in-law's phone number, and she picked up right away. Then Andre got on the phone, laughing as I told him my situation because he knew how badly I'd wanted to see a moose since we'd met.

"I'm okay, mi amor. Really, I am!" he reassured me. "The paramedics just left. They said to follow up with Dr. Garcia next week, but they're not overly concerned."

Well, I was worried. Hearing my husband's voice made breathing a bit easier.

The moose, massive with a floppy upper lip, decided he would mosey down the road and into the woods. I gawked at his textured antlers and wiry fur. The rest of the ride home was uneventful, other than my racing thoughts and pumping pulse.

I didn't bother taking off my filthy shoes in the mudroom.

"Andre? Where are you?" I asked, panic and relief washing over me after seeing my husband upright on the couch. Then I saw them.

Carmen's lips pursed and her hair was disheveled. Carlos stood with his arms crossed and shirt untucked. Andre seemed to be the calmest of the trio.

What am I missing?

"How could you keep this from us!" Carmen shrilled, her hands flailing hysterically.

Carlos stepped toward me with an expression I'd never seen before.

"Joy. I don't know what to say. After all these years—"

"Mami. Papi. Enough, please," Andre interjected, his voice wobbly and faint. I turned on my heel, dropped my bag on the floor, and hugged my husband.

"Oh honey, I was terrified. I am so, so sorry I didn't answer. Cell service at camp can be inconsistent," I cried, burying my head into his neck and squeezing his hand.

I'm the worst wife on the planet, I thought. We had a brief reprieve and then Carmen revved up again.

"How could you? My first born, mi hjio!" she crescendoed, and this time Carlos stayed silent.

I finally peeked at my in-laws, squinting, and inched closer to Andre. That's when I noticed the dried blood near his temple. He wrapped his arms around me. I had to say something.

"I am so confused. This has been a scary afternoon. But the paramedics said Andre is okay, yes?"

Carmen and Carlos nodded.

"Mi amor, it's the medication." I turned my head, searching Andre's eyes for an answer.

Why are they angry at me? Fear crept into my chest, and I shivered.

Andre cleared his throat and quietly began to explain.

"They know about me."

I was still flummoxed. Even Maple seemed distressed—she panted and her pink tongue looked paler than usual. I tapped my lap, and she leapt onto it, wiggling her tush until settling down.

As I stroked her ivory fur, I slowly lifted my head and finally looked directly at Andre's frazzled parents. My husband whispered the word that had changed our lives.

"Parkinson's."

CHAPTER 28

I hovered over Andre all night like a mom fretting about her newborn. Placing my palm under his nose to make sure he was breathing. Watching his chest rise and fall. Listening to him shout in his sleep. As if I could control, well, anything. My nervous system was frayed—the incident and the knowledge that my in-laws were livid while they still resided in my home.

Carmen had offered to sleep in our bedroom, which I politely declined. I told her just being in town for another few days was a gift (not really). Good thing she couldn't read my mind, or she'd be even more upset.

The next morning, Carmen prepared a buffet of hard-boiled eggs, guacamole, a bowl of berries, homemade whipped cream, and cinnamon toast. Andre gushed with gratitude, praising his mother's cooking and kindness. I might've gagged a little, thankful for the bountiful breakfast yet feeling a smidgen of resentment.

"Good morning, Joy!" she piped. "I set my alarm early, went to the store, and filled your fridge for the week."

Aren't you the perfect mother!

"Thank you so much," I said softly.

"I took Maple to *el baño, también*. My son needed his sleep," she continued as she sprinkled pink Himalayan salt on an egg. "Sit and eat—the puppy already had her breakfast. I am glad we're here for another few days."

Carmen hadn't worked a day in her life; she'd repeatedly boasted about raising her boys and now babysitting her grandchildren. Carlos provided for the family and, like his wife, believed women served others best by mothering and caregiving. He'd joke that he was the CEO of the business, she was the CEO at home. I pinched the upper part of my ear, the calming acupressure point my mom had taught me when I'd had panic attacks in high school. My pulse slowed, and I bit into the crunchy bread.

Andre yapped to his parents, talking about last night's soccer game and the volatile stock market—two subjects about which I couldn't care less. I stood and poured myself a cup of coffee, which amped up my energy. At least Carmen used the French roast beans from Artisan Coffee, my local favorite, instead of Bustelo.

"I made a reservation at Hen of the Woods for tomorrow night," Andre said. "It's farm-to-table, a perfect place to celebrate, and you'll love it." Carmen smoothed Andre's unkempt hair.

That was our special place. And tough to get a reservation. Loved my husband for how he cared for me, his parents, and everyone.

Oh my gosh.

Mother's Day was tomorrow.

My ear started ringing and everything became fuzzy. The trio of voices blended, a hum of background noise, and the buffet blurred into a streak of muted colors. I pinched the bridge of my nose.

Maple whined and scratched my calf with her paw. I ignored her, trying to ground myself by pressing my feet into the cool floor. She didn't relent and started to bark. Our camp veterinarian explained how farm animals can sense an impending storm hours before its arrival. Maybe Maple could feel my despair?

"I think Maple needs to do her business," I mumbled, standing to get the leash from the drawer. "We'll be back."

As I clicked the leash onto her collar, I whispered "lifesaver" into Maple's floppy ear. She wagged her tail and stared at me. I could swear she winked.

I'd lost track of the time, letting Maple lead me up and down the streets in our neighborhood. We stopped to admire the burst of white hydrangeas. We jogged toward the pond around the corner, and I took off my sneakers, sinking my toes into the spongy dirt. Dragonflies skimmed the water, flitting to cattail leaves and landing on the brown, tubular flowers. Maple sat next to me, rapt with curiosity. A squirrel scampered up the peeling birch tree beyond the pond.

Mom, this sucks. Summer is almost here and you're not here to see it. To smell it. To hear it. Right now, you'd be on a plane to Burlington, escaping the humidity and sweltering weather in Miami. You would be here with me.

Maple yipped and her ears twitched. That's when I realized I was talking to my mom out loud, again. Even my dog thought I was crazy. I wish I'd brought my journal.

My first Mother's Day without my mother.

My first, too, as a dog mom.

And I'd meet some of the camp staff next week.

I had to get my shit together.

Maple batted her long, auburn lashes and nudged me with her little damp nose. I put on my socks and laced my shoes. We ran back home together, and I dashed to my bedroom before anyone saw me.

CHAPTER 29

Dear Mom,

They. Are. Still. Here. As Andre would say, "Dios mio!" And you'd tell me to appreciate that I have such loving in-laws. I made it through Mother's Day; we went to Hen of the Woods. Remember we celebrated Dad's birthday there? He misses you so much.

He tells me he's okay. Golfing, having dinner with friends. Julian and I take turns calling. We have a schedule set every week. I feel awful I'm not there; and now with Kismet, I don't have the flexibility I once had. Julian and Uncle Jack will be with him for Father's Day. He still refuses to get rid of your stuff, even though we've told him it's okay and maybe would make it easier for him. Then again, you always told me that everyone grieves differently.

Andre's been so sweet and the meds, at least for now, are helping with the tremors. I can tell when they wear off—we are learning how to time and track when he takes them. Andre checks on Dad every day, sending him funny memes and jokes. Remember you wanted Dad to retire? Now I'm glad he didn't; numbers and spreadsheets are something he can control. It's also keeping him busy.

My therapist suggested I set a time, every single day, to grieve, remember, release. It feels super awkward and unnatural but I'm starting to see why it can be helpful. I cry almost every night and especially in the shower, though not as long. In the beginning, I wanted Andre to hold me as if I couldn't bear the weight, the shock. He propped me up like a two-by-four. Now I seek solace in being alone—I don't want to burden Andre with my sadness.

The campers arrive next month. You're missing so much. It's not fair. Fuck the five stages of grief—where's the sixth? The one that's not a phase. The part where you don't get over the loss but learn to live with it.

CHAPTER 30

SHAKEN TO THE CORE

WEEK ONE

It smelled like camp. Sweat, bug spray, sunscreen, and prepubescent hormones. As I stood at the gates, proud of the new logo I'd created, I remembered my first day at sleepaway camp. A junior counselor had taken my hand in hers and encouraged me to join my bunkmates at the lunch table. Terrified and timid, I didn't want to disappoint my mother, who'd loved her summers at Camp Intermezzo in Michigan. She'd spoken about it, sharing hilarious stories about her and her best friend, Ruby, since Julian and I were kids. After two weepy sessions, I didn't go back. It turns out even the most caring people can't stop a homebody from feeling homesick.

When I was a camper, I cried myself to sleep. Buried my head in books. I never understood why my bunkmates didn't miss their sand-free beds, homemade meals, hugs from their parents.

How'd I end up here owning a freaking camp?

I watched two girls—their pigtails swaying like swings—run toward each other. They shrieked in unison, reuniting after months apart. I learned later that one lived in New Hampshire and the other in Maine. They both already knew they wanted to be veterinarians—this was their fourth summer together at camp. They held hands, skipping toward the baby goats, giggling and connecting as if no time had passed.

A bunch of teenage boys had already started a game of ultimate frisbee on the sprawling lawn near the water. The lakeside staff watched closely. I'd confirmed that lifeguards would be on duty during all waking hours.

Another camper, probably about twelve years old, snuggled in a hammock and read a paperback book. Squinting to see her better, it seemed like she was content being by herself. She twisted her flaxen, blonde hair around her finger as she turned a page. Something about this camper reminded me of my younger self. I'd make sure to find her later tonight.

I greeted parents, some of whom were puzzled and wondered who I was. I'd anticipated confusion, even though we'd sent current and new families letters months ago. Dave had prepared me, at least for returning campers, for the typical questions I might hear.

My umpteenth worry weaseled its way into my psyche. The what-ifs surfacing like whack-a-mole—I'd answer my own question, and within seconds, another popped up. It was only nine in the morning, and my shirt was soaked. Definitely not the weather, as today was a balmy sixty-five degrees; my inner temperature blazed with anxiety.

Then it was time for parents, grandparents, and guardians to leave. Some kids said goodbye, trotting like horses to an activity, and didn't look back. Others lingered in long embraces. To my right, the head of the junior girls' division gently led a wailing ten-year-old toward the garden. I almost started to cry and could barely look at her parents, who held each other, heartsick at leaving behind their youngest of three kids.

Our camp therapist, Jenny, was available for campers and their families. The world had become an overstimulating, unpredictable environment. Even though our setting promoted a peaceful experience—no electronic devices allowed—I'd read, researched, and spoken to tons of camp owners about possible challenges. It overwhelmed my fully formed, adult nervous system. I could barely imagine growing up with the barrage of information these kids had to digest.

Mental health doesn't discriminate; I knew that as the daughter of a therapist. Being now motherless, I'd joined infinite others who'd had to navigate sudden loss.

During the year, Jenny counseled children with varying challenges, or as she said, "students who are LD—not learning disabled but souls who learn differently." Based on the camp forms, we were aware that about 10 percent of our campers had diagnosed anxiety. A few others struggled with depression. And a handful, we learned, were possibly in the autism spectrum.

Jenny was an integral part of counselor training. She'd coached the counselors and unit leaders about the signs of eating disorders and suicidal ideations. She rapidly established a rapport with them, offering times during the week in which she was available to support the staff.

My mom would've loved Jenny. The pebble reemerged in my throat, and I willed it to go away. I didn't have time for my own misery—these campers needed me. I knotted the end of my T-shirt, forest green with Camp Kismet in bold, block yellow letters in the upper right corner. The rainbow arched over the name like a hug. I retied my shoelaces, cursing silently that I'd worn white sneakers.

"Joy! I'm over here!" I heard Dave bellow from somewhere behind me. I accompanied the last parent to her minivan, another teary mommy, reassuring her that her little boy would have an amazing few weeks.

"Are you sure I can't call him? He is super shy and what if—"

"Ms. Jensen, it's our camp policy. We've learned that, especially for kids who are homesick, hearing parents and siblings from miles away can make it worse. I promise we'll be in touch if there are any concerns. And you'll see Brian's sweet face every day on the photo gallery!"

I handed her a few tissues that were tucked in the belt bag around my waist. She sniffed and tried to smile while thanking me.

Did I make a promise that I could keep? I waved as she drove away, trying not to panic at the thought that I was now responsible for these children. Not having any of my own. Zero experience as a parent or even a teacher. *What the fuck was I thinking?*

As I turned around, I rubbed the center of my chest with my pointer finger, feeling this mother's angst and missing my own mom.

After a quick stop in the bathroom, I joined Dave and the other camp leaders. He handed me the megaphone he'd been using all afternoon. My hand trembled, and I hoped nobody noticed. We were at the flagpole, the campers grouped by divisions.

"Welcome to Camp Kismet, everyone!" I yelled cheerfully. "My name is Joy, and we're so glad you're here. We'll gather right here each morning." My eyes briefly darted to Dave's, and he nodded, encouraging me to continue.

I introduced the nurses, waterfront staff, Jenny, unit leaders, and others. With every word that left my mouth, some of my earlier jitters began to dissipate. Then I saw that young girl again, with her bunkmates yet isolating herself with visible space between her and the other kids. She looked at the ground, digging the tip of her shoes into the dirt. We sang the camp song together, and I wished everyone a wonderful first night. Then I walked to the back of the circle, holding up my hand and signaling to the senior counselor that I needed to speak with her.

"Is everything okay?" Kate asked, her brows furrowing and brown eyes widening.

I pulled her aside.

"Yes, all is well." I lowered my voice. "What do you know about that camper?" I described her quietly instead of pointing.

Kate, the sprite grad student, smiled knowingly.

"It's her first summer—she hasn't said a word to any of us. I only know what we read on her forms. She doesn't seem too sad; when her parents left, she settled into a hammock," Kate explained. "I'll keep a close eye on her; she seems comfortable but not interested in engaging with me or the other kids."

I looked at my watch.

"You need to get going—it's almost time for morning activities," I said. The junior counselor had already corralled the kids. The young girl chewed on her thumbnail and swayed back and forth like a windshield wiper. I headed to the camp office, thanking everyone again for a fabulous first day. I reread each camper's file, trying to memorize their names and smidgens of information.

I called Andre. "Hi honey, I'm on my way home—I can't wait to tell you everything!"

He laughed and said he hoped I was starving. Carmen had cooked for hours as if it was our last meal. I'd made it through Mother's Day (barely), and I couldn't wait to have my house to myself again. Though I'd admittedly miss Carmen's lavish spreads.

When I entered the kitchen, I twittered about the campers, especially the new shy one, Simi, and how compassionate the counselors were with their groups. Carlos asked interesting questions; he said in Colombia, kids didn't typically go to sleepaway camp. Carmen continued to dote on Andre as if he was comprised of delicate porcelain. She'd made enough food for a month! I heaped the leftovers into individual glass containers and put them in the freezer.

After huge hugs and planting kisses all over my face, Carmen and Carlos left with Andre. I was thrilled about getting back into my pajamas and lounging around the house. I couldn't wait to roam from room to room braless or even topless. Andre didn't like Maple in our bed, but I broke the rules and cuddled with my growing fur baby while my husband schlepped his parents to the airport.

Maple nipped at my earlobe and eventually lay her head on my lap. I replayed each moment, playing images like a film reel—exhaling with relief that all the campers were generally happy, safe, and healthy. What more could I ask for? The horrific stories I'd read that haunted me—fires, illness outbreaks, lawsuits—must've been exaggerated and dramatized.

"Daddy's home, sweet girl. We better get you out of here!" I giggled and lifted Maple off our comforter. I let my legs dangle from the bed before standing up and throwing on a cotton, lilac robe. Since Maple's arrival, I'd rarely worn the silky ones that I preferred. Living with a puppy didn't pair well with wearing luxurious fabrics.

"Ah, mi amor—we're finally alone," Andre crooned into my ear. As if she understood, Maple pushed her paws into his shins and yipped. I wrapped my arms around Andre's trim waist.

"I think our girl doesn't agree." We both laughed and Maple barked loudly. She'd almost reached her full height and weight. It seemed she'd be on the smaller side. Her puppy fur had become curlier and coarser. When she was a baby, her ears and tail were tinged with strawberry blonde; as she grew, some of that faded to a pale rose. I reminded Andre that we needed to get her spayed.

"I know how busy you've been, so I didn't want to bring it up. The vet said we can wait a bit longer. What do you think?" Andre rested his chin on the top of my head.

I squeezed him tighter and inhaled his crisp cologne. Maple woofed in agreement.

"You heard the boss baby—let's make her an appointment for July," I said. "Speaking of plans, I made a few for us!"

Andre cocked his head.

"We haven't had a day date in forever. Get your workout clothes on—when can you be ready?"

"That sounds amazing, Joy! I'll be ready in thirty minutes." Andre spun on his heel and Maple trotted behind him, her tail wagging double time.

"Come here, sweet girl. We need to go for a quick walk!" She ignored me. I called her name, clapped my hands, and she finally responded to hearing her squeaky toy. Thankfully, Maple wasn't as stubborn when it came to doing her business. She devoured a crunchy treat, and I tucked her into the plush bed in her crate. Then I put the picnic basket I'd prepared in the trunk, before Andre opened the garage door.

"So where are we going?" he asked, his voice cracking and sounding hoarse.

"If I told you, it wouldn't be a surprise!" I grinned, knowing that my husband had a tough time letting go of control. "Trust me. You'll love it."

I'd thought about blindfolding him but figured that might be overkill. His left leg bounced up and down. I intentionally took back roads so he couldn't figure out where we'd land.

"You've stumped me—I have no clue where we're headed," Andre remarked.

"Excellent. Mission accomplished, sweetie!"

We rode down a one-way street for the last fifteen minutes. Andre showered me with questions—I didn't give in. I veered off to the right and parked the car in a spot where I hoped we'd still have a vehicle when we returned. I had to climb over my husband to exit the car because it was wedged between two boulders.

Andre tickled me while I tried to unlock the door.

"Stop! I think I just tinkled!" I cackled, prying myself off his lap and nearly landing on the rocks. He joined me, still wondering what our afternoon entailed.

I asked Andre to close his eyes. Then I took out the fleece, hunter green blanket we'd used during camping trips in college. I draped it over my shoulder and lifted the basket, which was filled with Andre's favorites—an açaí bowl drizzled with local honey and topped with cacao nibs, slivered almonds, and shredded coconut. A bottle of bubbly rosé that I'd found at a specialty shop from a small vineyard in Spain. Four types of cheese—two soft, two hard, and all from Vermont farms. I'd borrowed the woven basket from Mel; the one she'd brought home from her solo trip to India. I slung my camera bag across my torso.

"What is this for? Did I forget an anniversary or something else? I heard these freaking meds can—"

I held a finger to his mouth.

"Follow me and I'll answer after we get settled." I laughed, enjoying his adorable discomfort.

I led us to the meadow that overlooked a pond. Bullfrogs croaked in the distance, echoing off the water. I'd found this spot last year during a photo shoot.

"This is gorgeous!" Andre bellowed, his voice louder than I'd heard in months. I'd already taken the cap off my lens, snapping images of his expressions. His dimples that deepened when he smiled. The vertical lines in his forehead like a closed Japanese fan when he raised his thick eyebrows. His blue eyes that morphed from oval to wide circles, revealing glimmery gold flecks.

One day he may not be able to show these emotions on his face. I shivered even though it was eighty degrees, shaking away the depressing forecast of my meteorologist mind.

Andre grabbed the edge of the lid. I giggled and swatted his hand away.

"Not yet, Mr. Need to be in the Know!" I crossed my legs and motioned for him to join me on the blanket.

"You wondered about the occasion. There isn't anything in particular. I've been working around the clock, and you've been so supportive," I began. "If you told me this time last year I'd own a camp, and my mother would be gone and—" I pressed my lips together.

Andre tucked a curl behind my ear.

"And that you'd be dealing with a declining husband," he said softly, holding my gaze. "You didn't sign up for this—I should've come with a warranty." He traced the lines on the inside of my palm.

Shit, I think he can read my mind. Or am I that transparent?

I couldn't find the words, so I kissed him instead. When we came up for air, I pointed to the basket, indicating he could take a peek.

"This is amazing! You know me so well," Andre said, taking the top off the glass container. "And you even remembered to add pineapple to the açaí bowl!"

I rolled onto my stomach, beaming. I unwrapped each block of cheese, placing them on the round, walnut board. Then I strategically arranged the strawberries, forming a heart around the wedges.

After giving him the bottle of wine, I changed my lens and took close shots of his hands as he uncorked it and noticed his steadier movement. I continued taking photos as the bubbly liquid cascaded from the top and sloshed into the glass. Then I zoomed in on his relaxed, content mouth. I'd silenced our phones when we sat, cherishing our unplugged time together.

"How long have you been taking pictures?" He leaned back on his elbows.

"At least two decades. Thanks for remembering!" I snarked.

Andre chuckled then began to cough.

What if this is how it'll be? Will he be eating pureed food? Is he choking?

"Are you alright?" I uttered nervously, dropping the camera next to the cheese board.

Andre nodded and pointed to the thermos filled with water. He cleared his throat.

"I'm fine, worrywart. You pulled off this awesome surprise, and you're sneaky with the camera, too." He stroked my cheek with the back of his hand. I plucked the stem from a plump strawberry.

"You must try one!" I moaned, a trickle of rosé-tinged juice drizzling down the side of my mouth.

Andre agreed and asked where I'd discovered such delicious berries.

"At Camp Kismet! Isn't it amazing—these beauties are from our garden. Dave is so competent I could take a few hours off today."

"Joy! These are delicious! You must be proud of the campers." Andre pitched forward and popped two more into his mouth.

I refilled our glasses and asked if he was ready for the hike.

"HA! Are you kidding? I think we're a bit old to walk a trail all tipsy and buzzed," Andre snorted.

"Nah, I found a flat, easy one," I replied, rewrapping the remaining cheese and gathering the utensils. "We need to drop by Mel's on the way home; she picked up Maple after we left so we wouldn't be rushed. Then I need to head back to Kismet."

"You always think ahead—I bet that'll come in handy running the camp too," Andre said, adjusting his sunglasses.

We walked to the trash cans, separating the items to be recycled from those to be disposed. Andre placed the picnic basket in the back seat, then threaded his fingers through mine as we strolled to the start of the trail. I'd also packed Andre's hiking boots and light-wool crew socks.

Nature had awoken from her intermission. Birds sang in varying keys, a chorale of chirping. Peeling bark protruded from towering birch trees. Mossy mounds nestled between raised, twisty roots. I loved how the light shone from above, projecting shadows onto the path of clay-colored dirt layered with maple leaves and pine needles. A luna moth flitted by and stayed on a leaf long enough for me to capture it on my camera.

We walked in silence—the comfortable kind that comes from years of connection and growth. Andre stumbled on a stone as he strolled in front of me. I put my camera on silent, capturing photos of his footprints.

"Wow this is spectacular!" Andre crooned. I picked up my pace to join him. Water trickled with ease, pivoting between chunky and flat rocks. Concentric circles glimmered in the sunlight. Andre wrapped his arms around my waist and rested his chin on my shoulder. We stood like that for a while, soaking it all in.

Then I saw it.

A shimmering arc of red, orange, yellow, green, blue, indigo, and violet cradled the waterfall. Andre saw it too. He held me closer as I pointed the camera toward it, adjusting the aperture as the light fluctuated. Zooming in and out, I must've taken thirty photos before it disappeared.

Andre turned me around to face him and cupped my face in his hands.

"That was magical. And just after Mother's Day." His eyes glistened. It was the first time he'd been with me when a rainbow appeared.

Mom, this meant everything. He believes me now. You showed up at the perfect time, again, I thought.

I didn't want this moment to end.

CHAPTER 31

I cracked four large eggs in the cast iron pan. While they sizzled, I stirred the old-fashioned oats and added flax seeds with a dash of cinnamon. I'd read that eating an anti-inflammatory diet might be helpful for neurodegenerative diseases like Parkinson's. Dr. Garcia's office had been super supportive when I reached out. Andre didn't complain much, though he was reluctant to give up gluten.

We'd made it through the first week of camp—a short one as it began on a Wednesday night. I felt more at ease and excited as we kicked off week two.

"Good morning, gorgeous." Andre kissed the crook in my neck. Even sweaty after his workout, the man still smelled divine. "Thanks for making breakfast!"

I sighed contentedly and wondered if he'd notice the flax seeds that I'd hidden at the bottom of the bowl. We sat down and Andre spoke animatedly about a new building. The owners, originally from Bermuda, wanted to transform their workspace into an oasis. His hand shook slightly as he held the spoon.

"They're partners in business and met when they were in elementary school. They love snowboarding—we still need to try that!" Andre said, coughing. "Their ideas are wild, way beyond aesthetics. One of the women suggested knocking down the entire building and adding palm tree sculptures in the center of it." His voice sounded wet, as if the water he'd sipped didn't go down the right pipe.

"Why is the oatmeal crunchy?" he asked, inspecting the inside of the bowl. Then he took his pinky finger, pushed into the side, and studied the speck on the end of it.

"What on earth! Are these termites?" Andre exclaimed.

I spewed coffee everywhere.

"No sweetie, those are flax seeds." I snorted and wiped my face with a napkin. Maple licked the droplets that splattered on the floor.

"I'll grind them up next time!"

"No chance. These are gross," Andre retorted as he dumped the rest of it in the sink.

Maybe I'll blend them into a smoothie tomorrow, I thought.

After Andre left, I filled Maple's bowl with fresh water and couldn't imagine our home without her. Now technically a teenager, she tested us at night and seemed to have developed a bit of separation anxiety. It was hard to hear her whine and whimper; I wanted to scoop her up in my arms. But Andre encouraged me to ignore Maple's griping; he'd read that she'd eventually cease and self-soothe.

I'd started taking long showers to drown out her plaintive pleas. I remembered Mel telling me when her kids were babies this worked for her. Often, I finished drying my hair and Maple had conceded; I could hear her syncopated snoring when I quietly opened my bedroom door.

I turned on my desktop computer, smiling at the screen saver of the Camp Kismet logo I'd designed. The corner of a fluorescent pink paper caught my attention. I lifted the square mousepad and found a card.

Thank you again for planning the picnic, hike, and for being the best life partner.

I'd wish you luck on week two, but we both know you don't need it.

All my love,

Andre

I tacked the note to the bulletin board that I'd hung above my desk, grinning to myself and grateful for my husband. Then

I entered my password and started reading a slew of emails. Dave called a plumber because one of the toilets had backed up overnight. The counselors tried to use a plunger but no luck. Another message from the head nurse, Janet, who asked for my approval regarding an email that she wanted to send—a few campers had lice. I remembered my mom telling me about when she had it and reading the four-letter word made my scalp itch. The insurance company bill also landed in my inbox; Andre suggested I could put everything on autopay. I wanted to review each invoice manually.

My calendar pinged with a reminder of our weekly huddle. Dave said he had it covered, but I wanted to be immersed in camp operations, at least this first year. When it dinged again, it occurred to me that maybe I should set an alarm for writing to my mom; I couldn't believe it was June.

June. Her birthday was June 30th. I took off my smudged glasses and cleaned them with the edge of my shirt. The pebble reappeared, widening and making swallowing nearly impossible. I hadn't exercised consistently since camp started; I knew what I needed to do.

I hadn't been behind the lens since last weekend. I craved the solitude, creating without interference or interruptions. After pulling on leggings and a long-sleeve shirt, I sprayed insect repellent on any exposed skin. I filled a water bottle for Maple and found her favorite toy. Then I pointed to the car seat and said, "uppy," proud that I'd taught her this new command. She leapt into her nylon doggie bed, and we drove toward the water.

I smiled as Maple yawned, and I watched her in the rearview mirror. She itched behind her floppy ear, which flapped like a sail billowing in the wind. I found a spot and parallel parked near ECHO, Leahy Center for Lake Champlain. I marveled at Maple's inner compass as she sat on her hind legs and barked. Her sense of direction was definitely better than mine.

We walked around the lake, passing couples holding hands and college students reading textbooks. I thought about how much had changed since I'd been here with Mel in the fall. Life could be divided by BM—before Mom—and AM—after Mom. I should've brought my Nikon because Maple had also changed in recent weeks. At least I had the digital camera. I squatted and tossed her a red, rubber ball.

"Good girl!" I shouted as I clicked the button, capturing Maple midair. Then I threw it farther, trusting her to reliably respond to her name. My stomach started rumbling, and I was shocked that it was nearly six o'clock. I took a few more photos of my sweet pup under a canopy of trees. I loved how the light shifted as afternoon transitioned to evening, and Maple's shiny coat would range from cream to tan to taupe. Clicking the leash onto her collar, I ran my fingers back and forth through her fur and lifted my face to the setting sun.

CHAPTER 32

I'd noticed a nest in the corner of the wood eaves outside the health center. Only the mama robin had made an appearance. I wondered if the babies slept under her body, protected by her beady, vigilant eyes and blanketed by her soft feathers.

My car skidded as I drove up the hill, reminding me of the first time I'd driven in the rain. Scared and squirmy in my seat, my mom had repeated that it's best not to resist what is in front of us, but rather lean into the turns. Summer upstaged spring and announced her arrival with a litany of afternoon storms.

I clicked open the inverted, yellow umbrella—whoever invented this contraption was a genius. It covered most of the mail I held and folded into itself when I closed it. Droplets lingered at the tips of pine needles. Maple leaves bowed, soggy and soaked from the rain. A puddle formed at the side of the office; I sent myself a voice memo to ask Dave if the gutter needed to be serviced or replaced.

A group of teenage girls gathered under the pitched roof, giggling, chattering, and engrossed in conversation. A baby goat poked his head out of the low, aluminum house Dave had constructed. Two young boys poured fresh milk into jugs. I worried that the greens growing in the garden would be waterlogged and possibly wilt.

Taking the longer route, I weaved between bunks, ducking under beach towels and swimsuits that draped over clotheslines. I heard rock music blasting from one cabin and acoustic from another.

As I reached the entrance of camp headquarters, I saw Simi sitting on the step. She had her head down, a book flattened on her lap, and her shoulders hunched. The rain had finally stopped, though the mosquitos didn't get the memo. One flew near the tip of my nose, and I shooed it away before it bit me.

"Hi Simi," I said softly, hoping she'd reply.

She bit her pinky nail and flipped the book over.

I sat down next to her and asked what she was reading.

Still no verbal response, but Simi held it up and pointed to the title.

"I loved that series! I read it at camp too," I chirped, realizing I probably should lower the volume.

She inched backward and briefly met my gaze. Though Simi was only fourteen years old, her almond-shaped eyes, a striking ocean blue, seemed replete with wisdom. I sensed she had so much to say. And I was determined for her to feel safe enough this summer to speak. I thought often about this kiddo, wondering what would coax her from the world of solitude in which she lived.

I tried one more time.

"How's everything going?" Simi shrugged.

Oh. Right. I remembered our camp therapist said during team building exercises that it's best to comment, not question. And especially for introverts or nervous campers, when asking something, it can be helpful to offer choices.

"What's your favorite activity so far—gardening or taking care of the animals?" I asked, intentionally slowing my pace.

Simi looked at me longer this time. Then she held up two fingers like a peace sign. Confused at first, I stayed quiet and then understood.

"Oh, you like the chickens and goats!" Her ponytail, loose and low, moved as she nodded enthusiastically. I had much more to say but didn't want to push my luck. I stood up, cleaned off the muck that was caked on my rear, and wished Simi a wonderful day.

I'd ordered pizzas and salads for the staff. Dave and I met first. I silenced my phone, knowing Andre could reach me on the landline, which was now fully, dependably operational. Before we got to camp updates, Dave crossed his arms behind his head and studied me.

"What?" I asked. His biceps pulsed as he leaned back in the chair. I blushed and silently chided myself for even noticing.

"Wondering how you're doing. I know you want to get to the business stuff," he began, peering at me as he took off his weathered baseball cap.

His concern disarmed me. I took a deep breath and straightened the papers on my desk.

"I don't mean to pry. The emergency with your husband, then Mother's Day, and learning the ropes here." He rolled his chair closer and paused. "It must be a lot to handle."

Journaling had been healing. Yet it didn't feel like enough anymore. *How did Dave know?*

I twirled a damp strand of hair that'd escaped my loose bun.

"I appreciate you asking," I answered, my voice trembling. "It's been tough to be honest." I pressed the pad of my thumb into the corner of the chair.

Dave blinked and rubbed the back of his neck.

"I get it, Joy."

He cleared his throat and stretched his legs out in front of him.

"What I mean is that people at camp become like extended family. I care about everyone here. I know you're the boss, but that includes you," Dave explained. He twisted the cap off his stainless-steel thermos and took a swig.

I couldn't find the words. Instead, I tried to rearrange my face like Mrs. Potato Head. *This man didn't miss a thing.*

Emma knocked on the door.

"Come in," I shouted, grateful for the interruption.

"Is it okay to have Janet and Wendy join you now?" I waved my hand and nodded.

The two jolly women, both in their mid-fifties, sauntered into the room. I'd thought they were sisters when we first met.

"Great to see you!" Janet piped. She untangled a kink in her white wavy hair.

"The lice infestation has been extinguished!" Wendy quipped as she unzipped her raincoat. "We confirmed that not one little louse got away."

We all laughed, and the women winked at each other. Steadfast and calm, the two nurses had been fixtures at the camp. They'd been campers, counselors, and employees now for a few decades. Janet and Wendy had more energy than an entire bunk of teens. They updated us about the latest camp crud—this week it was the common cold—and they alerted me to a few kids about whom they were concerned.

"His counselor asked me to observe a camper in the cafeteria," Wendy began. "And it seems like he's been losing weight." I knew the boy she referenced; I'd also noticed he'd gotten thinner but figured it was a growth spurt. Besides, I thought it was mostly teen girls who were at risk for eating disorders. I clearly had much more to learn about child development. I'd peruse the internet and library shelves this weekend.

After Janet and Wendy left, Dave called the veterinarian and put her on speaker. A senior counselor, who also supervised the goat feedings, had documented a change in our mama goat's behavior. She was lethargic and not eating as robustly as usual. Who knew goats took the same antibiotics for a UTI as I did? I silently chuckled at the thought that we could've had a joint visit to the doc. Andre would crack up when I shared this with him later.

As I listened to the vet's insights, I thought again about the word *our*. We were almost halfway through the first session and all beings—animals and humans—had become like family. Dave was right.

Counselors and other staff members bopped in and out to say hello. They devoured the pizza, updating me as cheese melted and stuck to the plates. One confided that two of her junior counselors were dating, though it was on the down-low. A senior counselor needed a day off because his grandmother had passed away. I observed and listened to Dave guide the conversations with compassion and empathy.

I'd scheduled it to touch base with the unit leaders; each person gave a five-minute update. The first week of camp, thankfully, breezed by without any major mishaps. One child, a new camper who had significant anxiety, needed to go home. Dave met with the sweet girl and her parents numerous times. We determined that she wasn't ready to be away from her family. Although she especially loved feeding the sheep, nighttime terrified her; she'd started sleepwalking while screaming.

My younger brother, Julian, went through a similar phase. I'd wake up, hearing my mom or dad soothingly guide him back to bed. It turned out the camper had night terrors, aptly named, as witnessing them was deeply disturbing. When this nine-year-old walked right out of the bunk one night, I painstakingly realized this could be a risk to her safety. And that of the other campers.

Peeking at my cell phone, I saw three missed calls from Mel, but no message. Usually, she'd text me or leave a lengthy voicemail, which was more like a monologue. Dave had everything under control, so I jotted a note letting him know I needed to step out of the staff meeting.

"Is everything okay?" I asked nervously. "I just saw all the missed calls."

Mel groaned. "Nothing urgent but my little girl has been wailing all day. She had a low-grade fever last night; now she's burning up and I need to take her to the pediatrician. I didn't want to bother—"

"Can you get a later appointment? I can be there by five or so," I said.

Luckily Mel's house was closer to camp than my own. As I sped into her driveway, she opened the door and Charlie skipped toward my car.

"Auntie Joy! Did you bwing your camwah?" He craned his neck, bouncing up and down as if springs grew from the bottom of his little feet.

"Let's see what I have in my trunk." I winked.

Mel mouthed "thank you," knowing her voice was no match for her toddler's wails. Gracie's blonde curls framed her cherubic face. Mel had Gracie on her right hip, moving back and forth, trying to soothe her little girl. As I got closer, I saw the start of a rash on her pale neck.

"Go to the doctor, Mel. I've got this and my ringer is on in case anyone at camp needs me." I patted Gracie's damp, tousled locks and hugged Mel. Charlie tugged on the end of my T-shirt, eager to take photos in his backyard.

"Jake's away or I wouldn't have called," Mel said over her shoulder.

I waved her away with my hand.

"I'm so glad you did!" I handed the tripod to Charlie, which he proudly tucked under his arm. Then I talked about the ambiance and why cloudy versus sunny days affect photography. He listened intently when I explained how clouds can create soft, more even lighting.

When we arrived at the mossy slope toward the back of the house, he carefully opened the tripod as I marveled at his memory. Charlie loved puzzles and painting, too. Mel was worried he didn't like books as much as Gracie; I'd reminded her that she'd barely made it through English Lit 101. And how her brilliance manifested in the creations she crafted. Also, that the kid wasn't even five years old yet!

"Auntie Joy, can I take it off and put on the bigger one?" Charlie pointed his finger at my eighty-five-millimeter lens. I hesitated for a moment because it was new. Then decided to trust his dexterous hands, so steady and strong.

"Here you go." I handed him the base of my Nikon. He beamed and stood up taller, taking this task quite seriously.

"Can you teach me how to use it wight now?" He gingerly held it in front of him and examined the dial.

We spent the next hour snapping photos of the sunflowers Mel planted. I showed him how the same petal can appear different depending on the angle and position. I taught him about aperture settings and depth of field in general terms.

Then Charlie squealed and grabbed my hand.

"Look! Do you see the babies?"

I shook my head.

"Wight dere, Auntie Joy. Between the tall twees!"

A slight movement between the leaves caught my eye and a bushy tail appeared. Three baby deer tentatively took steps beyond the thicket, their slender legs like moving twigs. I brought a finger to my lips, which Charlie understood and he hushed immediately. We quietly inched toward the trio, and I wondered why the mother wasn't present.

As I switched the setting from auto to manual on the camera, a snorty strange sound bleated in the distance. I zoomed in and took a series of the mom reuniting with her family. She stood tall, staring at us protectively, waiting until her babies walked ahead before following them.

CHAPTER 33

WEEK THREE

My phone dinged at 5:45 a.m. Andre had already left for his work-out; he'd started boxing because Dr. Garcia suggested that it would be beneficial. Turns out like all other sports, Andre excelled at it and became obsessed after the first class. The noise startled me.

> Sorry to text so early. Our girls are scheduled to go on a hike today. Head counselor is with Wendy at the health center. She has the stomach flu. It's bad. Is there any way you can fill in?
>
> I'll be there.
>
> Thanks, Joy. I appreciate your flexibility—I tried others before reaching out.
>
> See you soon,
> Dave

Lathering my hair with shampoo, I inhaled the minty scent and drew circles on the glass door. After a cold rinse, I coated the coarse ends with conditioner. I still couldn't hear my mom's voice, but a scene from my childhood flashed in my mind. Sweltering, sticky South Florida turned my corkscrew curls into a matted mess. I closed my eyes and cried, my six-year-old self feeling my mom's loving touch as she'd spray detangler on my hair. She was patient and gentle; somehow it never hurt.

I yearned for one last time, even as an adult, to hold her hand, to see her face, to hear her breathe.

Stepping out of the shower, I thought about Andre's worsening condition, and how he'd ironically designed this space that could one day fit a wheelchair. I shuddered and shoved away the thought, vigorously towel drying my hair. About halfway through the blow-dry, a fuse blew and I realized it was pointless anyway—I'd be a sweaty, stinky disaster after the hike.

Maple scampered into the bathroom, her pink tongue lapping up the water that dripped from my hair and onto the floor. Then she followed me into the closet and burrowed herself on top of my growing pile of sweatshirts.

"Good thing Daddy suggested that we have our own closets. You know he's a neat freak!" I said, tying the string on my khaki pants. Maple cocked her head and wiggled her nose—further proof that dogs understand words. Then I buttoned up a powder blue shirt that allegedly provided protection from ultraviolet rays.

I packed breakfast—an apple, a nut-free granola bar, a few cheese sticks, and pretzels. Still ravenous from yesterday's Pilates class, I added vanilla protein powder to my oatmeal along with organic blueberries. Maple looked up at me, optimistic that I'd drop something on the floor. She didn't budge and kept staring—I now understood the literal meaning of puppy dog eyes.

"Such a sweet face, my *shayna punim*!" Maple's mouth hung open as if she had something to say. And our girl was trilingual—English, Spanish, and a bit of Yiddish. I lured her into her doggie bed with a crunchy chicken treat.

"I'll see you later. Have a good day—I miss you already," I called over my shoulder. *I had become that person. A dog mom. Talking to this canine cutie pie as if she were human. I couldn't believe it.*

I said hello to my neighbor, who was outside watering her lawn. Then I waited at the stop sign for a massive truck to move. I loved early summer mornings in Vermont. The crisp breeze whipping through the maple leaves. Sunlight dappling on spruce, fir, and birch trees—all shades of green adorning the mountains. I ordered coffee—a maple latte for Dave, a large dark roast with oat milk for me, and a double espresso for Emma. I bought the rest of the staff donuts and scones.

"It's good to see ya!" Sage piped, tucking a pen behind her ear. I marveled at her perpetually chipper mood. Just one of the reasons why she was my favorite barista.

I loved this place. An array of succulents lined the windowsills. Purple and fuchsia dahlias perched in dainty bud vases. Stainless-steel vats housed the beans harvested from Ecuador, Ethiopia, and Colombia. I once purchased several bags and shipped them to Uncle Jack and his husband for their anniversary. I also sent a grinder and French press; they'd teased me for years about my morning ritual. And now they, too, were hooked. They'd even purchased a portable version.

"Glad to see you smiling again, Joy. Send regards to Andre and the rest of your family!" she said, flicking her bright pink hair over her shoulder.

I'd declined Sage's offer to help me to my truck. I placed the scones and donuts in my bag. Juggling my wallet in one hand and the coffee in the other, I pulled at the door handle only to spill steamy milk all over my pants. I placed everything on the ground, grumbling and dropping an F-bomb along with my car keys.

I hope this isn't a prelude to the rest of today, I thought uneasily.

I cranked up the volume, jamming to my playlist that I'd labeled "Joyful Jams." Totally corny and clearly ridiculous, but it did the trick! Noah Kahan, the Indigo Girls, Joni Mitchell, The Counting Crows, and Sting accompanied me the rest of the way to camp.

"Hey there!" Dave jogged toward me. I was later than expected yet he always appeared—did the man have some kind of sixth sense?

"Thanks. Do we have any wipes left in the office? It's not even 10 a.m. and I've already stained my pants." I rolled my eyes and grimaced.

Dave chuckled. "You do realize you're about to roam in the woods with a crew of kids, right?" Fair point. My clothes would likely look like an abstract art project by tonight. I realized how silly it was to even bother washing my hair.

"I think the junior counselors are nervous—boss lady going on the field trip," Dave teased.

They probably knew way more than I did—where to go, what to avoid, how to keep everyone safe.

"Yea, I know I'm super intimidating," I joked, taking a sip of my coffee and wincing as it scorched the back of my throat.

Anticipating my needs, again, Dave handed me a bandana from his back pocket. I scrutinized it, and satisfied that it was clean, I thanked him while wiping my chin.

"It's going to be great—you've got this!"

"Of course. Easy breezy. I'm not worried," I lied, pulling up my socks and double knotting the laces on my boots.

"Everyone line up, please!" I shouted, holding a clipboard and marker in my hands. After making certain all kids were accounted for, I paired the campers with random buddies. I saw two girls wrinkle their noses. The senior counselor immediately caught the vibe and strode toward them.

"We have such a fun day planned. But before we begin, I want to be clear that Camp Kismet is a safe, welcoming space," I said while pointedly looking at the girls who'd barely adjusted their attitude. "We're here to connect, explore, and make new friends along the way."

I pointed beyond the tall, wispy grass.

"That board will be our guide; let's check it out and vote on the trail we'll hike!" I exclaimed, already knowing that only two choices were fitting. But I wanted the campers to be invested in our trip, to understand each of them had a voice. We gathered in front of the faded, beige board. I explained the differences between the options, and the group decided on the easier hike. (I sighed with relief!)

I led one group. The senior and junior counselors corralled the others. We sang the camp song while ascending the rough, stone steps. One of the girls, Leah, teetered on her heel; I couldn't discern if she was nervous or uncoordinated. After twenty minutes, we paused to hydrate. Two dragonflies hovered over a stream of water to our right, flitting back and forth, landing on a lily pad briefly before resuming their flight. I took a few pictures, and we continued walking.

Some campers chattered about a cute boy. Others were quiet. Leah stumbled and awkwardly stood up, her cheeks blazing with embarrassment. I smiled and encouraged her to keep going. Hearing a snicker from the back of the line, I stewed and vowed no kid would ever feel ostracized. Then I had an idea.

"Leah! I'd like you to lead us on a scavenger hunt," I said. She tugged on one of her dark brown braids.

"What do you mean?" she asked meekly.

I tightened the cap on my water bottle.

"I have a list of five things to spot during our hike. What would you add?" I motioned for her to stand next to me.

"Oh! What about a heart-shaped rock or leaf?" Leah said, her face flushing with excitement. Another snarky sound came from the back.

I was pissed. *Who was the lil stinker?*

Scanning the area, I settled on a blasé girl. Her wavy, sun-streaked locks (or possibly salon dyed) were gathered in a perfect ponytail at the base of her neck. I watched as she opened a pocket mirror and admired her own reflection.

Shit. I hadn't memorized which name went with which camper. I asked Leah if she knew the camper's name.

"Cami, please come here." I tried to keep my tone neutral. This pompous, petulant child was uncannily similar to a kid who'd bullied me in middle school.

Did she just roll her eyes at me?

"Perhaps you didn't hear me. Cami, I have a quick question. Respectfully, you are holding up the rest of the group," I spat through clenched teeth and a terse smile.

Reluctantly, she traipsed toward me and flung her hair over her shoulder.

She doesn't have an ounce of respect. This is the queen bee. I'm about to dethrone her.

"We are kind and inclusive at Camp Kismet," I whispered in her ear. "Just wanted to remind you."

Her huge, round eyes stared at me with a mix of deference and defiance.

"Are we clear?"

Cami nodded and I gave her pieces of recycled paper and tiny pencils.

"Please pass these out to your *friends.*" I emphasized the last word.

My mom had told me, all those years ago, that when kids are mean, they're usually unhappy or seeking control. I studied Cami's expression, which altered slightly, and she seemed engaged in her task.

"Does anyone want to guess what this is for?" Four eager hands shot up into the air. The second camper knew the answer.

"It's to write down every time we find an item!" she exclaimed. I gave her a high five.

"Way to go!" I cheered. "After we're done, we'll meet up with the others for lunch. Who's ready?"

The girls squealed in unison. Leah led the pack, and Cami, who was unsurprisingly competitive, squinted as she surveyed her surroundings.

"I found a four-leaf clover!" she shrieked, holding it up like a tiny trophy. Kids clapped and I beamed, proud of this supportive community. We continued exploring as the wind picked up. I listened to the campers collaborate, telling them not to rush, as they continued their search.

Suddenly someone up ahead screamed. Another camper ran toward me with wide, frightened eyes.

"What's going on?" I asked as my chest constricted.

"Vera fell and she's gushing blood!" She tugged on my hand and pulled me to the front.

I don't have a fucking nurse with me. I knew the spilled coffee this morning was an omen.

A few campers gasped. Another one started to rock back and forth. Cami's skin blanched and Leah shakily asked how she could help.

"Everyone please give Vera some space," I said in what I hoped was a calm tone. I got down on one knee and murmured, "You're okay, sweetie. Let me take a look."

Thank goodness I brought my just-in-case pouch from the glove compartment of my car in addition to the supplies Wendy had assembled in a first aid kit. I had gauze, antiseptic wipes, non-latex gloves, and bandages.

What if she needs stitches? My pulse quickened and panic rose in my chest. I quickly texted Emma that we'd need a bus to pick us up.

I asked Vera to hold onto my shoulder while I slowly poured water over the wound. Exhaling as I saw it wasn't a gash, I dabbed the area with a wipe.

She winced and took a sharp breath.

"I'm sorry, I know that must hurt. It's not too deep, but I think we should have Nurse Janet take a look when we return," I said soothingly. Vera nodded and squeezed her eyes shut.

"We need to put pressure on the area, okay? I'll bandage it when the bleeding stops." *And it better happen soon before I faint.*

Thankfully, it clotted quickly, and I put two wide, waterproof Band-Aids over the slit in her knee. I helped Vera stand up and she assured me she could walk. As we headed toward the meadow, where the others waited for us to eat, I learned that Vera was on the ski and lacrosse teams.

"I've broken bones before, Ms. Joy. This is nothing!" She grinned. *Well, it looked like a murder scene at first,* I thought to myself.

"You're very brave, Vera." Before we disbanded in different areas of the meadow, I praised the campers for being caring and compassionate.

As we rode on the bus back to camp, I realized we never finished the scavenger hunt.

I texted the nurses, so they'd be on alert, and sat in the first row with Vera to my right. *What a trooper, this kiddo*! Most of the campers were quiet; I looked over my shoulder and saw about half of them were snoozing. Leah was wide awake, listening to the music in her earbuds and bopping her head. Cami dabbed tinted lip gloss on her lips.

"What an eventful afternoon!" Janet greeted us. "Vera, please come with me to the clinic. You feeling okay?"

Vera nodded and looked up at me.

"Thank you, Ms. Joy, for cleaning the cut and everything." I beamed.

"You're welcome. You taught me and led by example; you were calm and even kept your sense of humor. Sometimes adults need that reminder." I winked at Janet as they walked away.

I washed up, checked in with Dave, and then headed home. I'd survived my first field trip at Camp Kismet.

CHAPTER 34

Andre met me at the door with a cold cup of bubbly cider. He chuckled as I yapped and yammered about my day. I plopped onto the leather couch and put my feet up on the tufted ottoman. Maple jumped up and licked the pads of my toes.

"Mi amor, those kids are lucky to have you lead them," Andre said, massaging my head with his long fingers. I yawned and relaxed into his chest.

"This won't be a regular occurrence, I hope! I had to fill in for the unit head who was hurling," I sighed, taking a swig of the cider. "Dave tried to find another person before reaching out to me."

Andre lowered his hands. I turned my head, noticing his brows nearly touching.

"What's up?" I asked.

"Nothing," he said.

"Honey, c'mon. What's with the sudden scowl?"

"It's Dave this, Dave that. When will I meet this guy?" Andre grumbled.

Oh my gosh, he's jealous, I thought. Wow. The last time my hubby grilled me about another man was when we first started dating.

I paused for a beat, turning to look at him, stroking his cheek while contemplating how to stroke his fragile ego.

"Andre, he's like a lumberjack. Flannels, burly, and never clean shaven." I chuckled, leaning closer and pecking his pouty lower lip. I noticed his hand shaking, and he tucked it under his leg.

"How was your visit with Dr. Garcia today?" I said, resting my head on his shoulder.

"It was quick. He wants to increase the dose of one of my Parkinson's medications—Levodopa; but the mood med stays the same," he said, coiling a strand of my hair around his finger.

"What else?" I hoped he didn't hear my heart hammering.

Andre inhaled deeply and hesitated.

"Mi amor, you've already had enough excitement for one day. We can talk about this later." His voice lowered to a whisper. Andre seemed apathetic. I silently reassured myself this was the Parkinson's—not a true reflection of his feelings—his facial expressions were less animated than before.

I folded my legs under me and Maple wiggled herself in between us.

"No. Full transparency or I am coming to the next appointment." I'd promised Andre not to badger him, trusting as he promised that he'd never keep information from me.

He sighed and hunched his shoulders.

"Dr. Garcia said it's progressing more rapidly than he expected." Andre's voice quaked. Maple climbed into my lap. I pulled her closer and scratched behind her ears.

In for four, hold for seven, exhale for eight. This will pass. I remembered my mom's calming words. A classmate had made fun of my squeaky voice—one of the first times I had a panic attack after a jerk shamed me in middle school when I'd finally summoned the courage to speak in class.

"Joy?" Maple and Andre stared at me.

"Sorry honey, I was processing what you said," I murmured. *This camp idea was a colossal mistake. I can't do this.* The pebble jammed into my throat, and I could barely swallow, its edges feeling sharp this time.

I finally lifted my chin and saw something I'd never seen before on my handsome husband's face.

Fear.

He needs me to be strong, I thought. I'll deal with my shit later.

I pointed to the wood and said, "Maple, down." Then I pivoted and held my husband's gaze.

"I've got you. We've got this and each other. Say the word and I'm selling the camp," I blurted. Damn, that was supposed to stay in my mind.

Andre shook his head.

"Not an option and don't ever say that again. I don't need a pity party or rescuing," he protested, his voice again fading at the end of the sentence.

My eyes moistened, and I blinked several times before responding.

"I hear you, honey. I don't pity you—never did, never will. You're one of the strongest people I've ever known," I said fervently. "I feel awful that I wasn't there today—for you to hear this alone…" I buried my head into his neck.

"It makes me happy to see you excited about your new venture!" Andre said. "Parkinson's isn't going away. In fact, I think we should start planning exotic trips. No more bucket lists—let's call it a fuck-it list!"

We laughed and he pulled me closer.

"Worrying about the future is futile. It is what it is," Andre said. *Had he been studying Buddhism?* My control freak hubby sounded serene, as if he'd accepted his fate. Our fate. I clearly hadn't.

He didn't even care that I double-dipped in the almond butter. After munching on celery sticks, we walked a few miles with Maple. Andre noted that our puppy had a pattern. She had no problem peeing at nearly every tree. But when it came to poop, Maple wouldn't go unless we turned around.

"At least our pup doesn't get acne or body odor," I joked. Then I told him about the bus and that we were able to crank open the windows. I'd heard counselors complain, especially in the boy's division, about the stench. Andre chortled as I continued chattering. Maple must've been amused also because she started to jump up and down. I swear I saw her smile.

I'd reserved a pickleball court for two hours; Andre and I hadn't played a match in a while. We'd stopped playing tennis—this sport had less running, and it felt safer (to me, anyway) as my husband's balance and coordination had gotten worse. Given the news he'd shared last night, I was even more psyched to volley and possibly let him win.

Before we left, Andre went to the gym for a boxing class. While he was gone, I let Maple run around in our backyard. My husband's logic and foresight never ceased to amaze me; he'd fenced in a strip of grassy area so we could let our puppy wander safely. I brought my journal outside and settled in the mesh lounge chair under the awning. Then I tossed Maple a toy with carrots and peanut butter stuffed in it, figuring this would keep her busy for a bit. I popped the cap off the purple pen.

Dear Mom,

Tomorrow's your birthday.

And you are gone.

You're not coming back.

I'm not ready to celebrate without you.

I still can't say the "d" word. My therapist keeps encouraging me to at least write it. Does the first letter count? I've found every synonym in the dictionary:

Passed.

Gone.

Transitioned.

Exited.

I'm not in denial. How can I be? I've made it a few weeks—a milestone—without dialing your phone number. But this day stings like someone is jabbing my heart with a scorching metal knife. I can't breathe. I can't think straight. I can't celebrate with you, Mommy.

How could you go so soon, so young? It's so fucking wrong.

And the irony of my name. When will I find my joy? High and low tides that are impossible to predict. It's like a tiny surfer pops up on the waves, reminding me to move forward, to stay afloat. Yet there are tides of gloom, days I can barely keep my head above the water. I run, doodle, hell, even meditate (can you believe it?).

I've been immersing myself in work. Or, trying to. Loving the smiles and wonder on these kids' faces. Oh! Did I tell you I rede-signed the camp logo? You would fucking love it—I sketched a modern, muted rainbow like a hug from above. I also rewrote our camp mission and vision statement to be clearer about inclusion and all that the spectrum of colors symbolizes.

We're already tweaking Andre's meds. We are also research-ing an implantable device used for Deep Brain Stimulation (DBS). It requires surgery, which frightens me. Reminds me of The Wizard of Oz and the Tin Man's heart. It can help the tremors, though I'm noticing it's his voice that seems to be worsening. Unless he's pissed off—lol—Andre's volume goes up and down, more so at the end of the day. Yet lately it's always happening. I think he's embarrassed, especially when he's leading a meeting.

It breaks my heart.

I try not to burden him with my angst. I snuggle with Maple, vent to Mel, go to therapy, and all the things that're supposed to help. Thank G-d for the pharmaceutical industry! Dave from camp thinks I should try weed. Of course, he and so many other Vermonters grow it in their backyard. They insist it's "natural." Ugh. I think I would get paranoid—I haven't touched the stuff in years. I'm not planning on it.

The campers inspire me. Had a close call with one of them but handled it! Poor kid was mortified after falling. And I also put a conceited, bully-in-training in her place. It's not her fault that her parents have made her the center of the universe, but I'm not allowing her to be the queen bee mean girl here. Hell no. I'm so grateful you taught me how to stand up for myself. And that every person matters.

These kids are imbedding themselves into my soul; I can't imagine being a therapist like you were. The whole "don't take your work home with you" mentality seems impossible. I don't know how you did it.

And this one young girl, Simi. I worry about her. She's withdrawn, shy, doesn't speak much. I am determined to boost her confidence; I want her to finish the summer not only verbalizing with ease but also knowing her worth. Her folks are hoity-toity, and her home environment must be so high *pressure. I heard she found our camp (I'm loving that word lately—our!); she loves animals. I wonder if taking photos would help her feel empowered, provide an outlet for expression without having to use her voice. It sure did for me.*

I'm ruminating about mortality since you departed, Mom. Mine. And now Andre's.

Time. Don't know how long we have or when ours is up.

What will I do with the time I—we—have left? Am I making an impact? Am I present enough? These kids give me hope.

CHAPTER 35

This morning, I decided to spend a few hours taking pictures of activities. I planned to start with the waterfront; we'd just surprised the campers with a new inflatable water slide. But on the way, I saw Simi near the chicken coop. A teenage boy peered at her from the other side of the area. I observed these two and slowly switched my lens from the wide angle one to the telephoto one. Simi didn't notice the boy staring at her. She balanced a tattered book on the edge of the wooden enclosure and pushed her glasses higher up on her nose.

The other day, I reread her file and learned that Simi was a Manhattan girl who seemed to be raised in a home with parents much like Vivienne. Spending part of the summer in the Hamptons, Simi counted the days until camp started, according to her mother.

Here she felt safe. She didn't feel the academic pressures to speak or answer questions—that's what our camp therapist shared with me. She'd feel embarrassed in front of her middle school peers. Simi must've worried about where she would sit in the lunchroom. What words she should avoid. Breaking out with pimples and getting her first period.

Caught up in my own thoughts and summer memories of when I got my period in the middle of the night at sleepaway camp, I didn't notice Simi had closed her book. I double-checked the lens, making sure it was on properly. Then I peered through it and saw Simi staring straight at me. Uh-oh. Crap. The kid had finally started speaking a bit more and I didn't want to screw it up.

I quickly lowered the camera and edged toward her.

"Hey there! Are you on chicken duty today?"

The teenage boy snickered.

"You said 'doodie!'" he smirked, proud of his pun.

I couldn't help myself, covering my mouth as I tried not to laugh.

"Funny! Not what I said, and what is your name?" I tilted my head.

His light hazel eyes nearly sprang out of their sockets. I suppressed a smile—the kid comically seemed like a cartoon character.

"Lucas," he replied, shoving his hands into his pockets.

Poor kiddo—maybe he thinks he's in trouble?

I held out my hand and he hesitantly shook it.

"It's lovely to meet you, Lucas. Quite a sense of humor you have!" His shoulders lowered and he smiled.

"Thanks, Ms. Joy!"

Simi stayed silent and studied the chickens, who'd begun clucking as if they wanted to join our conversation.

"That's a super cool camera!" Lucas exclaimed.

"Do you want to hold it?" I replied, looking at Simi through my peripheral vision and noticing she'd turned her head slightly toward us.

"Yeah!" I handed it to him and placed the wide strap around his neck.

I released the curls from the scrunchie that held them and redid my bun. Simi met my eyes, briefly.

"Why don't you join us?" I motioned for her to come closer. She did but kept a few feet between her and Lucas.

Simi already knew that she wanted to be a veterinarian. Her parents noted on the camp application that one of her hobbies was reading biographies about scientists; it seemed many of the books she'd brought from home had nature or animal themes. Though she excelled in academics, her parents shared that Simi never felt like she belonged at "the best private school in the Northeast" or in Manhattan. The taxis blaring their horns. The hustle and bustle of the city. The skyscrapers that felt overwhelming. My guess was she had no choice but to speak in that environment, otherwise she would risk disappointing her parents.

Simi completed the "about me" camper form, and she even attached an additional handwritten note, stating how nervous she was to come to camp and she was afraid of speaking. I could understand why she withdrew—she probably needed to recharge.

Milking the goats in the morning seemed grounding as little or no talking was required. The rhythmic squeeze and release was calming, a predictable routine. Simi also enjoyed a structured daily schedule. She got nervous during that hour before dinner—free, unscheduled time. And she'd already finished the seven books she'd brought with her from home. Simi sensed when a cow was sick. She knew by the way a sheep bleated if it was happy or sad. I was thankful Simi's parents had signed a release form, which was optional, giving Jenny permission to share information about the campers.

"Hey. Isn't this cool?" Lucas asked, his hazel eyes darting from Simi then back to the chicken.

Simi stared ahead, a rosy embarrassment blushing her ivory skin.

"What's your name?" The boy ran a hand through his shaggy, ginger hair.

Simi pretended like she didn't hear him.

"I'm Lucas." His voice cracked at the end. Then he took swift strides toward Simi.

"Do you speak English?" He smirked.

Looking down at her rubber boots, Simi's heart-shaped face reddened even more as she nodded slightly. I'd noticed that she usually retreated like a turtle into a shell. Maybe Simi thought Lucas was cute with those adorable freckles smattered across his face—I wondered if she had the beginning of a camp crush.

"Let's keep watching—I think she's about to lay eggs!" I sensed that Simi couldn't coax her legs to move. Like so many campers who lived in metropolitan cities, she'd never seen a chicken lay eggs before. I waved again, beckoning her a bit closer.

I supported the lens with a cupped hand, teaching Lucas what the different numbers meant. Then I explained about aperture settings and how it is similar to the pupils in our eyes adjusting to the changing light. I'm glad I'd looped the strap over his head. Either from excitement or lack of coordination, Lucas didn't have a steady grip on my favorite camera.

Unzipping the inside pocket of my bag, I searched for another roll of film.

"Please give it to me for a second. I want to show you how to load and change it," I said to Lucas. Simi stood straighter and stood on her tippy toes.

"Simi, right? Come over here and check this out," Lucas said. "We don't bite. At least I don't!"

I thought about Andre's dexterity—his strength that would one day be his weakness. I turned my body slightly, pleased to see that Simi seemed interested.

"It's like a puzzle," I uttered, hoping she'd ask to hold the camera.

"Oh," Simi murmured.

"Want to try?" I said gently.

Simi nodded.

I slid the tiny rectangle to the right and the area opened. As if she'd done this before, Simi took the shiny film between her slender fingers and slipped it into the notch, aligning it perfectly.

"Dang, that's impressive!" Lucas said, admiring Simi's precision. "I couldn't get it into that small space."

She shrugged humbly and pointed to the chicken at the back of the coop.

"I told you!" Lucas bounced up and down like a ball.

"Let's go over there, slowly. Please give me the camera," I said.

As we approached the corner, Simi squealed with delight.

"She's laying an egg!"

I'd never heard her say more than one or two words at a time.

"Here. Would you like to take a picture? I'll set it to automatic, so you don't miss this moment," I offered.

Simi nodded so enthusiastically that her glasses fell off her face and onto the dirt.

Lucas immediately swooped them off the ground, and he cleaned them with his uniform shirt.

"Here ya go," he said.

"Thank you," Simi replied.

I had a hunch that Simi's heart raced when Lucas was nearby. I remembered that feeling, those teen flutters, like before a big test or doctor visit. I wondered if Simi had noticed him the first day of camp. I'd overheard a few of the older girls chitchatting about Lucas. And he was the only boy with that fiery red hair.

He was going to follow her, but I signaled for Lucas to stay by my side.

We're about to have a breakthrough, I thought. I wished my mom could be here right now, witnessing this with me. I looked up at the cloudless sky, wondering if she was seeing this from wherever she was.

Click.

Click.

Click.

We watched as Simi captured each moment of the egg leaving the chicken's body. Another chicken flapped her feathers. The third clucked and pecked at the organic feed the campers from the morning session had sprinkled all over the area.

My mind drifted to a memory—the first time I'd held a camera back in middle school. It felt like plates in the earth shifted that day. My Uncle Jack, my mom's brother, was in advertising back then. Boisterous, bold, and a total badass, he was one of the only people who didn't overwhelm me despite being loud. He bought me a camera for Hanukkah, just before I'd entered high school, and my mom chided him for the extravagant gift.

It became a lifeline. Then and now.

I'd discovered that I could express my emotions and thoughts in photos. I'd go to the beach at sunrise on Sunday mornings and my mom would bring her yoga mat, holding poses while I captured the world waking up. I loved seeing the cruise ships in the distance, the phases of the moon, the sun spreading her light as she awakened. I, too, hid behind the lens. By the beginning of my senior year, I'd told my parents that I wanted to study photography and visual arts at a small college. And definitely in a different landscape from the tropical vibes of Miami, where I'd never really felt at home.

"Ms. Joy?"

I shook my head, realizing I'd totally spaced out.

"Look over there!" Simi said softly.

Tears pricked the corners of my eyes. A faint rainbow, not quite an arc and more like a brushstroke of paint, stretched between two puffy clouds.

"Please give me the camera," I said, sniffing quietly.

I took two photos before it faded away. It must've been drizzling in the distance.

"Thank you for pointing that out, Simi. And not even a drop of rain!" I mused. "That's what I love about taking photos—

moments are fleeting, and we can capture them, if we're lucky, before they're gone."

Her eyes met mine and held them for longer than in the past. Even Lucas stayed silent. No smart-ass jokes. A collective, shared, and at least for me, unforgettable experience.

She also signed up for the garden. Simi lived on the Upper East Side, and though her nanny took her to Central Park, she told Jenny that she'd always longed for a yard of her own. She learned about sunflowers, how they'd grow toward the light, and their stems so strong, seemingly unbreakable. And she wondered if they could be grown on her penthouse balcony. She'd written to her mother about sending books about this, which Jenny shared with me.

Simi volunteered to pull weeds from the vegetable garden. I wondered if it was satisfying, like something she could control. Jenny told me Simi felt freer at camp. At home, Simi's mother dragged her to cocktail parties, insisting her hair was shellacked with gel and making sure she wore fancy shoes. Her father, a well-renowned radiologist, understood Simi preferred solitude over swarms of people.

Her parents had only sent one letter on linen, embossed stationary. Simi recognized the flowery handwriting, which was her father's executive assistant. Other girls in her bunk got packages filled with treats and loving, handwritten notes.

———

I was psyched for Saturday—our annual "sleep under the stars." And I hadn't planned to be there because weekend nights were reserved for Andre. Now that Simi had shown interest in photography, I thought I'd bring my tripod and other equipment. It had taken me most of my college years to master nighttime images. Even with a point and shoot, an automatic camera, it could be challenging.

When I told Andre about the breakthrough with Simi, he encouraged me to go.

"Are you sure, sweetie?" I asked.

"Absolutely!" he answered.

"Do you want to come?"

He paused for a beat.

"You'll be so focused on the kids—it's best if I stay home," he said, lacing his fingers through mine. "Plus, I don't want to be up until midnight. I'll go to happy hour with Jake and then early to bed."

I studied him, making sure he meant it. I couldn't tell; his facial muscles were frozen in a neutral position.

"Why don't we have dinner, the four of us? The sun doesn't set until much later, you know." I offered.

Andre smiled. "Great idea—I'll make a reservation."

"Shouldn't we see if they're free first? And they need to get a babysitter," I laughed.

"Good point," he said.

The next few days flew by as I completed mundane tasks like paying bills and meeting with staff members. Dave had busted a junior counselor smoking weed behind the boathouse. He'd put him on probation. I touched base with Jenny, wondering about her observations and feedback about some campers. She shared that the kid who wasn't eating at the beginning of camp was increasing his portions and showing progress.

Then I asked about Simi.

"She still seems quieter than her peers. Not exactly reclusive, and I do see her hanging out with Lucas. He's here for his third summer on a full scholarship," Jenny said.

I animatedly told her about the chicken laying eggs and the kids connecting. Jenny laughed when I also shared that Simi corrected me, explaining hens, not chickens, lay eggs.

"Simi's an avid reader—I've heard from her counselors. Yesterday, she was so immersed in a book that I saw her plow right into another camper! Poor kid, she looked humiliated," she continued.

My heart sank. "How did the other camper react?" I asked nervously.

"You'd be proud. In the Camp Kismet way, she was kind and empathetic."

As Jenny spoke, I'd been doodling rainbows and sketching an image of a Polaroid. Then I wrote and rewrote KISMET. And suddenly had an idea.

Kind. **I**nclusive. **S**ynchronous. **M**indful. **E**mpathetic. **T**eamwork. What if I started a new tradition at Camp Kismet? A collaborative, community project that would be displayed in the art shed or dining hall?

"Thanks for everything!"

I reached for my sketchbook, which I hadn't felt inspired to use since my mom died. Then I untied the thin leather knot that held my pencil case together, opening the trifold material and laying it flat. I arranged each pencil like the colors of a rainbow. ROYGBIV—red, orange, yellow, green, blue, indigo, violet. I'd never forgotten that acronym, which ironically, I'd learned at summer camp.

I stacked them vertically. Then I tried horizontally. I drew rainbows in the shapes of farm animals. I also wrote "Kismet" in big, block letters. I looked out the window to my right, saw the cardinal and started to wonder if my mom had sent her, too.

CHAPTER 36

WEEK FOUR

Flashlight. Check. Extra blanket. Check. Binoculars. Check.

What was I forgetting? It'd been decades since I'd slept under the stars. Andre suggested it a few years ago, and I shivered at the idea, thinking I was too old (and would be too cold) for that type of excursion.

As I tossed my bag in the car, I laughed at the irony. Now I was the one in charge!

"Mi amor, are you ready yet?" Andre called from inside.

"Packing for tonight. I'm already dressed!" I yelled.

I didn't want to rush through dinner with Mel and Jake. We hadn't spent time with them in a while. I'd drive separately so I could go to camp right after.

It was the perfect Northern Vermont summer evening. A light brisk breeze blew. Thin branches bent but didn't break. Bronze-silvery birch bark peeled revealing new, younger growth—the cambium—beneath it.

As I drove to The Bistro, a cozy, mountain chic restaurant with scrumptious, savory cuisine, I saw lavender blooms, a blossoming lilac tree that only flowered for a few weeks. Rolling down the window, I inhaled the floral scent and wished I knew how to make perfume. I sat in my truck for a few minutes after parking it. Then I walked to the front of the charming, historic building.

Gazing at the mountains in the distance, I zoned out, studying how shadows played with the lingering lights and observing images shifting with the sun's waltz over the water. Today the mountains were a combination of deep greens, faded brown, a layered back-drop for the tranquil Lake Champlain.

I remembered the first time we'd gone sailing. We nearly cap-sized; Jake and Andre had bragged about their boating expertise. It turned out they'd collectively only sailed three times in their lives! Good thing we were all strong swimmers. The next time we went for a sunset trip, Andre hired a captain. He—and we—would need to soon learn to lean on others for tasks he might not be able to do. I quivered and heard Mel call my name.

"Where'd you go?" she asked, retying the red bandana on her head.

"I'm right here!" I retorted with a wink. The men were anima-tedly discussing something about a building project.

She didn't push, thankfully. We'd ordered fried artichokes and Brussels sprouts tossed with diced dates, which arrived at the perfect time.

"This is decadent!" I said, admiring the crispy vegetables and how they contrasted with the spongy, sweet fruit.

"And it pairs perfectly with the wine I brought from home," Andre chimed, bringing out a twenty-year-old Cabernet.

"What's the occasion? That's a special bottle," Jake remarked.

Andre shrugged and smiled.

"Being with you both. Being alive and healthy. Just plain being," he said, wrapping his arm around my shoulders.

Who was this Zen, philosophical man sitting next to me?

Mel tilted her head and Jake held out the goblet, motioning for Andre to fill it to the top.

"I'll have iced tea—I need to be lucid for the campers. And it's not a good look for the new owner to show up plastered!" I giggled. Andre's hand shook, and he quickly flattened his other palm over it. I pretended not to notice.

Two hours felt like two minutes. I was lucky to have friends with such a rich, shared history. They were like family. We barely took a breath as we bantered about politics, art, business, and everything in between.

I wished I could stretch time like a rubber band, prolonging this moment. I also wished the soul and psyche could bounce back quickly, returning to its original shape by simply letting go. Nobody warns humans about the hard work that's required for healing. If only it were easy.

I glanced at the rustic, round clock that hung above the bar. People gathered at the long, cherry wood plank, sitting on stools and sipping cocktails. One woman, probably in her late twenties, tossed her straight hair over her shoulder. A couple toasted, raising their mugs in the air, and hugged each other. The bartender took the rag that was tucked into his waist and wiped a spill.

I wanted to warn them, that one phone call could dramatically, permanently, change their lives. But would it matter? How can we prepare for a parent—or anyone we love—dying suddenly?

What a morbid thought. I zoomed back in and refocused my attention on Mel, Jake, and Andre.

"I'm bummed but I need to go," I said wistfully. "This was awesome—let's not wait so long to make it happen again!" Andre stood and pressed his lips to my forehead.

"So excited to hear about your evening—I'll miss you," he said. Ever the gentleman, he helped me into my windbreaker and walked me to the car.

"Thank you again for being cool with all of this, honey. It means so much to me." I threw my hands around his neck, kissing him deeply now that we were alone. "Tomorrow let's relax at home and—"

"I already have ideas." Andre smiled seductively.

"I'm glad some things never change," I snarked, settling myself into the seat. Then I lowered my window.

"Lemme know if you need me to be on bear patrol! Or protect you from other creatures—animals or kids. I'll have my phone on." Andre waved as I backed out of the parking lot.

I was nervous being away from him, which seemed irrational, yet I couldn't shake it. We'd all have our phones on silent; the adults needed to model and exemplify the Camp Kismet values, one of which was being present. I'd have to find a discreet way to check in with my husband. Ever since his diagnosis, I worried about him constantly.

Our campus at night was magical. Lights twinkled from the upper corners of the cabins. The flagpole shimmered, standing tall in all her glory. Wind rustled the leaves like the white noise setting on a sound machine. I thought about recording it to play for Andre; I couldn't adequately describe it.

In the past few months, his sleep (and mine as a result) was interrupted by nighttime awakenings. And his restless legs had gotten worse; Andre would get up frequently, walking to relieve the tingling and burning sensations. I'd feel the bed move when he'd toss and turn.

Yawning as I approached camp, I saw Leah and Cami, their heads bowed and close together. My first thought was that lice can jump like little acrobats. My second was *wow, I think enemies can become friends.* Then I smiled as I turned, leaving them to chat and, hopefully, connect with kindness.

Someone had already lit the fire—the smoky smell evoked memories from summers I'd spent with Andre in nearby Stowe. We'd spend weekends there, especially in August when Burlington's temperatures increased. Though only about forty-five minutes away from where we lived, Stowe had become our sanctuary in the mountains.

We biked on the recreation path, peddling over bridges and listening to the river. We waded in the water, rolling up our jeans to just below our knees. We built rock formations called cairns. We celebrated our five-year anniversary at the Stowe Mountain Lodge, luxuriating at the spa and ordering room service. I'd complained at the time about the extravagance, and how it was a bit bougie—not so "Vermonty." Now I'm grateful we spent that time together in our happy place.

We discussed the possibility of buying a home in Stowe but decided that was a waste of money. I wondered if we should revisit that idea, though the real estate market had skyrocketed. Plus, it wasn't fiscally wise after just purchasing the camp. Maybe having a place that was drivable would be healing for Andre as his disease progressed. And maybe for me, too.

I looked up at the cosmic portrait in the sky. I spotted the North Star and the Little Dipper. *Mom, I miss you so much. Are you up there?*

"Joy! Over here!" I heard Dave shout. *Shit, was I talking out loud again?*

As I neared the campfire, I saw Simi cross-legged with a pile of books on her lap. Her back was curved, and she held a flashlight. She wasn't wearing her glasses, which explained why she peered so closely at the pages.

"Good evening, Simi! What are you reading?" I asked gently, crouching down to meet her eyes.

She pressed her palm into the middle of the novel and looked up.

"I'm reading a biography about Temple Grandin," she said, her voice louder than I'd ever heard it.

"I've heard of her. Isn't she a scientist?" I asked.

Simi nodded excitedly.

"I would love to learn more about her!"

She explained that Dr. Grandin was autistic. And she always related more to animals than humans. She studied cows, learning about their behaviors, and had designed ethical and well-organized systems for them.

"Sounds like her story speaks to you in some way," I remarked.

Simi closed the book and balanced it on her navy sleeping bag, which was rolled up next to her.

"It does."

"May I ask why?" I held my breath, hoping I hadn't pushed too far.

She stayed silent and rested her chin on her fisted palm. Then she spoke.

"Honestly, I've always felt weird around people, especially kids my age. I never know what to say. And I don't always get the jokes they make. Animals accept me as I am."

My eyes got misty as I listened to Simi. Like a lotus flower, this young girl had begun to open, quietly, gracefully, and at her own pace. I had to resist asking the bazillion questions that mushroomed in my mind.

"Thank you for sharing, Simi. Isn't it amazing how we can see ourselves in others' stories?" Damn it. I couldn't help myself. A question, albeit a rhetorical one.

Her eyes widened and a smile spread over her face.

"Yes. You understand," Simi said.

I don't want to leave her. She's never spoken this much and with such conviction.

"Ms. Joy?"

"Yes?"

"May I sit next to you at the campfire? And maybe sleep near you?" she asked timidly, biting the cuticle off her thumbnail.

Now I was the one beaming.

"Of course, Simi!" I stifled a shriek. She didn't seem to like loud noises.

She ran a finger back and forth, tracing the crease in the binding of her book.

"We will all gather in about fifteen minutes for s'mores. I'll show you how to roast a marshmallow, so it's barely burnt but toasty!" Simi didn't look at me, but her posture shifted, and she'd stopped gnawing on her nail.

"Where did you go?" Dave asked as he added another log to the fire. Mesmerized by the cobalt hue around the flames, I didn't answer right away.

"Joy?"

"Oh sorry! I was talking to Simi," I replied sheepishly, embarrassed that I'd spaced out for the second time that night.

"Whoa. Did you use the words *talking* and *Simi* in the same sentence?" Dave stroked his beard.

"She's slowly starting to speak, and more than those one-word responses," I replied proudly. "And she's been expressing interest in photography. How cool is that?"

He raised his hand to high-five me.

"Damn, that's something. You have a way with kids—not just Simi. I overheard a few counselors chatting about it the other day," Dave said.

I blushed and shrugged.

"I get her, I guess. I was super shy at her age, too," I replied.

"No way—you?" He covered his mouth in mock surprise. "I don't believe it."

"It's true. I was bullied when I was a kid; that's when I realized I felt safe to express myself from behind a lens. Ask my mo—"

I almost said mother. I blinked back tears.

He handed me an orange bandana that was wrapped around his wrist.

"Thanks," I managed and dabbed at the corners of my eyes. "Let's get everyone over here. I'm ready to show you all my marshmallow technique!"

Dave chortled and shot me a look like "you've got nothin' on a native Vermonter!"

Leah and Cami skipped toward us, holding hands, their ponytails swinging in synchrony. Vera followed them; her wound had healed. Lucas joined the rest of the boys, who laughed at whatever joke he was telling.

And I felt happier than I had in months.

Dave brought all the supplies: long, sturdy sticks, Hershey bars (and dairy/nut-free chocolate for our allergy kids), graham crackers (regular and gluten-free), and sprinkles. That last ingredient I found strange.

"Why these for s'mores?" I held up the bottles of sparkly sugar.

"Well, I thought this year it would be neat to make the chocolate colorful—you know, like the new logo and Kismet vibe," Dave said.

I almost cried, again. *How thoughtful and creative!*

"What an amazing idea!" I exclaimed.

Simi looked at me and I waved for her to come closer.

I banged some sticks together that Leah had found on the scavenger hunt yesterday.

"Who's ready for s'mores?"

A chorus of campers shouted "me," and they lined up in a zigzag formation.

"Is this anyone's first time?" Simi raised her hand halfway. A few other kids did as well.

I smiled. "Let's make this a night you'll never forget. And this year, Mr. Dave had a brilliant idea—he brought sprinkles, which some of you call 'jimmies,' right?" More squeals and shrieks from the kids.

I sat on a stump about a foot away from the fire. As the newbies approached me, I demonstrated how to put the puffy, pillowy marshmallow in a place where you could get the flame to catch it. Then I showed them the importance of being mindful—and when to blow it out.

"I did it!"

"Ooooo, it's gooey!"

"Look how the chocolate's melting over the cracker!"

I picked up my camera, switched the settings, and started snapping photos. One camper showed another how to make taffy; she took a marshmallow and kneaded it, pulling and turning it between her middle finger and thumb. I'd forgotten about that! I took pictures of crumbs stuck in the corners of mouths. Chocolate streaked on shiny faces. Most of all, I tried to capture the kids' joy that kindled the campfire as much as our campers.

Settling a bunch of sugared-up, overstimulated kids was no easy feat. I stepped aside, admiring our counselors' patience as they coaxed the kids to calm. One counselor brought her guitar and started strumming what sounded like Joni Mitchell. Dave strategically placed lanterns in different areas of the field. After everyone washed their hands, faces, and hopefully brushed their teeth, we reconvened at the campfire.

The logs crackled and embers blanketed the decreasing flame. I continued taking photos and noticed both Simi and Lucas were watching. We sang the camp song and others like James Taylor's "You've Got a Friend," among other tunes.

Then the unit head, Sandy, withdrew a hardcover, hefty book from her backpack.

"Everyone turn on your flashlights, please!" she shouted cheerily. "Would anyone like to read the first poem?"

Six hands shot up in the air.

"Lucas, why don't you begin?" He scampered to the front, his gangly legs trying to catch up with the rest of his scrawny body. I continued to take photos.

Witnessing the connections and bonds formed in just a few weeks was nothing short of breathtaking. The campers listened attentively and patted their legs rhythmically like drums (another tradition instead of clapping). They took turns reading poems about empathy, friendship, and kindness.

All of a sudden, Simi piped up with a noise I'd never heard from her.

"Ms. Joy! Look over there!"

Even the campers seemed shocked at her enthusiastic exclamation. And how her typically timid voice cut through the chatter.

"What are those lights?" Her pitch rose at the end.

I walked toward the area she was referencing—there were clusters of shrubbery I hadn't noticed during the day. Flickering lights danced between the leaves. Chill bumps smattered on my forearms and warmth spread across my chest.

One by one, as if sensing something otherworldly, the kids followed me. I waited until everyone was nearby.

"Those are fireflies. Aren't they magical?" My mouth hung open like Maple when she smelled peanut butter. I turned my camera back on. Instead of capturing the fireflies, I backed up and took photos of the wondrous expressions on the kids' faces.

No matter how many times I'd seen them, fireflies fascinated me, a reminder that we need the dark to appreciate light. Thank goodness I'd brought my digital camera tonight because I'd defi-nitely be out of film already.

"Can we catch them, Ms. Joy?"

"Do they have superpowers?"

"Can they see us?"

I didn't know who to answer first. Dave looked sideways at me.

"It's amazing, right?" he answered.

Well, that was a smart answer, I thought. Kinda covers it all.

I sensed somebody was behind me and turned around. Simi stood there with her hands clasped in front of her.

"There must be a logical reason the fireflies light up, right?" She glanced from me and back to the bushes.

I nodded, though hesitated to inform her. Somehow it might feel less magical if we brought in science.

Simi didn't stop there.

"How does it happen? Is it phosphorous or some other chem-ical reaction?"

I remembered when Mel's oldest learned that the tooth fairy wasn't real. It devastated him. I didn't want to diminish Simi's won-der—or any of the campers.

But I wasn't going to lie, either.

Simi stared up at me and tapped her foot like a bunny, politely yet impatiently awaiting my response.

"You're so smart, Simi. Yes, it's something similar. When oxy-gen and other molecules mix, it creates a chemical reaction that releases energy in the form of light. Still, aren't they beautiful?"

Simi twisted the end of her ponytail.

"Understanding how they light up makes it more meaningful. Thank you, Ms. Joy!" She wrapped her arms around my waist and squeezed me.

I froze. We had guidelines about hugging children and respecting each child's boundaries. (I found that counterintuitive, especially because I was a tactile person!) I yearned to hug her back.

Of all the kids in our camp community. This quiet, reticent, reclusive child. Who was speaking in sentences. And now a hug!

I didn't know what to do, so I offered my two palms and gave her a double high five.

All night I tossed and turned. And had to pee every hour. I'd blame it on too much water but that's bullshit. I think my bladder mimicked my mind—excited and energized.

I wasn't the only one awake into the wee hours of the night. It was Dave's turn to make the rounds, checking on the staff and campers. I'd finally relaxed, halfway asleep.

"Hey there," Dave whispered at 3 a.m. "You good?"

Startled, I stifled a scream and tucked my knees into my chest.

Dave's upper torso bellowed in and out as his eyes crinkled in the corners.

"I didn't mean to spook you!" he said, trying not to laugh.

"Well, you did!" I retorted.

"Guess you're not used to camping, eh?" He tilted his head.

"Not like this, I'm not. My husband and I love camping. But in recent years, I guess it's more like glamping—we have a premium tent." I chuckled.

I didn't mention his Parkinson's. Or that Andre was the main reason I felt like I'd consumed an entire pot of coffee. I'd been present earlier in the evening, especially jazzed after witnessing the kids' astonishment when they saw the fireflies. But when the sounds of snoring mixed with a few campers talking in their sleep, my mind wandered and went from wonder to worry.

I tried to meditate. Then I read a few chapters of a novel. I sprawled out on my blanket and gazed at the stars. Nothing distracted me from my noisy, inner turmoil. I finally snuck a peek at my cell phone, slipping my body into my sleeping bag so nobody would see me.

> I can't wait to hear about your night.
> All is well here. Quit worrying and enjoy!
> Love you!

He knew me so well. I sent Andre a pink heart emoji then put my phone in the pocket of my backpack.

What if he wasn't telling me the truth?

What if he needed me?

What if I couldn't get there in time?

CHAPTER 37

'd finally dozed an hour before sunrise. I raked my fingers through my knotted, frizzy hair before I resignedly gave up. My faded Middlebury cap would have to do. The sweet scent of maple syrup and campfire smoke drifted toward me. It'd make the perfect candle! Maybe I'd design more camp merch for next summer. After brushing my teeth with bottled water (Dave teased me), I joined the rest of the counselors at the makeshift kitchen.

"I am impressed! Were you all in Scouts? And I thought my s'mores skills were something," I exclaimed, gawking at the buffet of scrambled eggs, French toast, and leafy greens adorned with sliced radish and cherry tomatoes.

"It's the Von Glad way, Ms. Joy! Oops, I meant Kismet," Sandy piped as she pressed a silicon spatula into the thick challah bread. The counselors checked on the kids, sprawled out in their sleeping bags. Some had limbs sticking out. Others were tucked away like burritos, and I could only see the top of their heads.

My smile broadened and I stretched my arms toward the brightening sky. I surveyed the area, noticing an array of wildflowers in a vase. My eyes roamed and landed on a tower of stones. When Andre and I attempted to make them, ours were simple and not as high. I'd seen elaborate cairns like this one in rivers. Damn, I'd left my camera near the rest of my stuff.

I turned around and ran smack into Dave. Literally.

"Whoa, do we need to get you a helmet?" he asked, laughing. "Maybe your next profession you could be a linebacker."

I pulled my cap lower to hide my humiliation, wishing it were still dark outside.

"Sorry! I was just going to get—"

He held up my camera bag.

"This?"

Unbelievable. Now I was certain Dave had some kind of psychic abilities.

"How'd you know that's exactly what I needed?" I stammered.

"It's not rocket science. You take it with you like Linus and his blanket!"

"True. Fair point. Thanks so much," I slung the strap across my body.

I couldn't decide if it'd be creepy or cool to photograph the few teens who still slumbered. I could intentionally shoot toward the sunlight—then the images would be silhouettes. When I wasn't worrying about Andre, I brainstormed, envisioning other ways to enhance the Kismet camp experience. A dormant part of my essence—my creativity—had awakened. Ideas formed an ever-growing collage of ideas for our Kismet community. It was hard to believe the first session was almost over.

Kids heaped piles of food on plates, chattering and twittering between bites. I'd promised Andre we would have brunch together, though now I wished I was eating with everyone here. Reluctantly, I plodded back to my area, packed up my things, and said goodbye to everyone. I noticed Simi sitting with Lucas as I walked to the car.

———

"Hey there, sweet girl!" Maple scampered toward me and put her squishy, soft paws on my belly when I returned home. She licked every inch of my skin, starting with my face and then moving to my neck. You'd think I'd been gone for a year. Andre stood in front of me, grinning.

"It's a shame she doesn't love her momma," he snorted, taking my hands in his and pulling me upright. My entire face was wet with puppy slobber. And I couldn't believe Andre didn't wipe it off before pressing his lips to mine.

"Hello there," I said huskily. Maple made her way to my ankles. "Does she think I'm breakfast?"

Andre brushed my bangs away from my eyebrows and smiled.

"Can you blame her? You are mouthwatering," Andre teased. "I'm guessing she's also enticed by the sweat and sunscreen."

I giggled as Maple barked in agreement. She'd had a growth spurt the past two months; her head almost reached my knees.

"Alright, my two favorite beings. I need to shower! Give me a few minutes and I'll be back," I said.

Warm water cascaded from the top of my head and down my back. I dawdled in the steamy shower, relishing the solitude and shampooing my hair three times. Then I ran a razor up and down my calves after applying a hair mask that Mel swore was a miracle treatment.

The pads of my fingers, wrinkled like raisins, signaled it was time to turn off the faucet. No clock in our bedroom, other than the tiny alarm next to Andre's bed. My stomach growled, and I reluctantly dried off. Then I lathered my legs with lavender lotion, thinking about when my mom and I bought it on one of our last spa trips together. I squirted mousse into my palms, rubbed them together, and scrunched my hair.

After taking Maple out for a quick walk, we put her in the crate, which she loved, as she'd learned that a tiny treat would be waiting for her inside. We drove toward Lake Champlain, and I appreciated the quiet. Andre's right hand rested on the console between us, shaking ever so slightly. I wondered if he took his meds on time today.

He parallel parked near Skinny Pancake, but we ate at a different cafe. I watched that same hand shift the car into park, worried about how much longer Andre would have the steadiness and strength to do something as simple as that action. I squeezed my eyes shut and reopened them as if that would change what lay ahead of us.

"You haven't said a word since we got in the car," Andre noted.

Crap. Are my thoughts all over my face?

I bit my lower lip.

"I appreciate the silence. It's not you. Just processing all the moments from the sleepover," I replied.

I need to write in my journal, I almost said. Andre ordered for us, knowing exactly how I'd like my eggs fried. Over easy but not too runny. And my sourdough bread lightly toasted but not burnt.

"What's so funny?" Andre asked.

"Listening to you order the food for me. I sound like Goldilocks—not too big, not too small, just right," I cackled.

Andre raised an eyebrow.

"You just realized that?"

I poked him with my elbow.

"Tell me about the night! Your appendages are attached—that's a good sign," Andre said. He took a sip of water, and his voice sounded the way a pixelated photo looked—unclear, scratchy, uneven. I needed to bring this up at his next doctor's appointment.

"These kids and counselors are incredible. Even the new campers seemed in sync with the seasoned ones. No nightmares or sleepwalking. Harmony—while we sang songs around the campfire—and in general," I chattered.

Andre leaned forward in his seat.

"Tell me more," he said, placing the napkin on his lap.

"Oh! Speaking of newbies, remember the shy girl Simi? She spoke with confidence, loudly, and in front of the Kismet community for the first time!"

He nodded and his eyes widened.

"She was captivated by fireflies that flickered in the bushes. Then in the morning, the counselors prepared such a scrumptious spread, as if they do this on the daily," I continued. "I can't believe the session is over next week."

The waitress stood behind me. I didn't notice until Andre glanced above my head. I turned around and salivated at the sight of the full plate.

"Here you go!" she shrilled.

"Love your ring," I said.

"Which one?"

"The amethyst and silver on your pointer finger. My best friend makes jewelry," I beamed. *My mom would love that piece, too.*

"Is she local?"

"Yes!" I answered.

"I'm a senior at UVM. Kinda obsessed with gemstones. Where's her shop?" She blew air upward to move her wispy bangs out of her eyes.

I gave her Mel's website, and the young woman's jaw nearly dislocated.

"No way! I purchased a pendant from her—what a coincidence!"

We grinned at each other while Andre stuck a fork in his blueberry gluten-free pancakes.

"Let me know if you need anything else. Enjoy!" she said.

"Only you, mi amor," Andre remarked.

I sipped my coffee and scorched my tongue.

"I still have a hard time imagining you as a quiet kid," he teased.

"Clearly I have lots of words that I've stored up and now they need to be used!" I chuckled.

Andre broke off a piece of the crisp turkey bacon and popped it into his mouth. Then he started choking. I rubbed his upper back. He shirked away, embarrassed as he continued to cough.

"Honey? You okay?" I handed him water then withdrew it, remembering what I'd learned in the CPR course before camp started. If someone's making noise, it is best to wait. If a person is totally silent, that's another story. I twiddled with my fingers under the table and tried to appear calmer than I felt.

Water gushed from his eyes and nose. Andre held up his hand, signaling for me to chill.

The pebble lodged itself into my throat—its first visit in a while. Now I couldn't swallow either. Andre finally stopped coughing.

"Just don't, okay?" he grunted.

What's he talking about?

I stayed put, lips pursed and arms crossed.

His shoulders lowered, and he was about to finish the rest of the turkey bacon.

For goodness' sake. Really?

"That melon looks juicy," I said. *What I wanted to say was, Are you fucking insane?*

Andre huffed and looked at the plate.

"I'm not a child, Joy," he retorted.

I changed the subject, asking him if he'd like to take Maple on a hike later on. Our girl always made him happy.

"That's a great idea. We'll have to see how the weather is because I think it may be stormy," Andre replied.

I wish I could forecast our future.

We stood, paid the bill, and headed to the car.

———

As Andre predicted, heavy clouds congregated in the sky a few hours later. Maple whined when she heard thunder, so I snuggled with her on our couch.

"You're okay—it will pass," I murmured, wishing somebody would do the same thing to me when I felt anxious. Maple nestled her furry head underneath the blanket. Tufts of fur looked like cotton, matching the champagne color of the chenille throw on my legs.

I told her I'd be right back. She dove off the sofa and followed me into my bedroom.

"Well, hello there!" I laughed, looking back at her tail between her legs. Poor girl. Maybe we needed to try giving her the CBD treats the vet had recommended. She climbed onto my bed.

"You know I'd love if we stayed here," I said. Maple cocked her head. "Daddy doesn't like it, and it's already been a bumpy morning."

I grabbed my journal, the purple pen, and a pillow.

"Come! Let's go back to the den." Maple licked my heels as she followed me.

The thunder stopped and the sky cleared. Andre was shredding some old documents. After spinning in circles, chasing her own tail, Maple settled into her poufy bed. I threw her a bone, which she began chewing immediately. Then I opened the journal, surprised at how long it'd been since I'd written in it.

CHAPTER 38

Dear Mom,

I don't even know where to begin! I guess with an apology. Sorry I haven't written lately. So busy with camp, Andre, our new puppy, and life stuff. I miss our chats. Real ones in person. Hearing your voice. I always will.

I'm still trying to accept this is the closest we'll get to an actual conversation. And I notice that when it's been a while, I feel inflamed with emotions. Sometimes my body even swells, quite literally. After a run recently, I took off my socks and saw a line around the top of my ankles, like indented into my skin. A few days ago, I couldn't button my jeans and didn't even have my period.

I'm trying to "tune in" as you'd say. After I take photos or write to you, the swelling lessens, and clothes get looser. Wild, right? Acupuncture seems to help, yet, honestly, I haven't been consistent with it. Who has time to be a human pin cushion? There's also a salt room that just opened in Burlington. I need to get there soon! A few of our friends went and said it's super serene.

Anyway, enough about my bodily musings. I'll share some good stuff! I slept under the stars. The annual Camp Kismet (love how that sounds!) sleepover on the field. It was magical.

Do you remember the shy kid—her name is Simi—anyway, she spoke in sentences, maybe even a paragraph! She'd never seen fireflies before. They lit up the surrounding bushes like that old Lite-Brite game from the eighties. She opened up and shared more about herself. She's letting me in. Simi is also intrigued by photography. Even the other campers noticed, a few smiling at her in surprise. Simi escapes her thoughts (and likely insecurities—sound familiar?) by reading books. I get the sense she's not seen or understood at home, and here at our camp, she is accepted for who she is. This teen boy, Lucas, is so sweet and seems interested in her—maybe it's becoming a crush. Simi's totally clueless about his attempts at flirting. She'd rather study patterns in a garden or observe animal behavior.

The first session is almost over. With each day, I feel more confident and I'm starting to have flickers of happiness again. Every new experience, every ending, and everything in between makes me want to call you. Share with you. Vent to you. Listen to your insights. I still can't hear your voice.

And Andre is losing his. We've had a few close calls—he choked at a restaurant and recovered on his own. His hands are tremoring more; we're looking into surgery and not sure yet if he's a candidate for it. He thrashes all night, so I don't sleep. I finally joined an online caregiver support group. I know you'd suggest it. Usually, I find that the forums and chats make me feel less alone. Spouses, partners, and others have shared about how meds stop working, recurrent UTI's, and other scary shit.

It worries me.

Based on everything I've read, along with input from Dr. Garcia, it's become clear that there is no definitive way of predicting what symptom might occur next. Like one thing may calm down or is managed. Then another thing appears.

Andre agreed to see a physical therapist twice a week. He's also going to start speech therapy—we found someone phenomenal! She's trained in the Lee Silverman Voice Treatment (LSVT LOUD) method. Andre will learn strategies to project his voice and what to do when it gets more challenging. He's still charming, a total smart ass, and working out daily. His gait has changed. Like he can't get started, stumbling or stiff when he walks.

I'm terrified, Mom. I know this is just the beginning.

We don't have kids.

Who will take care of us?

Of me?

CHAPTER 39

We'd almost made it without any incidents.

Almost.

The last time my house phone rang at 3:30 a.m., my father's devastated sob was on the other end of the line.

Deep in slumber, I didn't hear it ring.

"Joy. Joy!" Andre shook the side of my body.

Our room was completely dark. *Why was he waking me?*

I pried one eye open, rolled over, and smushed the pillow over my face.

"Mi amor, it's an emergency," Andre whispered. "Get up. Dave's on the phone!"

My throat narrowed. I couldn't move. My limbs wouldn't cooperate.

No. No No.

I can't do this again.

Andre shakily held the receiver to my ear.

"The firetrucks are here. Nobody was injured. Lucky the bunk was empty. Kids on an overnight trip," Dave said, his words sounding like another language.

My legs felt like cinder blocks, my chest felt clammy and sweat dripped down my spine.

I heard murmurs. I think it was Andre.

"Dave, I'll drive us over there. I can help assess the damage for the insurance company. We'll be on campus as soon as possible."

Something cold and wet was on my forehead. It wasn't Maple.

"Joy, we need to go. The kids are safe. Everyone is okay," Andre said, assuring me while pressing a cool washcloth into my temple.

He remembers. He knows. The trick my mom had taught me years ago when I froze in fear, back in high school when those bitchy bullies terrorized me. I'd only had a few panic attacks in the years Andre and I had been together.

Is that what was happening right now? A faint, high-pitched ringing in my ears. The tips of my fingers tingled. I still couldn't get myself vertical.

Andre took my hands in his and pulled me upright.

"Breathe with me, Joy. I've got you," he said, rubbing my back in slow, calming circles.

This must be what an epidural feels like, I thought. My legs dangled from the bed, numb and limp. The digital clock on Andre's nightstand was hazy. Our tall, pine armoire looked like a Dali painting—curvy and abstract.

"Maple. Is she safe? Did someone die? What's happening?" I tried to inhale but couldn't catch my breath.

Andre faced me and pressed his warm palms into my knees.

"In for four, hold for seven, out for eight," he said rhythmically. "Let's sit on the floor for a few minutes."

He remembered that, too. The wood that grounds me. The wall that stabilizes me. His voice, somehow strong and steady today, reassured me that all was okay. Objects became clearer and so did my awareness.

"Better now?"

I nodded tentatively.

Andre wrapped his arm around my waist and guided me toward the bathroom. He even remembered to keep the lights low. When my mom died, for weeks afterward, loud noises or bright lights bombarded my nervous system. He handed me the dry towel that was draped over the bathtub.

I couldn't eat. Not only was it practically the middle of the night, but nausea and nerves roiled in my belly. Even Maple stood silently in her crate, staring up at me with her tail down.

"Mommy's okay, sweet girl, just a bit scared. We'll be back soon," I whispered. Andre gently ushered me toward the garage.

———

As Andre drove to camp, what-ifs invaded my mind. I conjured images of smoke and screaming children. How could this have happened?

A mélange of orange spread like marmalade across the mountains. As we pulled up to the entrance, amber and apricot hues from the sun backlit the maple trees. Light peeked through the leaves, momentarily morphing my fear into reverence. Andre turned off the car and squeezed my shoulder.

"I'm right here," he said as I tried not to hurl. Andre unbuckled my seatbelt and walked around to the passenger side. He ambled in jagged steps in front of the car. The sunrise cast a shadow; the silhouette of his upper back curved and his head jutted forward. I'd started to carry a day's worth of his meds, in case we'd ever needed it.

Who knew we would so soon?

Before we reached the camp office, nurse Janet, Dave, and Jenny darted toward us.

"Nobody is hurt."

"The fire is out."

"No major damage."

Normally my hearing was hyper acute. Today I couldn't discern who was talking. I hoped my countenance appeared composed and confident. Andre's palm pressing into my upper back boosted my strength.

"Let's go to the bunk now, please." My voice wobbled like a newborn calf learning to walk.

A squirrel scampered up a pine tree. A few birds chirped as the sun rose higher. Other than the world beginning to wake up, the humans for whom I was responsible still slept.

It was eerily quiet.

Until I saw the ambulance.

Suddenly I was back months ago, racing through the sliding doors of the emergency room in Miami. The log cabin in front of me loomed like the ICU. I saw the tubes, ventilator, machines, everything that kept my mom alive so I could see her one last time.

I shook my head, trying to erase the images that assaulted my brain.

"Joy? I know it's shocking to see the burnt door. Thankfully, the sprinkler mechanism Bernard installed worked perfectly," Dave said.

How the fuck is he still calm?

I couldn't speak. Andre nudged me forward—I thought I'd literally collapse if he weren't here. I took a few breaths, now able to inhale more deeply and fully than earlier this morning.

"Ma'am? Are you the owner?" A buff, young man with the face of a doe-eyed boxer looked down at me.

"Yes, I am."

"I want to reassure you that no children were harmed. Your staff is amazing, and the counselors managed to keep the kids calm," he began. "By the time we arrived, along with the firetrucks, the flames were already almost extinguished."

I pushed my palms together and exhaled.

"Thank you so much. Forgive me, I'm trying to absorb all of this. I'm grateful nobody was hurt—that's the most important thing." Jenny moved closer to me and touched my forearm.

Forget the campers. I may be the one needing therapy first, I thought.

My neurons started firing, and so did the directives.

"Dave, please contact our insurance company now. Tell them that it's urgent."

"Janet, I'd like all the kiddos checked. Lungs and breathing— whatever you think is best."

"Jenny, let's meet with the campers in small groups. Who saw or smelled the fire? Lucky this bunk is newer, and it's a bit removed from the others."

Their heads bobbed in unison. Dave took out his tiny notebook from his back pocket and wrote as I spoke.

"Flagpole isn't for another hour. Let's meet and make sure our messaging is uniform. Speaking of which, we need to write an email to our parents and—"

Dave looked at Jenny.

"We already have a draft. I'm waiting for your approval. I also reached out to a few confidants in the camp industry. Surprisingly, bunk fires are not as uncommon as you'd think," Dave said.

Andre cleared his throat.

"I'd be happy to assess the structural damage," he offered.

Dave replied immediately. "That would be amazing. Joy is always talking about how talented you are!"

If my husband had feathers, they'd fan behind him like a peacock.

I looked at Dave. *Perfect timing and response, buddy.*

Then I thought about Andre's lung capacity, and if inhaling even minimal smoke could cause a problem. Before I uttered a word, Janet said she'd grab a few masks.

I read and reread the email Dave had drafted. The gravity of what could've been catastrophic jolted through me. I tweaked the language, softening the tone in some areas and inserting reassuring words in others. Then I texted Bill and asked him to review it ASAP.

While I awaited his reply, I squeezed my eyes shut and curled my toes inside my sneakers. The adrenaline from earlier faded as my pulse slowed. A screen door banged nearby, likely from the arts and crafts hut. I didn't smell the smoke in here, thankfully. I massaged the upper corner of my ear cartilage, trying to press into the area that my acupuncturist needled, the calming channel. When I opened my eyes, a cardinal landed on the ledge outside the window right above the computer screen. It perched there for a few minutes, peered at me, then flew away.

Somebody lightly rapped on the door.

"May I come in?"

I nodded.

Jenny handed me a mug filled with chamomile tea. She even brought a piece of honeycomb from our beehive near the garden; this was a new addition, and kids of all ages were fascinated with it.

"How kind of you," I said, breaking off a piece with the metal spoon. As I chewed on the comb, tiny tunnels burst in my mouth and honey coated the back of my throat.

"Isn't it amazing how brilliant the bees are? They're the architects of the insect world." I smiled and thought about Andre.

I stirred the rest of the honey into the steamy water, breathing in the calming concoction.

"I'm here if you want to talk—now or anytime," Jenny said softly. I patted the stump next to me, a remnant from the eighties that we'd converted into a seat.

After another sip, I moved my chair closer to her.

"Thank you for being here," I began, unsure how much to share. "Our campers will need you soon."

Jenny pitched forward and waited patiently. I still wasn't sure what to say.

"It's normal to feel scared. And I hope it's okay that your husband told me a bit about your mom," Jenny said.

That's all I needed to hear. I quivered as a tiny tear trickled down my cheek. I turned my head to the right and avoided Jenny's eyes.

She handed me a tissue from her pocket.

"This incident on its own was traumatic. I can't imagine how triggering this may have been for you personally. We—our Camp Kismet family—are all here for you," she continued, enunciating each word and pausing between sentences.

Her cadence would be perfect for a meditation, I thought. Maybe next year we could incorporate that into the schedule. First, we needed to finish this session, which sadly ended in a few days.

"Joy?"

Suddenly, I wanted Jenny to know my mom, who would've loved her. Other than Andre, Mel, my dad, and a few others, I hadn't spoken about my mom often. It hurt too much.

"My mom was a therapist, too. I think you would've really connected with her," I began. The pebble returned, though smaller this time. As I spoke, it began to soften as if responding while I shared about my mother.

Jenny nodded slowly, encouraging me to keep talking. I told her about the journal and how finding the entry inspired me. I shared about my heartbroken father, who said he'd never remarry as my mother was his bashert. I even told her about the rainbow and its significance since my mom died and why I'd incorporated it into the new Camp Kismet logo.

As I spoke, the pebble flattened and dissolved. That had never happened before.

The bell sounded, signaling it was time for flagpole. I loved the rusty, brass structure and hearing it reverberate across the camp. I blew my nose, rubbed my eyes, and pulled my frizzy hair into a bun. A ding from my laptop sidetracked me.

"Joy, this is well done. It's good to send!" I read Bill's email, relieved he'd replied so quickly. I needed to get this out before the day began.

We stood up together and as we reached the exit, I turned to Jenny.

"I didn't realize how much I've been holding," I whispered. Then I gave her a tight, quick hug.

"Thank you for sharing; I'm always here to listen. Your mom sounded like an extraordinary woman," she said. "It's tough to grieve while birthing this camp, right?"

Birth.

Birthing.

Rebirth.

A warm sensation spread throughout my belly. I suddenly understood what my mom had tried to teach me for years—trust your inner knowing. It will guide you in the right direction. Jenny and I joined the circle of campers that had already gathered. I spotted Simi digging her heel into the dirt, her lime and lilac pajama pants rolled up at the bottom.

Thank goodness she wasn't here last night. Vera, Lucas, Cami, and all the older kids had been on the overnight trip, too. They'd just gotten back to campus. The other bunks were thankfully far from the one that could've burned to the ground. Jenny and I agreed that she would kick off today's morning meeting. She calmly and candidly spoke about the fire, beginning with the reassuring news that our community was safe.

Simi raised her hand.

"What started it? Was it a short in the electrical system?" Her voice had grown much louder since last week. I beamed at her.

Lucas interjected.

"It doesn't matter—everything is okay. Can we talk about something else now?" he said. Simi had more questions, as always.

"Every person here matters. And Lucas, while it's true that all is well, I want everyone to know I'll be on campus all day," Jenny said. "Please stop by anytime—I'm here for you. Some of our campers' clothing was destroyed; we've sent emails to your families."

I felt his presence before he spoke.

"Hey there," Andre whispered behind me.

"How bad is it?" I groaned, spinning to face him. I hadn't yet processed what I'd seen from my earlier glimpse at the bunk.

He gently touched my arm.

"Oh G-d. Can I afford to fix the bunk? Is it awful?"

Andre held up a hand.

"It could've been worse. I know that's not your favorite phrase, but it's true. The walls are intact, the beams are solid, and the toilets still flush." He paused. "Seriously, it is a miracle the bunk didn't burn down."

I nearly crumpled with relief.

"I've already thought about where the kids can sleep for the next few nights; we can move the beds into that extra cabin, which used to be where the Von Glads stayed," I said.

My husband smiled almost imperceptibly.

"What's on your mind?" I stared at his stunning eyes.

"You are amazing," Andre replied. "It's as if you were born to do this." His smile spread and his cleft deepened. "I'm going to head home; call me later and I'll pick you up."

I looked to the left, right, and behind me. I tugged Andre's hand, pulling him behind a cluster of pine trees. Then I stood on my tippy toes, wrapped my arms around his neck, and kissed him until we were both gasping for air.

"I've always wanted to make out at camp with my forever boy-friend," I cooed, fluttering my lashes and running my tongue over my top teeth.

We giggled like two teenagers about to get busted. I heard movement behind us and turned around. Simi stood with her feet planted in the dirt, staring at us like we were aliens.

Oh shit. How humiliating: She saw us smooching!

"Hey there! Are you on your way to the garden?" I put on my sunglasses.

"No. That is the other direction—I'm going to feed the goats," Simi replied. From another child, that would've sounded rude. Her tone was simply matter of fact.

"Any interest in helping me in the photo lab later? Between your photos and Lucas's, I'd appreciate an extra hand; we need to print the images before Friday's final circle," I said.

Simi nodded eagerly.

She pointed at Andre. "Is he coming?"

Thankfully, he stayed silent instead of making a smart-ass remark.

"He's leaving now. We needed his expertise—did you know my husband is an architect?"

Simi's mouth opened and her eyes widened with astonishment as she gaped at Andre.

"Guess what? If I don't become a veterinarian, that was the other profession I wanted to learn more about! Maybe I could do both— design more efficient ways for animals to coexist with humans!" Simi chirped, even louder than the choir of birds above us.

Andre took a tiny step forward.

"I'm happy to tell you all about the field, if you'd like," he offered hesitantly.

My heart squeezed in my chest, knowing what an incredible father Andre could be, knowing we'd never have children.

Simi looked up at my husband. "Really? That would be amazing. Thank you so much!"

As if she'd depleted her word quota for the day, Simi slouched over and slunk away. I noticed that she needed time to recharge her social battery. I worried about how she'd do that back in New York City. My mind wandered as I thought about saying goodbye to Simi and the other kids.

When Simi disappeared, Andre cupped my face in his hands, his earnest, azure eyes searching my own.

"You've created something so special here. Especially with Simi—what a brilliant, unique kid—I see the connection. I can tell you've impacted her in a huge way," Andre said, coughing.

I blinked rapidly and gazed at him.

"Oh honey, that means everything to me. These kids have nestled themselves into my heart—I'm going to miss them." Andre hugged me, rubbing his damp cheek on my shoulder.

CHAPTER 40

THE LAST DAY OF SESSION ONE

I curled my body into a fetal position. Then I wriggled to the edge of the bed, finally laying flat on my back. Andre's restless legs were shaking our mattress. I couldn't imagine sleeping separately, yet I understood why some people might choose to on a night like this one.

Staring at the ceiling, I wished I could stretch time like a wad of bubblegum. Just for today. The kids and our entire Camp Kismet community had become family to me. Timid hellos a month ago turned into tender goodbyes.

My mom described her last day of Camp Intermezzo each summer as total torture and extremely emotional. I reread her diary this weekend, now filtered through the lens of my experience this summer.

I didn't expect, especially as an adult, to connect deeply with a bunch of strangers.

Then again, I also didn't expect my life to unfold as it had.

Another boom outside; lightning illuminated the headboard. Andre thrashed then mumbled something in his sleep. I gave up and crept into the bathroom. Maple whimpered in her crate, so after brushing my teeth, I joined her in the family room.

"The noises are scary, huh?" I murmured, sliding the metal bar to the left. "Shhhh, sweet girl, I'm here." Maple bounded out of her crate. She nuzzled her furry face into my lap, quivering when a branch hit the side of the house. I missed the short season when

Maple was a puppy, her tiny tongue tickling my toes and her paws too big for her body.

She'd grown so quickly. We both did this year. As if reading my mind, Maple's ears twitched and she repositioned her head to rest on my knee. She looked up at me under her long, reddish lashes. The thunder returned for an encore, but thankfully the lightning stopped. I wondered if the goats, sheep, and chickens were nervous, too. I bet Simi would know.

I checked the time, shocked to see it was already 6 a.m. I poured food into Maple's bowl and filled the other one with fresh water.

"I'll be back soon—I need to get ready!" Maple tucked her tail between her legs, refusing to eat or drink.

Standing in my closet, I surveyed the stacks of T-shirts and shorts, each one threaded with memories. The one from our trip to Tahiti. Another from a camping trip with Mel and Jake. Dozens of others from college, a few from vacations with Andre. My eyes landed on the silk, purple pajamas—my mom bought us matching ones for my thirtieth birthday.

As I pulled a Camp Kismet staff shirt over my head, I knew I'd need to add this to the favorites pile. I slathered sunscreen on my face, neck, arms, and legs. Then I sprayed my hair with detangler and pulled it into a smooth ponytail.

Andre tripped walking into the bathroom and almost hit his chin on the edge of the countertop. I looked down, about to say we needed to get grips for the bathmats. He'd tripped on his own feet.

Shame blazed his cheeks, and I figured my commentary would only make him feel worse. I said nothing and instead rested my head on his chest.

"Mi amor, today may be tough," Andre murmured into my hair.

I brought him closer.

"Thank you for believing in me and—"

He held a finger to my lips.

"Let's get those packages in the car. We'll talk later," Andre said wisely. He handed me the overnight oats, a spoon, and a mug of iced coffee. Then he hoisted the heavy bags into my trunk.

I grabbed my yellow, knee-length raincoat from the mudroom. Umbrellas would be useless with the torrential downpour. As I backed out of the garage, Andre held Maple and waved at me with her paw. I giggled and waved back.

Though I drove slowly, the ride didn't feel long enough to prepare myself for whatever would greet me.

Could you please come to the car?

Sure. Be right there. Dave replied.

He sloshed through the puddles in rubber boots and held an oversized umbrella over me as I opened the door. I popped open the trunk and walked around the car.

"Gosh, what's all this?" Dave's eyes widened.

"I'll show you soon!" I exclaimed.

As we approached the camp office, I heard sniffles and sobs. I looked ahead, seeing three girls holding each other in a huddle. As if dipped in mud, my legs suddenly felt stuck.

Dave paused before we went in.

"Even after all these summers, I still get sad seeing these kiddos part ways. It's heartwarming and also heartbreaking, right?" he said, lightly squeezing my shoulder.

I nodded, thinking about my own heartache, understanding now what he'd said weeks ago about the camp community becoming like family.

"Bummer we couldn't have the final campfire. This weather isn't helping the mood around here!" I groaned.

"We'll have the morning meeting in the arts and crafts hut; I asked the junior counselors to rearrange the tables so there's room for everyone," Dave said.

Of course you did. Dave thought of everything, I'd learned.

"And I checked the radar; the rain will lighten up soon, in time for the parents' arrival. Brace yourself, cause that's the toughest," he said, shoving his hands in his cargo pant pockets.

"Good morning!" I said to whomever was listening. I heard murmuring in the other room. I walked in that direction and a collective "surprise" resounded from the area.

"What on earth?" I stammered. Streamers, balloons, and a "happy birthday" banner draped from the wood rafters. Emma chuckled, Jenny smiled, and the unit heads along with Janet and Wendy chortled.

"We couldn't let the session end without celebrating you!" Emma exclaimed.

"We know you're a health nut, so the cake's organic—nothing artificial," Dave added.

I stood there, speechless and stunned. I'd honestly forgotten that my birthday was soon. I was so focused on the campers and their experience.

Emma motioned for me to come closer. I willed my legs to move.

"Oh my gosh, this looks homemade!" I squealed.

Emma beamed and signaled for the group to start singing. I covered my mouth with my hands, grateful and also a bit embarrassed. Jenny gently encouraged me to get closer to the cake.

Holy crap, she made a rainbow out of fruit! Blueberries, raspberries, bananas, kiwi, strawberries, and mandarin orange slices. Juice trickled into the fluffy frosting, which tinted it like tie-dye. After blowing out the candles, Emma proudly sliced into it. She'd even continued the theme—sprinkles dotted the inside like edible confetti.

"This is beautiful—I need to take a photo before it's devoured!" I shrieked, hugging Emma before grabbing my phone.

"You stay there. I've got it," Dave said, holding a Nikon I'd never seen before.

I grinned as he snapped photos of the cake and all of us.

"One more thing," Janet said. "We have a little something for you!"

Now I was convinced that invisible sprinklers lived in the corners of my eyes. They had a timer out of my control, turning on and off on their own schedule.

I wiped my cheek on the corner of my shirt.

"This was not necessary—each of you is a gift," I said. They insisted I open the rectangular, cardboard box. It was signed by every staff member and wrapped in twine I recognized from the craft hut.

A thin, wood plank with CAMP KISMET etched into it covered the handmade scrapbook. I held it and slowly flipped each page. Drawings, poems, notes, and photos filled the paper, a textured paper like our birch trees near the lake.

"Wow. This is beyond words, truly," I said. "We need to head over to the hut. I can't wait to really soak this all in when I get home. Speaking of which, you've all touched my heart, and the heart of every child here, this summer. Family's taken on a new meaning for me."

Jenny linked her arm through mine. Dave lugged the large bags in a wheelbarrow, covering it with a green tarp before pulling it toward the hut. Again, I thought about how I wished we could stop time to cherish the magical moments, or speed it up during heartbreak or tragedies.

Now's not the time for my morbid musings. Get your shit together—these kids need you.

Overstuffed, canvas duffle bags lined the walls of the room. One young girl was braiding her bestie's light-brown hair. A group of boys cloistered in the back corner. I couldn't hear what they were saying, but they were slouched forward, looking at the floor.

I spotted the top of Simi's head, her hair perfectly parted, and she seemed deeply engrossed in a book. She had a remarkable ability to tune out the noise and ambiance around her. I approached her carefully, so I didn't startle her.

Simi glanced up, and I sat next to her.

"Hi there. How are you today?" I asked.

She shrugged and looked down at the pages.

"Simi."

Her lower lip jutted out, trembling slightly.

"I don't want to leave," she said softly.

I tried to swallow the pebble that lodged in my throat. Then I remembered what happened when I shared, rather than dismissed my feelings.

"I feel sad, too," I began.

She closed the book and placed it beside her.

"You do?" Simi asked.

I nodded, not trusting myself to speak. So, I looked at her instead, encouraging her to keep talking. The pebble shrunk to a sensation the size of a pea.

"Camp feels more like home than where I live. I feel safe here. I have friends for the first time, and they don't judge me," Simi said woefully.

I get that more than you know, I thought.

"I understand. I'm happy you found a home away from home!" I said, my pitch higher than usual. "I hope you'll keep taking photos during the school year."

Simi smiled and straightened her back.

"I wrote letters to my parents telling them all about the dark-room! They said I can get my own camera!" Her words stitched together like a quilt.

My throat relaxed, and joy replaced my earlier sadness. I peeked at the round clock on the wall.

"Can you please help me and tell everyone to take a seat?" Simi nodded.

Dave and the head counselors got everyone quiet. I pointed to the massive bags in the wagon. Then I took the megaphone and began.

"I'm so proud of our Camp Kismet community. Each of you has been kind, empathetic, and truly embodies what this place is all about. I hope you'll tuck all these experiences in your heart, taking with you lessons learned, growth moments, and forever friendships," I said, my voice steadier with each sentence.

"And I know I'm a grown-up, but goodbyes are hard for me. Anyone else?" Hands popped up from every inch of the room. "This isn't farewell—it's see you soon!"

The kids stood, clapping and hugging each other. I smiled at them, waiting for them to settle. They got louder.

"Everyone, I have a surprise! Please quiet down," I shouted. The youngest campers responded immediately. The preteens and older ones gabbed, totally ignoring me. Dave pointed to the megaphone.

"Hey hey hey—respecting others is the Kismet way!" he bellowed. Of course, they listened to him. Other than the light pitter-patter of rain, it was quiet.

"Some of you know I am a photographer. It's been a delight to witness you all flourish this summer—even with the bunk fire, colds, conflict—we worked through it all. I love capturing memories in pictures. The past few months, I learned that writing down thoughts and feelings is powerful." I paused, looking at each camper before continuing. Then I asked Dave, Jenny, and the head counselors to distribute the gifts.

"Ms. Joy, this is incredible!"

"Wow!"

"So kind!"

The campers unwrapped the paper that covered the journals I'd created. I wrote a note on the first page and glued a photograph of each child on the inside cover. I hadn't slept in days, yet an exhilarating energy coursed through my veins.

Dave joined me at the front with the empty bags. I pulled his journal from my backpack.

"No way. You made me one too?" he exclaimed.

"Yep! And one for each of the staff members," I replied.

"Joy, this is amazing. These kids—all of us—are lucky to know you," he said, pulling his baseball cap lower. He rubbed the tip of his nose, and I handed him a napkin.

Jenny, Janet, Wendy, and the others echoed Dave's sentiments. The sound of tires rolling over gravel got louder—I knew it was time. I inhaled slowly, breathing in a mix of damp pine needles, perspiration, dried paint, and the unmistakable smell of camp. The kids were signing journals and exchanging numbers (and likely social media handles). We'd give them back their cell phones soon.

Dave asked everyone to line up next to their belongings. The Camp Kismet bubble burst the second parents stampeded into the room, eager to hug their babies. I tried to talk to every parent and caregiver, but it was impossible. Shorter than other kids her age, Simi could camouflage in a crowd like a deer in the woods. I started to worry when I couldn't find her.

"Mrs. Stern, may we speak with you?" a clipped, baritone voice said. I pivoted and nearly collided with Simi's father.

Is she missing?

I looked down, noting six pairs of shoes, two of which were petite, periwinkle sneakers. I exhaled slowly and shook hands with Simi's father.

"Sure! Please come with me," I said, leading her parents to the photo lab. "I'm sorry there are only two stools in here. It's the only place that's relatively quiet."

Simi's mom adjusted her strand of large, lustrous pearls. I thought about Vivienne and our first meeting about Camp Von Glad and stifled a smile. Those two would be fast friends, I thought.

"We wanted to thank you personally. We've never heard our daughter speak with confidence around so many people," Simi's father said. "Jenny has been updating us—we are immensely grateful."

I beamed and waited for him to continue, surprised by his emotive words.

"Our little girl, we know she has so much to say, yet at home she rarely speaks. And especially at school, that's always been a struggle," he continued.

Simi's mom touched my hand with her long, bony pointer finger.

"You changed our Simi's life. Do you know what her full name is, actually?"

I shook my head.

"It is Simcha, which means 'joy' in Hebrew. We're not religious. But it took us years to conceive—Simi is our miracle. She gave us hope, filled our life with happiness," she said, unable to finish talking. Her husband took off his glasses, moving closer to her.

Those sprinklers came on full force, soaking my shirt. The pebble in my throat never returned. But my joy did. We walked outside, together, and found Simi sitting crisscrossed on the floor. She jumped to her feet, threw her arms around me, and I hugged her back.

Then we all stepped outside—almost everyone had left already—and looked up at the slate-blue sky. A double rainbow peeked between the clouds. It was kismet.

NEXT SUMMER

The Deep Brain Stimulation (DBS) procedure went well, and Andre healed quickly. The device helped control the tremors, though he continued to have difficulty projecting his voice. He stopped going to the office, which had been a big adjustment for us. But we knew, after Mom's unveiling in Miami, that we could get through anything. Seeing her headstone, surreal yet final, really rocked us.

We'd already been shaken to the core, first when she died, then with Andre's diagnosis. After finding Mom's journal, Camp Kismet finding me, and the months leading up to this summer, I couldn't wait to hug those kids. My kids. Our kids.

Speaking of kids, Simi's parents had reached out in December, sharing that she'd like to work in the photo lab or help take care of the goats. After discussing it with Dave, who shrieked with excitement, we decided Simi could split her time and assist in both areas. In another email, Simi's mother wrote about how much her daughter had blossomed this year, even joining the diving team at her school.

Mel would be a surprise guest and teach campers how to polish rough rocks. Special ones from Lake Champlain, when polished, look like abstract zebra stripes. Andre had a brilliant idea, and Simi would be his assistant, to come to camp twice a week and share about sketching for architects. He'd created a syllabus (of course all formal and I laughed), bringing in photography along with ways to design drawings. Because we were a no-tech environment, he'd purchased a special angled desk and thought it'd be fascinating for the kids to design their own bunk.

Carmen and Carlos had come around, especially when their eldest expressed interest in becoming involved with the camp community.

I still couldn't believe how quickly this idea gestated—in the best way—growing in just a few months. My marriage, strengthened by solidarity and support, allowed me to accept that life doesn't always go as planned. The detours forced me, and us, to recreate life on our own terms. I still couldn't hear my mom's voice, but I felt her presence. She appeared in the sky as a double rainbow just before opening day at camp.

I'd mothered these campers—I now understood that mothering and motherhood transcended biology. I didn't need to grow a child in my womb, something that I'd always yearned for, to become a parent. Or, to feel whole.

—THE END—

ACKNOWLEDGMENTS

This is one of my favorite parts of writing a novel—expressing infinite gratitude to the incredible people in my life. It's also admittedly anxiety provoking. I don't ever want to leave anyone out.

I dedicated this book to my husband's late mother, Terri Levan Katz. Just six months before our wedding, she died suddenly and tragically. For over two decades, Terri visits us in rainbows. Every milestone, significant moment, birthday, life decision. It's seriously mind-blowing. Her young passing, unconditional love, and spirit inspires me how to live. Thank you, Terri, for birthing such a special soul. My real-life bashert, Jarett.

In my first novel, *It Could Be Worse*, I saved the best for last—not this time! My love, life partner, my everything—you've inspired me to create characters who are loyal, loving, passionate, and with a strong sense of integrity. Thank you for supporting me during all phases of this wildly exhilarating career. When our lives are shaken to the core, you're my anchor. Jarett, you are an extraordinary dad and father. As this story explores, I believe motherhood and mothering transcend biology. Same for fathers. You exemplify what it means to parent; I am forever grateful for the life we've created together. It's not easy living with an author, especially when she's on deadline!

Speaking of children, I'm the luckiest mom. Todd and Madeline—pride is an understatement, and being your mother is the greatest gift of my life. You're empathetic, authentic, hilarious, and I love you forever. You both make me a better person.

Jay Levan inspired a core theme in this novel. What I didn't expect is that I'd have to revise these pages, to write about our beloved uncle in the past tense. He battled Parkinson's with quiet grace, rarely complaining even as he declined. I'm thankful I told him about Andre, an athlete and charmingly stubborn, much like Uncle Jay. A former skier, cyclist, and adventurous spirit, he was shaken by Parkinson's, yet always steady in his friendships and for his family.

To Gretchen Young for taking a chance on me not once, but twice. Your wisdom, humor, and guidance are unparalleled—I'm beyond grateful. Thank you to Anthony Ziccardi, Caitlin Burdette, and the amazing team at Regalo Press.

To the author and reading community—I wish I could list every single person. Not only would that fill enough pages for a novella, but now that I'm in menopause, I would likely forget someone. So many people have impacted and supported me; I appreciate each of you. Please forgive me if I missed anyone! Samantha M. Bailey, Meredith Schorr, Kristy Woodson Harvey, Annie Cathryn, Jill Santopolo, May Cobb, Jane L. Rosen, Jamie Brenner, Patricia Sands, Heidi Shertok, Leah Grossman, Julie Valerie, Stacey Igel, Harper Kincaid, Debbie Fischer Reed, Corie Adjmi, Sara Goodman Confino, Dan Blank, Jean Meltzer, Gila Pfeffer, Meghan Riordan Jarvis, Deborah Goodrich Royce, Dina Aronson, Cindy Cunningham, Julie Fingersh, Rachel Sobel, Cari Fund, Francene Katzen, Ali Wenzke, Mel Greenberg, Lauri Schoenfeld, Linda Rosen, Kara Kavensky, Tamara Schweitzer Raben, Renee Weiss Weingarten, Julie Maloney, and the late MJ Rose.

To the Instagrammers, bookstagrammers, podcasters, bloggers, reviewers, librarians, booksellers, and those in all areas of publishing—I am thankful for your literary passion and support. Girl Well Read, Aimee Fogel, rachels.booknook, kaylareadsbooks, Books

Turning Brains (Andrea J. Stein), The Book Club Mom, Renee's Reading Room, Thoughts on Plots, Beauty and the Book (Jamie Rosenblit), Liz Gerke, Jenn Bouchard, Book Cook Look, The Joyful Book Blogger (Arielle), The Real Book Keeper (Traci Benedon), Pinkish-Perla, Beachandbookgirl2 (Kayla), Adina Reads, The Grateful Read (Katie), and countless others. To organizations including the Jewish Book Council, Women's Fiction Writers Association, the Authors Guild, and so many more.

To my incredible friends who inspire me to write about chosen family. My Village Girls—Robyn Gottlieb, Ilona Mandel, and Ronit Neuman—you've been there through it all. Samra Vogel, Natalie Haywood, Brad Meltzer, Robin Landau, Zameer Kassam, Forrest Nelson, Diana Levy, Bari Norman, Brian Kopelowitz, Susanne Hurowitz—dear friend, cheerleader, and sounding board about Parkinson's and its impact on caregivers. Natalie Silverstein— grateful books brought us together and thankful for your nuanced insights about this disease. *Mil gracias a mi amigo,* Ray Bakalarz, for verifying the Spanish phrases in this book are correct and for explaining the difference between plantains and patacones.

They say friends are not the best beta readers, but that's not always true. Special shout out to two people who read early drafts—honest AF, discerning, and direct—Rachel Frank and Nikki Kopelowitz. Rach, I can't express how much it means to me that you took the time to read my book. You mined minuscule moments I might've missed, finding timing errors (unsurprisingly related to math!) and much more. Terry, I appreciate you schlepping drafts to Rachel, who I'm still convinced should be an editor. Nik, you always understand the ifs and what-ifs, asking why with honesty and always love. And my Indiana University college bestie and fellow creative Dana Kaufman—you get me. Thanks for always showing up. Tricia Warford—warrior, soul sister, my ride-or-die—I hear your wisdom echoing in my mind when self-doubt tries to crash my creative party. I love you all.

To my family and fur babies—past and present—you will always be part of me. I'll love you forever. My hilarious Goldendoodles, Auggie and Melody, sparked the idea to make Maple a main character. Thank you for the puppy kisses, crazy antics, and unconditional love.

To Dr. Ihtsham ul Haq MD, FAAN, professor and Division Chief of Movement Disorders Department of Neurology at the University of Miami Miller School of Medicine, who took the time to share his expertise about Parkinson's Disease.

To BookSparks—Crystal Patriarche, Reilly Warner, Hanna Lindsley, Emani Glee, and the whole team—you all rock!

A special shout out to my friend, fellow podcaster, writer, and publisher, Zibby Owens, who has amplified authors' voices around the world. And who published *On Being Jewish Now*. I am honored to be a contributor to this *USA Today* bestselling anthology.

As a former camper, who'd still be there if it were allowed, and the mother of two kids who attended sleep-away camp, the formative experience of weeks in the woods is indescribable. I spent eight summers at Interlochen Arts Camp in Michigan, but I didn't fully grasp the dedication, breadth, and responsibility a camp owner inherits. What an amazing group of human beings—thank you to camp owners, directors, staff, and all who make summer camps magical. Thank you to The American Camp Association for the plethora of information on your site, which broadened my knowledge—the resources and kind community you foster is extraordinary.

Vermont has been a healing sanctuary for me. I wanted to set this novel there, hopefully whisking you away, not only into Joy's story, but also the magic of the Green Mountains. Camp Kismet, though totally fictional, was loosely inspired by Shelburne Farms. I have vivid, fond memories of my kids feeding goats from baby bottles and milking cows. My husband and I still go to Shelburne to walk, taking time away from technology, connecting with nature and each other.

And for every person who's taken the time to read my books, you are why I write. I hope Joy's journey is a reminder that we all have the reserves necessary to pivot and live a meaningful life, even when things don't go as planned. Sometimes those detours become our destiny, leading us to a path we never expected to take. Perhaps one even better than we could've imagined.

RESOURCES

The Parkinson's Foundation
Resources & support. (2026, January 20). Parkinson's Foundation.
https://www.parkinson.org/resources-support

The Michael J. Fox Foundation for Parkinson's Research
Parkinson's 101. (n.d.). The Michael J. Fox Foundation for
Parkinson's Research Parkinson's Disease. https://www.michaeljfox.
org/parkinsons-101

American Parkinson Disease Association (APDA)
https://www.apdaparkinson.org/

ABOUT THE AUTHOR

Photo by Alison Frank Photography

Dara is an author, podcaster, and the creator of Every Soul Has a Story. She interviews guests from around the globe. Her award-winning novel, *It Could Be Worse*, published in 2024 with Regalo Press. Dara's work appears in the *USA Today* Bestseller, *On Being Jewish Now*.

A graduate of Indiana University with a BA in English and certificate in journalism, Dara earned her MS in communication sciences and disorders at Nova Southeastern University. She stopped practicing speech therapy to return to full-time writing.

Actively involved in her South Florida community, she is an executive board member of the Joe DiMaggio Children's Hospital Foundation/Memorial Hospital Foundation. Dara is also a Trustee for Interlochen Center for the Arts. She served as a board member of the Community Foundation of Broward, the Hollywood Art and Cultural Center, and Junior Achievement of South Florida.

Dara is a founding member of the Circle of Friends for the Alvin Sherman Library Research, Information, and Technology

Center at Nova Southeastern University. She is also a member of the Authors Guild, the Women's Fiction Writers Association, and the Women's National Book Association.

Her husband, two children, and finding meaning in everyday moments are her greatest sources of inspiration. When she's not writing in Fort Lauderdale, you'll find Dara with her family and fur babies, traveling, capturing moments through photos, and talking to strangers who become friends. Learn more at daralevan.com.